A LOVE TO KILL FOR

A MEADOW OAKS NOVEL

JEN MCGEE

LilyPad Publishing, LLC

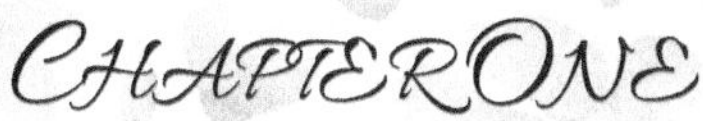

S he had killed her fifth unfaithful lover only moments before when she finally found "The One." She was absolutely sure this time. What was that old saying? It went something like, "You'll find what you're looking for when you're not looking." Well, that was exactly what happened to her.

She walked away from behind the darkened office complex where her latest paramour had taken his final breath. When she made it to the front of the building she stopped and took a deep breath as she felt the breeze from the nearby ocean lift her hair and whisk away the sweat from the back of her pale neck. She closed her eyes and focused inward to the adrenaline coursing through her bloodstream, the pounding of her heart. She envisioned the look in his eyes when he realized he had underestimated her and that he was about to die. She opened her eyes and smiled brightly. "Time to celebrate," she spoke aloud to the cool night air.

She made her way over to Broad Street, the click-clack sound of her heels on the sidewalk in time with the beat of her heart. Her cross-body purse gently bumping against her left hip with every step. Ahead she spotted the lights of Brasserie La Banque, but instead of making her way into the fancy French restaurant she went below to Bar Vaute'. The dim atmosphere of her favorite speak-easy style bar in Charleston welcomed her like an old friend. Sliding onto a stool at the corner of the bar she nodded over at the bartender.

As she waited for him to come over, she placed her hands on the dark bar top and thought about what had led to the necessary violence. *Who did he think he was cheating on? Smiling at his coworker like that. Touching her shoulder. And he said he was a gentle-*

man. Just like the others. Sure, he was all good manners and graciousness, until a shiny new option caught his eye. Well, he learned his lesson. Just like the others.

She glanced down and noticed a few drops of blood drying on her tan suede pump. *Whoops! Made a bit of a mess,* she playfully chided herself.

"What'll it be tonight?" the bartender asked.

She looked up from her bloody shoe with a private smile to order her favorite cocktail. "Goose and tonic with a lime twist. And if you don't mind, may I please have a couple of napkins and some soda water? I seem to have gotten something on my shoe."

"Sure thing," he answered, tapping his knuckles on the bar and turning away to fill her order.

He returned with her drink and a small glass of soda water and the napkins. "You stopping by for an after-work drink or is it a special occasion?"

"Oh, definitely celebrating."

When she didn't elaborate, he gave up on his effort at small talk. He checked on his other patrons and left her to her drink. She sipped on the smooth concoction, the alcohol helping loosen up her muscles and dissipating the adrenaline. She dreamily relived every gory moment of getting her revenge. As she remembered what it felt like when her knife slid past the barrier of his skin into his insides and the blood ran red down the blade, she was reminded that she needed to tend to her shoe. She dipped the small stack of cocktail napkins the bartender had provided into the small glass of soda water and proceeded to dab at the rusty red spots on her shoe.

When she sat back up straight on her stool, her attention was completely taken over by the gorgeous, rugged hunk of a man sitting down a few barstools away. *Normally I like to take a break before moving onto another lover, but hot damn! This one is too good looking to pass up!* She patiently waited for him to look over at her, sipping on her drink. Finally, he looked her way, and she gave him her biggest, flirtiest smile and a come-hither stare. *Oh yeah, you're mine.* He smiled slowly back and came to sit on the stool next to her.

"May I buy you a drink?" he asked smoothly.

"Perfect timing. I was just finishing up this one."

"Lucky me," he said as he motioned for the bartender. "So, tell me about yourself."

She couldn't believe her luck. A man that didn't immediately start bragging about himself or boring her with whatever stupid hobby he was into. She told him a little bit about her work and interests. *Oh my gosh, he is so perfect. This one is different. Finally! He is so focused on me. No wandering eye here. I need to lock this down.*

After half an hour of really hitting it off she decided to make her move. "So, do you live around here?"

"No, I'm just in this area for work."

"Oh, well I'm staying not too far from here. If you'd like to keep getting to know each other, we could go back to my place," she suggested, trying not to sound too eager.

"Yeah, sure. I could follow you there. But I do need to be up front about something. I'm not looking for a relationship. This will be a one-time thing only. Are you ok with that?"

Her smile faltered for a second, but she brushed it off. *I'll change his mind. All men that say that end up falling for someone. Why couldn't it be me in this case?* She had convinced herself.

"Fine by me," she answered. "I don't have my car here, though. I could call us an Uber and have one bring you back to your car later."

"Sounds like a plan."

She pulled out her phone and requested an Uber while he paid the tab. He put his hand on the small of her back as they walked out of the bar together. *He's so romantic. His touch makes me shiver.*

They held hands in the backseat of the car as they were driven to the address she had given. They pulled up to a little cozy cottage in the woods. She felt like she was the star of a romantic movie. While he tipped the driver, she walked over to unlock the front door. She stepped over the threshold into the interior and turned on the overhead light, but decided a fire would be much more appropriate for the occasion. She flipped the bright light off and went over to the fireplace. She used the light from her cell phone to find the lighter and ignite the kindling. The fire slowly started to come to life, and she could feel the warmth spread across her face.

She turned to find her new lover standing inside the front door. He had closed it and was watching her. She rose from her crouched position seductively, using the firelight to accentuate her figure. He gave her the sexiest smile she had ever seen, and she flushed with a heat that had nothing to do with the fire. *This is going to be life changing,* she thought to herself. She couldn't stop herself from closing the distance between them, jumping up and wrapping her legs around him. She thrust her tongue in his mouth and moaned in pleasure at the taste of him. *Bourbon, yum.*

A long time later, she lay on the floor in front of the fireplace completely spent. He was a very generous lover. Her needs were well tended to, unlike the times with those selfish men before who had only been concerned with their own pleasure. The selfish men that she had been forced to teach a lesson before she watched the life drain from their eyes. *He is so perfect. He is so charming and romantic. He couldn't have meant what he said back at the bar. Not after this. I've done it, I've changed his mind. I'm going to be the one that he settles down for. This is true love.*

"Is it ok if I use your shower before I head out?" he asked, bringing her out of her daydream.

"Yes, of course," she replied lovingly, running her fingertips along his bare shoulder. "You can stay the night if you want."

"I left my truck near the bar; it'll get towed if I leave it there overnight."

"Ok, I'll order another Uber and ride back with you, so we have a little more time together."

He smiled and placed a peck on her cheek before getting up and heading down the hall to the bathroom. While he showered, she went through his jeans that had been discarded carelessly on the hardwood floor in their rush to get naked. In his back pocket she found a well-used brown leather wallet. She looked through the contents touching everything, thrilled to be touching things his hands had touched. He had cash, credit cards, the usual grocery store discount cards, and a picture of a young blonde boy that looked a lot like him. Lastly, she pulled out his driver's license. She stared lovingly at his picture on the little laminated card. The shower down the hall turned off, so she quickly took note of his full name and memorized his home address. *I'll do whatever it takes to make you mine. Forever.*

CHAPTER TWO

P aige Collins stood leaning her hip against her kitchen sink, looking out the window to her backyard. She admired the blooming azalea bushes and noted that her small vegetable garden was coming to life on this bright Saturday morning. She waited patiently for her coffee to finish brewing, the strong scent of her favorite blend filling the kitchen.

Her best friend Faith was coming over for their usual weekend cup of joe. Usually, Paige looked forward to her friend's arrival. Lately, however, all of their chats turned to Paige's love life or lack thereof. She didn't need the reminder of how lonely she had been feeling recently. And guilty. Her husband had been gone for a little over two years, a tragic accident when he was repairing downed power lines during a storm. Her heart had shattered and for a long time it didn't even cross her mind that there could ever be anyone else after him. That was starting to change. She found herself yearning for companionship. She had an ache in her chest that wouldn't go away. The problem was that she had no idea how to make that happen. Her life was busy with her kids and her work. *Where would a man fit in?*

"Good morning, my favorite little family," Faith's singsong voice called out as she let herself in the front door, interrupting Paige's pondering.

"Good morning, Auntie Faith," Paige's children, Henry and Chloe, called down from their rooms upstairs.

Paige smiled. Even though her children were without their father, they certainly did not lack for people who loved them. Paige walked over to the coffee nook she had created in the corner of her countertop and got two mugs down from the rack.

"Perfect timing as always," Paige said to Faith as she entered the kitchen. The two women poured their coffee and had a seat at Paige's rustic farmhouse table.

"I spoke with Sadie on the way over. Her shift at the hospital ends at noon. She said she'd be up for hanging out tonight after she got some sleep," Faith began.

"That sounds good. Chloe has a soccer game in a little while and then we are free. We could do a movie night over here at our house."

"I was thinking that your parents would probably love a grandkid sleepover and then us grown folks could go out for a night on the town," Faith suggested.

"I'm not sure I'm up for all that. How about a quiet dinner?" Paige countered as she brushed her long raven hair off her shoulders..

"Well, aren't you just a bag of fun," Faith retorted sarcastically.

Paige chuckled into her coffee mug as she took a sip.

"Seriously sweetie, you need to get back on the horse. Widowhood does not suit you."

Paige set down her steaming cup of coffee just as it was about to reach her lips, looked across the table at her best friend and replied, "What on God's green earth are you talking about? How does discussing a night out with you and Sadie take a sharp turn into my widowhood?" Paige knew exactly what Faith meant, *no beating around the bush today.*

"You know, get out there in the world, among real live people. Maybe wear some clothes with a little color in them. Make an effort. Have a little fun." Faith's piercing blue-eyed stare never faltered over the top of her own coffee mug as she drank.

"I'm around people all the time and I happen to like my clothes," Paige muttered sullenly, looking down at her black yoga pants and grey t-shirt.

Faith rolled her eyes as she got up from the table and walked over to the coffee pot for a refill. After getting the oat milk creamer Paige kept just for her out of the fridge, she doctored up her coffee and took a sip. "Perfect," she said appreciatively into her mug. Then it was back to business. Setting her mug on the counter to let it cool off a little, she turned back to Paige, popped out her left hip and crossed her arms. "I mean going out somewhere other than to school events or work stuff."

Paige stared blankly at her friend hoping she'd give up, but Faith was nothing if not persistent. "Don't look at me like that with those beautiful bright green eyes of yours. It's been two years, Paige. It's time for you to be social with someone other than me."

"Hey, I went to lunch with Sadie in Charleston the other day," she answered in her haughtiest voice from where she was still seated at the table.

"She doesn't count either and you know it, smart ass." Faith took another sip of coffee. "Look, I know you miss Matt, but it's been two years since he passed. I'm not saying run out and get married to the first guy you meet. I'm saying get out and date. Play the field or whatever. Have fun getting some *male* attention. I know you must have needs. You're still young and vibrant. Stop acting like some blue-haired lady at the retirement home." Faith paused for a second, tapping her fingernails on the side of her mug. "Actually, I shouldn't say that because according to that segment on the news the other night, they get a lot of action. Apparently sexually transmitted diseases run rampant in the old folks' homes!"

Paige couldn't stop herself from laughing so hard she had to hold onto her side to keep it from cramping. "I keep picturing a doctor having to give those results to the old folks and I can't stop cracking up! Well Ethel, you have the clap!"

"There's that beautiful smile I've been missing!" Faith breathlessly exclaimed, struggling to control her laughter. "Don't you want to feel that rush you get when a man touches you for the first time? Or the butterflies of a first kiss? I know you are a perfectly capable independent woman, but I also know that you have a lot of love to give. Don't you want to go on a date or two and see if you find someone worthy of that love?" Faith questioned animatedly.

The huge smile Paige was sporting disappeared. "I did. Go on a date that is. It was absolutely terrible and I'm not in any rush to do it again, thank you very much," Paige admitted begrudgingly.

Faith immediately went ramrod straight. "Wait, what do you mean? How did I not know about this?" she asked. "Did Sadie know?"

"No, I didn't tell her either."

"We're supposed to tell each other everything. We've been best friends, the three of us, sisters even, since college and you don't tell us about your first date since your husband died?"

"Well, I didn't want to tell you beforehand in case it was a total bust. Which it was," Paige replied softly. "I didn't mean to hurt your feelings. I'm sorry."

Paige took a deep breath to try to slow down her rising heart rate, a practice she had learned from her grief counselor. As she released the breath, a shudder ran through her just thinking about what a complete waste of time that date had been. She got up to unload the dishwasher. Thinking about the crappy date made her antsy and she needed to move around.

"Well, maybe I can forgive you this once. I guess you have been through a lot. Just don't let it happen again," Faith teased lightheartedly. "So, who was he? How did you meet him?"

Faith hopped up on a stool at the kitchen counter to get out of Paige's way while she stress cleaned, putting her elbows up on the granite, eager to hear every last detail.

"We were set up by Cora Rae from work," Paige began.

Faith cut her off, "Well no wonder, Cora Rae is a moron. Bless her heart."

Paige laughed despite herself. "Yes, I probably should have known better. Anyways, he works in high finance, or something else that requires a designer suit and tie daily. Not my usual type, but I was trying to be open minded. I must admit, I have been feeling lonely in the romance department and Cora Rae caught me at a weak moment." Paige shook her head as she recalled the disaster of a date. "He ended up being very snobbish and judgmental. The man even tried to order for me at dinner, even though I am perfectly capable of reading a menu. And to top it all off, he was rude to our server, and you know I don't condone that kind of highfalutin' attitude."

"Does Cora Rae not know anything about you after working with you for what, like ten years or so? I know y'all are over there running your mouths when you are supposed to be working. Any halfway decent friend of yours knows that you like those blue-collared men. Strong hands and whatnot." Faith gave Paige a knowing sly smirk.

"Yes well, this guy did not change my mind about that. I ended up missing Matt more and going back and forth between being sad that he's gone and angry that he was taken away from me."

Even comparing her late husband to that too-tight suit wearing douche bag felt like an unforgivable insult to Matt. The whole date felt like a betrayal to his memory.

"I'm sorry girl. That really sucks. But don't let one bad experience stop you from trying to find love again." Faith leaned forward, resting her forearms on the counter. "I personally believe that everyone has more than one soulmate. And depending on where life takes them determines whether they cross paths with just one soulmate or more than one."

Faith the philosopher, ladies and gentlemen, Paige thought with a smile.

"I'll think about it," Paige said to get Faith off her back for a little while. She knew it wouldn't be the last time the subject of her romantic prospects came up in conversation with Faith.

Paige felt herself sinking into the discouraging thoughts that seemed to creep up on her from time to time. *What if I never meet another person I could possibly spend the rest of my life with? I'll die alone. But I doubt I'll ever find a man that I could trust completely around my kids, so what am I supposed to do? I'm a protective mama bear, but I'm also a woman with certain needs. How the hell am I supposed to balance the two?* Suddenly, Faith's voice snapped her out of her downward spiral.

"I'm going to take you thinking about it as a win and leave on a high note before the tide takes another turn," Faith said. She gathered up her huge green Michael Kors purse off the kitchen counter, gave Paige a tight hug, and headed towards the door.

"Call ya later, girl," Faith said over her shoulder as she walked out the bright yellow front door. The door had been one of Paige's many attempts at making her and the kids' world cheerier after Matt died. But it was just a door.

What Faith had said about having more than one soulmate stuck in Paige's mind, and as she stood in the middle of her kitchen holding a clean pot, she couldn't help but remember the other man she had thought was her soulmate...

The young driver of the little Honda Civic parked on the street curb in front of the house party and the four seventeen-year-old girls filed out, straightening clothes and running fingers through their hair. They wanted to make sure they looked perfect before heading inside.

"Ooh, there's Jake!" one of the girls exclaimed as she waved frantically at someone down the street.

"Jake who?" Paige asked, turning to see who her friend was so excited about.

"You know, Jake Bennett. He's from Summerville. Used to date Courtney Lee until he caught her cheating on him. He's nineteen, so I practically had to beg him to come to a Meadow Oaks High School house party," she explained.

"Uh huh," was all teenage Paige could get out. The boy, well technically young man, coming towards them was tall and lean muscled. She had recently gotten out of an unhealthy relationship with her manipulative asshole boyfriend, Brad, and the absolute last thing she wanted was to be attracted to another guy. But she couldn't deny feeling a tug in her chest as she watched him. This is going to be trouble, was all she could think.

The girls started walking towards Jake, with Paige bringing up the rear. They met up with him under a streetlight before going into the party. Paige tried to stay hidden behind one of the other girls while also sneaking glances at Jake. The glow of the streetlight illuminated his light blue eyes and slightly crooked nose. Paige eyed his sharply chiseled jawline and noticed that his bottom lip was a tad bigger than his upper lip. Dirty blond hair peeked out from under a worn-out baseball cap. He was gorgeous. Her stomach started doing flips.

Jake had noticed her as well. While the other girls led the way up to the house, he hung back and didn't start walking until she was next to him. "Hey, I'm Jake. We haven't met, I would have remembered," he said, smiling down at her.

"Um, I'm Paige. Nice to meet you," she answered nervously. She mentally chastised herself for the lame reply, but her self-esteem had taken a hit thanks to her ex, so she was unsure of herself. However, he continued to smile sweetly at her whenever she made eye contact and followed her into the party.

"Oh my God! Paige, Brad is here with his new girlfriend. That jerk promised me that he wasn't coming," her friend declared indignantly. She turned to Paige with pitiful puppy dog eyes. "Are you going to be okay? Do you want to leave?"

The other two girls followed her lead by giving Paige pitying looks and after a few seconds Paige wanted nothing more than to make herself as small as possible. Not because of Brad, but because the girls were making her seem like such a loser in front of Jake.

"Brad is looking over here. Quick...laugh or something so he doesn't know you're upset," one of the other girls said loud enough for the whole party to hear, even over the blaring music.

"I'm not upset at all. I honestly don't even care about Brad and his new girlfriend," Paige replied, feeling her face flush with embarrassment.

"Oh honey, it's okay to be feeling hurt. He literally just dumped you so he could date her instead," they continued mercilessly.

Paige really wanted to crawl in a hole and die. Suddenly, Jake pulled her against him in a tight embrace. She looked up at him in question, but he wasn't looking at her. He was looking over her shoulder at Brad, quietly giving him the stare down. Challenging him. Paige felt her heart melt a little. Her friends had made her feel foolish in their attempts to be supportive, but this stranger did not.

Paige laid her head on his chest and listened to his heartbeat. She allowed herself a moment to indulge in feeling safe with a guy for the first time in a long time. Wrapped up in his strong arms, against his rock-hard chest, being lulled by the steady rhythm of his heart was making her second guess her conviction to stay away from guys for a while. She put her hands on his biceps and felt heat rise up inside of her.

"That guy's an idiot if that's who he dumped you for," Jake said when he finally looked down at her. He had the sexiest deep voice Paige had ever heard. It sent shivers down her spine.

"It's nice of you to say that, but," Paige began as she lowered her gaze before she was cut off by Jake gently putting his finger under her chin, making her look back up at him.

"No, I'm being serious, he's a moron," Jake insisted, staring at her hard.

Paige noticed that he had green specks in his blue eyes, and for a minute let herself be bold as she kept the eye contact. With every passing moment she felt more and more sure that she needed him to be a part of her life. Needed his hands on her. It wasn't even a question of want. Her body felt like it was on fire, and she could feel her heart pounding in her ears. She had never felt anything so powerful.

"MOOOOOOM!"

Paige came back to the present startled by the scream of the pre-teen girl standing in front of her in a bright pink soccer uniform with her hand on her hip and an annoyed expression Paige was seeing way too often lately.

"Geez mom, I have been standing here forever trying to get your attention!"

Oh, the dramatics.

"Sorry Chloe, but I was having a great daydream," Paige teased in her best valley girl voice because she knew it got on her daughter's nerves.

"Mom, you are so weird. I'm gonna be late for my game," Chloe said exasperatedly, rolling her eyes.

"Well, you better go get in the car then. Where's your brother?"

The stomping of feet coming down the hardwood stairs gave her the answer. "In the car Henry before your sister throws a fit," Paige called out as she put the pot she had absentmindedly been clutching to her chest in the cupboard.

Six-year-old Henry laughed as he jumped down the last two stairs. He ran into the kitchen and threw his arms around her waist. "I think Chloe's mood swings are getting worse, Mom," he confided to Paige.

Paige sighed and looked down at her son. Henry was a miniature version of his late father with his curly brown hair, deep brown eyes, and cute button nose. *I'm so happy I get this obvious part of Matt to hold onto,* she thought. She kissed the top of his head and nudged him gently out the door.

Chloe was impatiently waiting buckled in the front seat of Paige's white Volvo SUV. Paige looked over her daughter as she had Henry a moment before. Chloe had also inherited the curly brown hair from her father but got her mom's bright green eyes and sharp nose. She was a beauty. Paige admired her daughter's strong sense of self and prayed she never lost it. Especially because of some boy. Her reminiscing about the past brought near future worries to the forefront.

Paige put in extra effort at Chloe's soccer game to socialize with the other parents in between plays. She knew that wasn't precisely what Faith had meant when she said Paige should "get back out there", but a little practice couldn't hurt. She had to admit that she was a bit rusty at socializing. She smiled when it was expected and laughed at jokes even when she didn't really find them funny.

During the plays, while the other parents were occupied with watching their kids run up and down the field, she contemplated her situation. *I'm not depressed, just sad sometimes. Damn Faith for making me talk about what is missing in my life. Yes, there is another side of me besides just a widowed mom. Of course I miss having male companionship. That daydream sure didn't help. Freaking Jake. Chloe interrupting was a blessing. No need to go back down that road with its sharp turns and blind curves. Freaking Jake.*

"Can we spend the night at Nana and Pop's house tonight? Nana is supposed to teach me how to make her molasses cookies," Chloe stated as she plopped down on the grass next to Paige to take off her cleats after her game.

"Well, good game to you, and yes I suppose if it is okay with them, then it's ok with me."

"Yes! Yes! And I'll taste test the cookies!" Henry declared, jumping up and down.

"You should have a girls' night with Aunt Faith and Aunt Sadie," Chloe suggested.

Paige looked down at her daughter, a little puzzled and then it clicked. "Were you listening to my conversation with Aunt Faith this morning?"

"Maybe just a little. But I still think it is a good idea. The going out with your friends part. I stopped listening when she started talking about you dating. That's just icky," Chloe said as she crinkled her nose in disgust.

"Serves you right for eavesdropping. It might not be a bad idea though. The whole going out with the girls. It has been a long time since I've done that."

"Oh, we know," Chloe and Henry said in unison.

"Alright, enough from you two wise guys," Paige chuckled, leading her kids back to their car. On the way home, she listened to the local pop station, getting herself pumped for a night out with her two best friends.

Paige woke up abruptly the next morning to her cell phone ringing way too loudly, setting off a splitting headache. She rolled towards the obnoxious ear-piercing noise and blindly threw out her hand trying to find her phone on the nightstand. She knew better than to try to open her eyes all the way. Paige squinted at the screen long enough to see that it was her mom and answered the call.

"Hey Mom. Are the kids alright?"

Sherry Hawkins chuckled at the sound of her daughter's voice. "I haven't heard you sound like this since your early twenties."

Paige knew her mom had been worried when Matt passed away that Paige might turn to drowning her sorrows in alcohol like people do sometimes, but that didn't happen. Sherry had said many not so silent thank-yous to the heavens above, in front of Paige, that Sadie was a doctor and made sure she sought proper treatment to help deal with the loss of her husband.

"The kids are perfectly fine sweetie. It is almost noon though so I just wanted to know if I should feed them lunch in a bit or if you were on the way, but I think I already know the answer," her mom teased.

"Sorry, mama. I slept in."

Paige covered her eyes with her arm to block out the light trying to sneak through her closed eyelids. She desperately needed some water and a couple of ibuprofen.

"Oh, no worries, honey. I just didn't want to interfere with any plans you might have. Take your time and we will see you later this afternoon."

As they hung up, Paige pictured her mom in her mind. Her mom would go to the kitchen to see what she had to make for her grandchildren for lunch. The kids were probably outside helping their grandpa in the vegetable garden and would be starving by the time he finally gave them a break. It made her heart happy to think about her dad bonding with her children over churned soil and making things grow that would eventually nourish their bodies.

As the throbbing in her head regained her attention, Paige seriously considered throwing a pillow over her head and going back to sleep. *Ugh! How did I let myself get so bad? I am way too old for such nonsense,* she reminded herself.

Knowing that she should at least get up and drink some water, she threw off her covers and stumbled downstairs to the kitchen. The first glass of water went down fast so she got a second one to take back to her room. She got the much-needed ibuprofen out of her bathroom medicine cabinet and tucked herself back under the blankets. As she laid there waiting for the throbbing in her head to subside, she began to recall the events of the night before and jokingly blamed Faith and Sadie for her current condition.

The three friends had decided to go all out since it was the first time Paige had agreed to a girls' night in years. There wasn't much to do in their small town of Meadow Oaks, so Paige and Faith decided to meet up at Paige's house and then Uber into Charleston to meet Sadie for dinner and drinks.

When Faith arrived at Paige's house, she walked right in and stopped cold in the foyer at the sight of Paige cleaning her living room coffee table. She was completely bummed to see that Paige was wearing a faded t-shirt and old stretched out jeans.

"Dang girl, I thought it's supposed to be a fun girls' night out, not a sad night in," Faith exclaimed, not bothering to hide her disappointment. "Why did you even bother putting on make-up if that's what you are going to wear?"

"Ha-ha, don't worry, I know better. I couldn't decide between two dresses, so I wanted to wait and get your opinion," Paige reassured her friend. She led Faith up the stairs to her walk-in closet.

"Oh goodie, you have finally come to your senses," Faith cooed cheerfully, her mood turning around instantly.

Since one of the dresses was practically the same color as the bright fuchsia one Faith was wearing, it was a no-brainer for Paige to wear the emerald sundress that really brought out her eyes. It also showed a good amount of skin with its low cut back.

"Ooh la la! That dress is such a gorgeous color, and it gives a little peek at that dragonfly tattoo you have on your lower back," Faith commented as Paige did a little twirl for her.

"Yes well, eighteen-year-old me thought it was a great idea," Paige scoffed.

"I thought you always said you didn't regret it?"

"I don't regret the tattoo itself. Just the placement. I can't really see it back there and there's the whole tramp stamp thing. Oh well, that's spring break in Myrtle Beach for ya," Paige shrugged.

Outside a car horn beeped. "The Uber is here! Let's go have some fun!" Faith grabbed Paige's hand and pulled her through the house and out the front door.

Half an hour later, they met Sadie in front of Florence's for dinner. She was looking fabulous as always in a deep blue strapless dress with super high silver heels. The bold colors looked amazing on her smooth dark chocolate skin.

"Damn, Sadie! You look smokin' hot!" Paige exclaimed, smiling ear to ear at her other best friend.

"Oh, you know me, I always take advantage of any event where I don't have to wear scrubs and sensible shoes! I may cut people's chests open for a living, but that doesn't mean I can't walk a sidewalk like a supermodel on a runway!" Sadie replied sassily.

"I know that's right!" Faith chimed in.

"Girls, let's get us some jambalaya in our stomachs so we can go man-hunting!" Sadie shouted with a big mischievous grin.

"Oh no, this is a girls' night. I didn't say anything about finding a man," Paige shrieked, a look of faux horror on her face. "I knew I should have worn those old baggy jeans instead," Paige teased.

Faith and Sadie busted out laughing and continued to do so all the way through the door of the restaurant. Quite a few patrons turned to look at the three beautiful ladies and smiled.

Once they had been seated at their table and ordered their jambalayas and cocktails, Sadie and Faith started grilling Paige about what kind of man she'd be interested in dating, and they jokingly began to point out possible candidates among the men nearby that were not sitting with a woman.

"Seriously y'all, I didn't come out tonight to talk about men. I came to spend time with my two best friends and to not have to worry about anything for a little while," Paige insisted.

"And what about the secret date you had that Faith told me about? You know that's not safe. Someone needs to know where you are," Sadie went on without acknowledging what Paige had said.

"Cora Rae knew where I was, so that wasn't an issue," Paige replied.

The drinks arrived at that moment and Paige practically chugged her lemon drop martini. When she got done coughing and sputtering from the burn of the alcohol down her throat, Paige continued to defend herself to her friends.

"The date wasn't a big deal, but I knew if I told you two it would make this random guy mean more than he should at that point," she argued.

"First off, you know that Cora Rae doesn't count, it has to be one of us," Sadie started to reply back.

"And it's not about the guy," Faith interjected. "It's about *you*. Even if it was just a toe dipped in the water it is a big deal. You've been through so much and to take that step and put yourself out there is huge. We are so proud of you. We want to be there for you, for the good dates and the bad," Faith explained as she reached over and gave Paige's hand a reassuring squeeze.

"I get it, I do. And thank you guys for always being here for me."

Paige was already working on her second martini, and it was starting to loosen her tongue. She found herself telling them about the memories of Jake that her earlier conversation with Faith had brought to mind. Around mouthfuls of the best southern food, she told them about the high school party and the amazing friendship that bloomed from that first meeting with Jake.

"Just friendship?" Faith asked, wagging her eyebrows.

"Best friends. We talked on the phone every day. If I had a bad day, he would find a way to leave a sweet note on my car, even though the drive over to Meadow Oaks would be out of his way. He even watched a few episodes of Buffy the Vampire Slayer to try to understand why I was so obsessed with it that I would stay up late and risk getting in trouble with my parents. He even had my picture in his room and would tell any guy that noticed it to back off. I'll admit that I was smitten."

"He sounds like the perfect guy. Why didn't you just go for it?" Sadie questioned.

"Well, my previous relationship was with Brad, so I was more reserved around Jake than I normally would have been, especially in person. Over the phone I was more myself, but still."

"Ugh! I remember you telling us about Brad. What a jerk," Sadie grumbled.

"Yeah, he's lucky we never met him. I would have kicked him in the shins," Faith added.

"*I* should have kicked him in the shins back in high school," Paige agreed.

"Back to Jake please," Sadie requested to get them back on track. "So nothing ever happened romantically?"

Paige grinned. "As a matter of fact, something did. I used to sleepover at his house almost every weekend. Platonically, of course. But one night after a couple of months of hanging out, he turned to me while we were laying in his bed, and I could tell by the heated look in his eyes that things were about to change. He gave me a sweet sexy smile that melted my insides and slowly leaned in to kiss me. Then he leaned back a little to ask me if that was okay. I knew that I was supposed to say that we shouldn't risk ruining our friendship, but that's totally not what I said. I said 'yes, definitely' and then we just went for each other simultaneously, deepening the kiss." Paige paused to take a sip of her drink.

"And then what happened? We must know!" Sadie cheered.

Faith and Sadie were practically sitting on the edge of their seats from all the anticipation. It had been a long time since any of them had experienced that giddy feeling of early love and attraction. Remembering the rush of lust that had gone through her that night with Jake when she had realized what was about to happen sent heat through her entire body.

"Oh, it was so long ago, I'm not sure I can remember," Paige teased her friends.

Paige hadn't had this much fun in a long time. The drinks didn't hurt either. She rarely got to drink alcohol, so she was enjoying the buzz.

"Come on girl, don't leave us hanging! Was it just a kiss or two, or was there more?" Sadie was never one to shy away from getting the juicy details.

"I'll only tell y'all if we can go to Red's and get more drinks!"

Paige wasn't ready to go down that road quite yet. She also wasn't ready for the night to end. They settled their checks and headed to the waterfront in a taxi for more drinks and girl time.

Sitting outside at a table overlooking the water bathed in silver moonlight, Sadie and Faith could hardly wait for their first Hurricanes to come before they started trying to pull more details out of Paige.

"You can't do this to us. You can't tell us that you were in bed with a hot guy you'd been crushing on for months, who sounds pretty amazing by the way, and not finish the story," Sadie urged impatiently.

"Everything definitely started out amazing, but it didn't quite end up that way. That's a different story for another time. Only happy memories tonight." Paige dismissed the thought with the wave of her hand. "Anyways, kissing turned into...well, more. *A lot more.*"

Paige got a little thrill as her friends did a little happy dance and clap move.

"I don't think either one of us expected to have as much chemistry as we did. It was so hot and intense. With Brad, it had been kind of... methodical, you know? With Jake, it had been primal, like we were both in desperate need of what only the other one could give." Paige paused to take a sip of her drink before continuing. "Without getting too graphic, let me just say he was a genius with his tongue, and when we were done, he lit his cigarette backwards."

Paige smiled at the memory that had played on her highlight reel more than once. Seventeen-year-old Paige had been very impressed by her own sexual prowess.

"I think I need a cigarette now and I've never even smoked before." Faith giggled and fanned herself. "So why didn't it work out?" Straight to the point as always.

Paige's smile faltered. "I said only happy thoughts tonight."

"Fair enough, but why is this the first time we are hearing about Jake? We've been friends for years and shared so many stories. How did this one not come up?" Sadie asked.

Too smart for her own good, Paige thought to herself.

"Well, I believe y'all know him as Bennett," Paige admitted.

"The guy you went home to see on the weekends back in college? The one that you swore up and down was just a friend? It might be the alcohol, but I am so confused right now," Faith exclaimed, shaking her head side to side like she was trying to clear fog from her brain.

"Explain yourself please," Sadie simply said.

"Hmmm, where to start." Paige stalled a minute trying to come up with a reasonable explanation for her past deception. "To explain the whole situation, I would have to go into the not happy details of what happened with Jake, and I'd rather not do that tonight. Long story short, when things didn't exactly work out we spent some time apart, but later we became friends again. One of his new buddies called him by his last name, Bennett. Jake hated it, so I would do it whenever I was not feeling gracious towards him. Honestly though, calling him Bennett helped me hide my feelings about him from y'all. Just saying or hearing the name Jake makes me have some kind of emotional and physical reaction. It's hard to explain."

"Is that why you never invited us to go home with you on the weekends? I always thought that was a little weird," Faith said, pointing her finger at Paige.

"No, that was not it at all. You forget what overachievers you two were in college," Paige teased, trying to change the subject off of her history with Jake.

"Uh-huh. I see what you tried to do there, and that's ok. I'll let you get away with it this time but know that we will be continuing this conversation later," Sadie declared.

"I'll drink to that!" Faith said, lifting her glass in the air. The three friends tapped their glasses and broke out in laughter once again.

The friends had another round of fruity drinks and spoke of work and Faith's husband Travis and his obsession with his fantasy baseball league. Paige knew that Faith and Sadie were both keeping a close eye on her. She tried her best to look happy on the surface, and for the most part she was. The part that wasn't happy was haunted by the past with Jake and plagued with guilt since it was her first time speaking about lusting after another man since Matt died. But maybe that meant she was making progress in the process of moving on with her life.

***

When Paige and Faith got back to Meadow Oaks, Faith's husband was waiting in Paige's driveway to take her home. Travis laughed as the two friends stumbled out of their Uber, giggling, and clinging to each other for balance so that they wouldn't face plant in the bushes. He was ecstatic to see that the women had fun on their night out. Faith loved what a good sport he was about everything.

Travis had been to a buddy's house to watch an Atlanta Braves baseball game and was giving Faith a play by play in the car on the way to their house. She was nodding and smiling like she usually did when he went on and on about baseball. Personally, she found the sport dreadfully boring, but she knew how much it meant to Travis, so she acted interested in it for his sake.

When it got to the point that Faith knew Travis wouldn't realize she had zoned out, she laid her forehead on the cool window and started thinking about Paige's story. *Obviously, something had happened between Paige and Jake that had spoiled their relationship. They had been pretty young, so maybe it was the sort of conflict that could be attributed to something as normal as immaturity,* she reasoned.

Faith thought back to their college days remembering how Paige spent almost every free weekend with "Bennett." *What a trickster that Paige is.* She would need to find out exactly what happened. Not that she thought Paige should end up with Jake or anything serious like that. The past was the past for a reason. However, if they had that much chemistry, maybe running into him would jumpstart her friend's libido and therefore increase her efforts to try to date. The bad date Cora Rae had set her up on didn't count. Maybe she'd do some snooping on social media to find out a little bit more about this Jake fellow. The rest of the way home Faith formulated a plan.

CHAPTER FOUR

On Wednesday morning, finally fully recovered from her girls' night out, Paige was sitting behind her desk at the offices of the popular South Carolina Society Magazine, where she held the Editor-in-Chief position, when Cora Rae walked in. They were hired onto the magazine around the same time about a decade ago. Back then, Paige had written for the travel section.

Cora Rae covered weddings and had no desire to ever change that. She loved everything about the big showy weddings that merit an article in the magazine. Paige had to admit that Cora Rae's passion for the flashy events helped make Cora Rae better at her job than would be expected of the good-natured, but sometimes dim, woman. Brides all but promised their first-born child to get Cora Rae Summers to feature them.

"Hey, can you look at this piece I am doing on the McKenzie wedding? I don't feel like the wording is quite right in the fourth paragraph and I'm having a bit of writer's block," Cora Rae asked as she held out a printed copy of her article towards Paige.

While Paige read over Cora Rae's work, she tapped a red editing pen on her lips. Her coworkers that had been around a while would teasingly tell the new hires that when she tapped her pen on her lips like that it meant she was in an amiable mood and would be open to getting chatty. Being as Cora Rae had been around a long time, the woman took it as her opening to ask about the date she had set Paige up on, much to Paige's dismay.

"So, you haven't really told me much about your date with Gary. I was hoping that you two would hit it off," Cora Rae began cautiously.

Paige paused the pen tapping and pursed her lips. She was trying to think of a diplomatic way to tell Cora Rae that Gary was an ass.

"I think you need to switch these sentences around here and add a few more mushy details about the groom's face lighting up when he first saw his blushing bride coming down the aisle, and then it will be perfect," Paige said as she made some notes in the margins on the paper and handed it back to Cora Rae.

"As for Gary, we didn't really have a connection. I appreciate the thought though."

Paige sent up a silent prayer that Cora Rae would let it go without trying to convince Paige to give Gary the ass another chance. She had no desire to hurt Cora Rae's feelings, but she wasn't going to discuss her love life, or lack thereof, with Cora Rae anymore. She had slipped up and done so once and ended up on a miserable date. Not going to happen again. Ever.

Luckily, Cora Rae nodded and said, "fair enough. I'm just so proud of you for getting out there and trying. I figured Gary probably wasn't the one for you, but I believe that you deserve to find a forever kind of love again, like what I hope to have with a special someone sometime in the near future." Cora Rae smiled dreamily, then shook herself back to the present. "I'll make these changes and get the article finished up by this afternoon. Thanks, Paige."

Paige simply smiled at Cora Rae in response. Cora Rae started to leave Paige's office, but her path was blocked by another staff writer entering the doorway.

"Oh, hey Stacey! You coming to bend Paige's ear too?" Cora Rae chirped. "Paige, that reminds me, would you like to join me for lunch in a bit? I was going to ask Stacey here to come too."

"Thanks for the offer, Cora Rae, but I brought mine today so I can keep working on getting this month's issue out while I eat."

"Sorry Cora Rae, but I'm going to have to pass this time too. I want to get a jump on researching my next article," Stacey added. "I'm just dropping off an expense request form for Paige to sign."

Paige silently took the form from Stacey, hoping to politely discourage further conversation. She didn't know Stacey very well on a personal level. Stacey had only been at the magazine for about a year and kept to herself mostly. Since Paige didn't know how much of the conversation with Cora Rae Stacey had overheard, Paige wasn't choosing that moment to get personal. Luckily, Stacey handed over the form, turned on her heel after giving Paige a little nod, and headed back to her work area.

Paige sat back down at her desk and tried to focus on the layout she had been working on before Cora Rae walked in. After multiple failed attempts to get back on track, she gave up and let her mind drift. Sadie and Faith had been dropping not so subtle hints that she should set up one of those online dating profiles so that they could help her pick out men on the internet. It seemed kind of shallow to think of it like that. What would she even put in her profile? "*Sad widow with two kids who are her whole world, so you probably won't get much attention?*" Wasn't exactly going to have the fellas lining up for a chance to date her. She didn't think she could ever let a stranger she met on an app anywhere near Chloe and Henry. But how else was she supposed to "get back out there" as they say? Would she even know how to date?

The dating scene seemed even more complicated than it used to be when she was in her twenties. A couple of nights before, while nursing her hangover, she watched a Netflix documentary about catfishing. She thought she had chosen an innocent, relaxing movie about actual fishing and ended up learning something she never wanted to know that amped up her anxiety about dating even more. Now that she had gone down that rabbit hole and sufficiently freaked herself out, she decided to call Faith to see if she could get her mind on something else.

"Hey girl! I just walked in my office to call you!" Faith answered cheerfully.

Faith was sitting in her office so she could have some privacy at the daycare center she owned in Meadow Oaks. Happy Littles Learning Center was her dream come true. Faith might not have been able to have her own children due to infertility issues, but she found joy in making sure other kids got a great start in life.

"Oh yeah? What's up?" Paige asked as she got up out of her chair and walked over to the window and peered down at the busy city street below.

"Oh nothing, except that I met the man of your dreams only a few minutes ago!" Faith teased.

"Funny you say that. A few seconds ago I was thinking about what it would be like trying to online date and about had a panic attack."

"Ugh, I know what you mean. I don't envy you having to try to date these days. But anyways, this single dad recently moved here with his daughter, and he is a real catch. I just got done giving them a tour of the center. He is hot. Like Rip from Yellowstone hot. Paige, I am telling you, he is exactly your type, bearded and blue-collar. He was a little shy, but polite and it was obvious that he is an amazing dad. His little girl was literally the sweetest thing. I've only met him this once, but you know I can tell these things right away. Not to toot my own horn, but I am an excellent judge of character."

"Wouldn't it be unprofessional of you to try to set up one of your clients or parents or whatever you call them with your friend? Isn't there some sort of rule or code about that?"

Paige wasn't sure she wanted to be set up again. It had to be better than internet dating though, right?

"This is a small town, and you know it doesn't work like that here. You better scoop him up before some other hot mama does. Women are going to be all over him like flies on honey," Faith replied.

Paige could hear Faith toss a file on her desk and then she got serious.

"His name is Mason Pruitt, he is thirty-four, he works in construction, his daughter is three years old, and her name is Anna-Grace. He has been divorced a little over a year and has full custody of his daughter. He didn't say what happened with that but give me time and I'll find out," Faith assured Paige.

"Ok, well you find out and I'll consider it. Would you and Travis want to come over later for dinner with me and the kids? This is the only night we don't have to be at soccer or karate or one of the other million activities these kids have going on," Paige said, expertly changing the subject.

Paige hoped she said yes. The kids loved spending time with Auntie Faith and Uncle Travis. "We're having tacos!" Paige added excitedly, knowing Faith's love for tacos.

"Yeah, we'll be there. I better get back to work, the after-school crowd is coming in," Faith answered hurriedly.

"Ok, see you later!" Paige replied just as quickly, knowing her friend was about to have her hands full with kids burning off energy after sitting in a classroom all day. With a heavy sigh, Paige tried to get back to work.

***

Faith hung up with Paige and went out to greet the elementary school kids as they filed one by one off of the bus. While she smiled and ushered kids inside, she thought about how to get more information out of Mason without scaring the guy off. She hadn't forgotten about her plan she had decided on with Jake, but options were always a plus and Mason was too good to pass up.

Faith had been doing some digging on Jake over the past couple of days. She could tell from his social media that he was good looking in a rugged sort of way, divorced, had a teenage son, and owned his own surveying company. She tried to reconcile the information about Jake with what she knew about "Bennett" from back when her, Paige, and Sadie were in college. She remembered seeing a picture of "Bennett" and thinking he was smoking hot. Faith also remembered teasing Paige about having such an attractive guy friend and asking if she was sure that's all there was to it. Paige had sworn that there was nothing going on and seemed a little defensive, so Faith had let it go. *She wouldn't get away with that these days. I know her too well,* Faith thought.

Paige had been right about Sadie and Faith being overachievers in college. They both spent their weekends studying or volunteering somewhere near campus. Not that Paige had been a slacker, she did all of her weekend studying at home in Meadow Oaks back in those days. Sunday night she would always show up in the dorm with clean laundry, her assignments done, and tales of bonfire parties out in the woods with friends. It had sounded like so much fun, but Faith loved spending time with children who needed their day brightened.

Faith was not originally from Meadow Oaks like Paige, or from Charleston like Sadie. She only moved to the small town to be near Paige and Sadie after graduation. She ended up loving the small town and put down roots. Then she met Travis, fell in love and got married. Faith smiled to herself thinking of the beautiful life they built together.

The next night, Paige was sitting on a bench at the local dojo watching Henry run through his karate drills when Faith popped in.

"Hey! I wasn't expecting to see you tonight. I figured you got enough of my crew last night," Paige said as Faith sat down next to her on the bench for the parents and siblings.

"Never. I have the most exciting news for you and couldn't wait another minute to tell you!" Faith exclaimed in hushed excitement trying not to disturb the kids down on the mats.

"Well, don't keep me waiting, tell me!" Paige whispered back.

"I set you up on a date with Mason!"

Faith watched her friend closely to gauge her reaction, which was Paige sputtering up the water she was sipping on.

"What do you mean? When?" Paige questioned warily, wiping the water droplets off of her chin.

"Well, I wanted it to be tomorrow night so you wouldn't have time to talk yourself out of it, but I know you'll be working all night to get next month's issue finalized to perfection, so next Friday at Lorenzo's Italian Restaurant. He'll meet you there at seven-thirty sharp. That gives you plenty of time to make any hair or waxing appointments you feel necessary. And anytime you feel yourself trying to come up with excuses to get out of it, call me, and I'll remind you of all the reasons you should go," Faith finished, and smiled at her friend trying to encourage her to agree to the date.

Faith could see that Paige was quickly thinking of a hundred different ways to decline or delay, but in the end, Paige gave in.

"What do you think I'm going to be doing on this date that I will be needing a wax, huh? What kind of lady do you take me for?" Paige said in her best proper southern belle voice, raising a hand to her chest and widening her eyes in mock offense.

"Yes! I promise you won't regret it. He seems great. When I was telling him about you, he didn't ask any of the shallow questions some guys ask. Or at least what I've heard watching my stories. Anyways, Mason says that I seem like a smart woman and therefore he trusts my judgement." Faith couldn't help but grin remembering that fine looking man smooth-talking her.

"Oh, that's why you like him so much. I see now." Paige laughed good-naturedly and shook her head at Faith.

Faith loved that Paige was having a great time "talking boys". It was like their old college days. Well, except for back then Paige would apparently omit the truth about the only "boy" that really mattered to her. Until she met Matt that is. *I'm sure she had her reasons,* Faith reminded herself silently.

"Ok, well let me know if you need help deciding what to wear. And you already know that you are going to have to tell me and Sadie everything afterwards! Now that I have accomplished my mission, I gotta go meet Travis for supper," Faith said as she hopped up from the bench.

Faith waved goodbye to Henry down on the bright red mats and made her way out the door to meet her husband for sushi over in Charleston.

Faith felt a little guilty that she had failed to mention to Paige that she was the one who suggested Lorenzo's to Mason for their date. Normally, that would not be a big deal, but she had actually gotten the idea from Jake's Facebook page. She had been lightly snooping and came across a post he was tagged in, that luckily was set to public, with comments from some of his high school buddies who were coming back to their hometown for a visit and were meeting there at seven the following Friday. Faith was absolutely rooting for Mason. Her curiosity about Jake and Paige was getting the best of her though. She could hardly wait until next Friday to come and go so that she could get Paige to give her the scoop on both men.

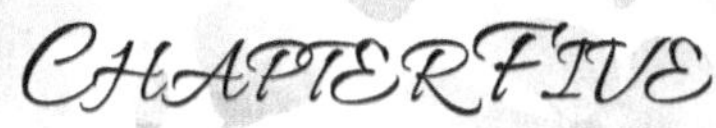

CHAPTER FIVE

On the way back into Meadow Oaks from her office in Charleston the following Friday night, Paige tried not to think about the fact that she was off to have dinner with a man she'd never met before. A man that her best friend thought was perfect for her. It felt like there was a lot of pressure for the date to go well. Her kids were staying with their grandparents, so to keep herself occupied she worked right up until time to leave for the date so she couldn't talk herself out of going. Faith would never let her hear the end of it if she cancelled.

Paige had to admit that she looked hot. She had followed Faith's advice and made that hair appointment. And the waxing appointment. A proper southern woman had to be prepared for anything, right?

As Paige approached the restaurant nestled in-between a used bookstore and a bakery, it was hard to miss the tall, ruggedly handsome man waiting outside. Damn, he made a Henley shirt and jeans look way more provocative than they should. Paige sent Faith a mental thank you and found a parking spot. A quick peek in the visor mirror to check her hair and make-up one last time and she was ready to go. She was suddenly super excited about the blind date.

***

Jake saw her walk into Lorenzo's. He was sitting in the bar area with a few of his old high school buddies and some inner awareness pulled his glance towards the entrance the moment she came through it. He couldn't take his eyes off her. He felt that familiar ache deep in his chest that he got whenever he saw her. Somewhere in the back of Jake's mind it registered that she was there with a date, *tall lucky bastard*, but she was all that mattered at that moment. He took a swig of his beer, but the taste of the IPA didn't even register.

As far as Paige knew, it had been many years since they'd seen each other. That was not the case. They both lived in the same small town, so it was inevitable that they would be in the same place at the same time. Her working in Charleston and Jake travelling around the area for work did help him keep his distance a bit, but he would see her around town every now and then. When that would happen he would wait in his truck with his chest aching and his stomach turning until she drove away before he would get out. It's not that he didn't want to talk to her. He was dying to. But the urge to touch her anytime she was near was way too strong and he had been trying to do right by her since she was a married woman.

When she lost her husband, Jake had wanted to be there to comfort her, but things were complicated. His reminiscing about the past didn't keep him from remembering that her situation had changed, and she was no longer off limits. Something that felt like hope bloomed in his chest.

Jake kept an eye on her while she sat with her date in the dining area. Both Paige and her date, *tall lucky bastard*, seemed a little stiff and awkward, so maybe it was only a first or second date. Nothing too serious, hopefully. Dang, she looked tempting in those tight jeans and her almost sheer top. Paige had always been talented at toeing the line of seductive yet classy. After a while he saw her get up from her table to go to the ladies' room and before he knew what he was doing, he was following her to the back hallway that led to the restrooms.

***

Paige was actually having a fantastic time! Mason was sweet, smart, and funny. It didn't hurt that he was sexy as hell either. She was definitely going to have to thank Faith for the setup. Faith was right about Mason seeming perfect for her. She could see herself possibly having a future with him. She checked her make-up in the mirror in the ladies' room and headed back out to her date. As she opened the door to exit the restroom, she turned her head and stopped dead in her tracks.

Before the days of social media, when a person would run into a past love they hadn't seen in a long time, it would be a surprise or a shock. Their heart would race in their chest. They would measure them up, note the changes. In the age of Facebook and Instagram, people see the faces of their past and what was going on in their lives almost daily. They'd become desensitized. However, that was not the case when Paige saw him. Thanks to the internet, she already knew about the crow's feet around his eyes and the grey hairs at his temple; the changes making him even more attractive, more like a man than a nineteen-year-old boy. Seeing Jake up close made Paige feel like a flustered seventeen-year-old girl again, not the self-assured woman she had become.

"Hey stranger," Jake said as he put his hands in the pockets of his jeans.

Paige tracked the movement and drank in the sight of him in the well-fitted denim. And that voice. That deep, sexy as sin voice with that sensual southern drawl. Paige was an absolute sucker for it. Whenever he spoke it was like smooth whiskey spreading warmth through her all the way down to the tips of her toes. His voice might actually be what she had missed the most about him.

"Hey yourself. How have you been?" Paige mentally kicked herself. Was that really the best she could come up with after more than ten years of not seeing him? Damn, he looked hot.

"I've been alright. Started my own business doing surveying. I get to spend my weekends fishing and tinkering in the garage with Caleb."

Paige stood frozen as Jake took a few seconds to look her over before he continued.

"I was sorry to hear about Matt. I wanted to reach out to you so many times, I just wasn't sure what to do," Jake said, almost pleadingly as he took a step towards her.

"Thanks for saying that, Jake. My friends Faith and Sadie took care of the house and kids. Other than that, there wasn't really anything anyone could do. It was pretty rough for a long time."

Why was she telling him all that? She hadn't spoken to the man in years, so why did it feel like she was talking to her best friend in the whole world and could say exactly what she was thinking?

"I definitely want to hear more about Caleb. He's almost all grown up now and I hate that I missed it. But I do need to be getting back to my table. He's going to think I climbed out the restroom window or something."

Paige turned to look over her left shoulder as she sensed someone walking by the entrance to the hallway, but no one was there. *Maybe Mason is looking for me,* she thought as she turned back to face Jake.

"Oh yeah, sure." He paused, never taking his eyes off her. "Can I ask you something really quick?" Jake requested as he took another step towards her.

Jake seemed to be losing some sort of inner battle as their time together was coming to an end. He looked a bit frantic. Afraid that her voice would reveal the surge of emotion that she was suddenly feeling in her chest, she looked at him with wide eyes and nodded her assent.

He asked softly, "May I hug you?"

Paige didn't say anything. She still didn't trust her voice to not betray how much she wanted, no, *needed* to be held by him. She simply closed the remaining distance between them and reached up to put her arms around his neck. As Jake slid his strong arms around her waist, Paige laid her head on his chest and closed her eyes. They were still a perfect fit. He felt like home. Her heart started racing in her chest. Her body came alive like a hotwire. It felt like every nerve ending was tingling. The only part of her body not going crazy was her head. Paige's brain was very clear on what it wanted her to do, which was to run her tongue up the side of his neck to nibble on his ear while her hands explored his thickly muscled arms and chest.

Jake moved his mouth next to her ear and whispered, "I've missed you, Paige."

Paige sighed and pulled away from Jake's warm embrace. The spell had been broken.

"I really should be heading back to my table now. It was great seeing you, Jake," Paige said as she turned away and headed back towards the dining area.

Paige risked a glance behind her to look at Jake one more time, and he was still watching her. When she met his eyes, he nodded and gave her a sweet smile and headed back to the bar area. Jake's words had been like ice water dumped on her head. She felt guilty for letting herself get caught up in her old feelings for Jake while she was on a date with another man. A seemingly amazing man who hadn't broken her heart over and over.

Paige sat back down across from Mason in the cushy booth and pleaded, "Please forgive me for taking so long. I ran into an old friend. I didn't mean to be rude."

"That's small-town life, right? It's part of the reason I moved here from Charleston. I figured it had to be a great place for Anna-Grace to grow up," Mason replied cheerfully.

Paige wanted to know more about Anna-Grace, so Mason told her all about his high-spirited daughter and her "threenager" antics.

"Anna-Grace is a backseat driver. She's always yelling at me that I'm going the wrong way or that I'm driving too slow. It's such a trip!"

"Oh my goodness! That reminds me of Chloe at that age. She might settle down for a few years, but it will definitely be like that when she is a pre-teen too. It will just be less cute and more angsty," Paige laughed. But then the ever-present mom worry creeped up to the front of her mind. "I can't get Chloe to relax and have a good time to save my life. Everything is *so* serious at her age, but she's just a child."

"Oh, I'm sure with a great mom like you she'll find her way just fine. Those middle school years are tough. What about your son? How old is he?" Mason asked.

"Henry is six and is resilient for sure. He misses his dad of course, but he's young enough that he still finds joy in the things he should. He's quite a jokester. Keeps a smile on my face." Paige smiled thinking of her sweet boy.

Mason had begun talking again, but Paige's mind had wandered to another precious little boy who she had cared deeply for. Jake's son, Caleb.

"Uh, Paige? Everything ok?" Mason asked nervously.

"Huh? Oh yes, fine. I guess I zoned out thinking about the kids. I'm so sorry," Paige said sweetly, attempting to recover the situation.

Paige was trying her best to give Mason her undivided attention, but she kept catching her mind wandering. She felt restless and couldn't seem to regain her composure. She was sure Mason could tell the change in her demeanor since she had come back to the table from the restroom. She couldn't stop herself from fidgeting as she struggled to not look over at the bar area. Paige could feel eyes on her, and the sensation was making her warm all over.

Paige was relieved when the check had been paid and they finally walked outside into the cool night air. It had taken every ounce of her willpower to not look back at where Jake was sitting one last time before walking out of the restaurant door. Once outside where Jake couldn't possibly see her, Paige felt like she could finally take a deep breath.

Mason insisted on escorting her to her car like the perfect gentleman that he was, his hand pressing gently on the small of her back.

"I had a wonderful time tonight, Paige. I would love to see you again. If that would be something you are interested in of course and maybe next time I'll do a better job of talking about something other than my daughter. She's my whole world right now, you know?" Mason said earnestly as he turned towards her and took one of her soft hands in his rough callused ones.

"Oh, don't worry. I completely understand. I'm constantly having to remind myself that I am more than just Chloe and Henry's mom. Even though that definitely comes first. But yes, I would love to go out with you again. I've been telling myself all night that I was going to have to thank Faith for setting us up."

"I was thinking the same thing. You live up to everything Faith said about you. I've been looking for a woman who was intelligent with a kind heart. I'm also not above noticing that you have a backside I'm dying to get both of my hands on."

Paige blushed and gave Mason her best coy smile. It was flattering to be noticed in a womanly way again. She hadn't done the dating thing in a while, successfully that is, so between that and the interaction with Jake she was feeling a little nervous and off-kilter. Seeing Mason again, however, was one thing she was sure of.

Paige glanced around the parking lot, out of nowhere getting that creepy feeling one gets when their instincts are telling them that they are being watched. When she made eye contact with Mason again, he leaned in towards her slowly and the wary feeling was forgotten. At first, he softly kissed her cheek. His dark, full beard scratching pleasantly along the side of her face. Paige turned her head to the side towards him and their lips met. He was a talented kisser. He put one hand firmly on her waist and pulled her in a little closer. Paige had to admit that he was crazy hot and there was definitely a spark. *With Jake it's Fourth of July finale fireworks,* her traitorous mind whispered. Paige pushed the intrusive thought from her mind and focused on the present.

"Wow! Well, I'd say we definitely have chemistry," Mason exclaimed when they finally pulled away from each other. "Goodnight, Paige. I hope to see you again soon so we can continue getting to know each other better."

He hugged her close one more time and opened her car door.

"Ooh, a true southern gentleman. I like your style," Paige teased as she climbed into the driver's seat.

"I'll call you tomorrow," Mason said happily as he closed her door and waved her off.

Paige felt giddy as she headed home. She replayed the highlights of the night in her head. When Jake's face popped in her mind, her giddiness turned to confusion, and if she was being completely honest with herself, a deep feeling of longing washed over her. How could she still feel so intensely about him after all this time? She had no clue what to do about that or even if there was anything to be done about it. Thinking of Jake when she should be thinking only of Mason and their date made her feel guilty. It was only their first date though, and she had a lot of history with Jake. Complicated history.

Paige wanted to enjoy the rest of her ride home, so she cranked up the upbeat Bruno Mars song playing on the radio and tried not to overthink the situation. There would be plenty of time for that later when she rehashed it all to Faith and Sadie.

As Paige started to drive across the old narrow two-lane bridge over Muddy Creek, headlights came on at the other end. She didn't think much of it at first until the big dark SUV started coming across the bridge at a very high speed. Paige switched the radio off and started to slow her car down. She could hear the angry roar of the other car's engine. Suddenly, the other car jerked over the yellow center lines and was coming straight towards her.

"Shit! Shit! Shit!" Paige shouted as she swerved to the other lane to avoid a head on collision, but the other driver swerved towards her as she went past and clipped the back end of her car and sent her spinning. Paige tried with all her might to regain control of the car. She managed to narrowly miss slamming into the bridge's concrete barrier with her front end. Her heart was racing a mile a minute as the adrenaline coursed through her. Her fingers were bone white from clutching the steering wheel so hard in her panicked attempt to not end up in the creek.

"Jesus, that was close," Paige said aloud when she thought she was in the clear.

No sooner were the words out of her mouth when she felt her car sliding down the embankment. Slamming on the brakes had no effect on the slick, muddy ground, and the last thing she saw was a giant looming oak tree with branches covered ominously in Spanish moss right before her car crashed into it.

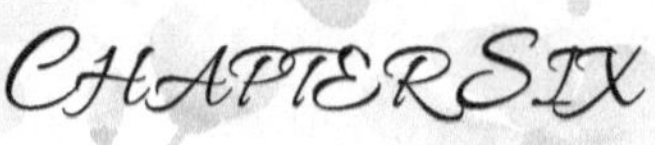

J ake left the restaurant around ten pm. When Paige and her date left a half hour or so before, he had completely lost the desire to stay, but didn't want to follow them outside to the parking lot either. He didn't even want to think about that tall lucky bastard putting his hands on Paige. Even an innocent hug would have been too much to witness. Hanging with his buddies at the bar had lost its appeal. They were all married and complaining endlessly about their wives and children. His son was the best thing that had ever happened to him, and he would give anything for a good woman to spend his life with; well, one particular good woman, who had just walked out of the restaurant with another man.

Jake climbed up in his pick-up truck and sat for a few minutes reliving his time with Paige in the restaurant hallway. The way she had said his name was what broke his resolve to keep his hands to himself. As soon as he heard it pass her lips, he knew that he had to touch her. No matter what pain and longing he might feel later.

He thought about when he had pulled Paige to his chest and put his face in her hair. She always smelled so heavenly, just a subtle hint of lilac and honeysuckle. Her soft body felt so perfect up against his hard one. He had wanted so desperately to put his hands under the back of her shirt like he used to so he could feel the smooth skin of her back. He hadn't wanted to scare her off though. He wanted to do things right this time around. Holding her like that, Jake knew he was home and didn't want to ever let go.

He shouldn't have been surprised when she pulled away from him after he told her that he missed her. Jake knew he had messed up with her many times before. He had said countless sweet things to her that his actions hadn't backed up. There were so many regrets when it came to how he had treated Paige in his younger days. Jake's heart had sunk watching Paige back away from him with her eyes on the floor.

With a deep sigh, he cranked up his truck and headed home. So, what if he was taking the scenic route? He wasn't going to drive by Paige's house, that would be creepy, but he was heading in the general direction she would have gone. If she had gone home. What if she had decided to make a night of it with her date? It was none of his business and he had no right to be jealous, but he was burning with it. He was well aware of what she could do with that beautiful curvy body.

Jake's thoughts were cut off as he approached Muddy Creek Bridge and saw the flashing lights of a couple of police cars, a firetruck, and an ambulance. It looked like someone had slid down the embankment and crashed into a huge oak tree. A huge branch had landed on the roof, crushing into a V-shape. The first responders were using the jaws of life to cut an opening in the mangled metal.

As Jake got closer, he recognized his buddy John Avery as one of the police officers at the scene. Jake rolled down his tinted window to ask John what happened and that was when he got a good look at the white Volvo SUV with the dragonfly sticker on the back glass. He didn't even remember getting out of his truck when his momentum was stopped by three officers holding him back from running to the crash site.

"PAIGE! PAIGE!" Jake was screaming, frantically trying to break free of the grips the three large men had on him. He had to get down there to her. His head felt like it was spinning out of control. She just came back into his life; it wouldn't be fair to lose her the same night. Jake could not imagine a world without Paige in it.

"Jake! Jake! She's conscious, man. Settle down. She's the one who called us. We are trying to get her out so we can get her over to the hospital to get checked out. Let us do our job, please." When Jake started to ease up a little, John Avery took his hands off of Jake's shoulders and continued, "Thank God for all of those Swedish safety features. Her tires are a little bald, which is probably why she couldn't get any traction on the mud."

Officer John Avery tried his best to calm Jake down. "I knew as soon as I saw your truck pulling up to the bridge that you were going to freak out when you realized whose car had gone off the road. I called the other guys over to assist with holding you back before you even got out of the truck. I felt like a damn rodeo cowboy trying to subdue a damn wild bronco."

Jake briefly recalled how John knew precisely what Paige meant to him. He had told John their whole story a couple of years ago over a bottle of Gentleman Jack shortly after

Paige's husband had passed away unexpectedly. John knew all of the regret and longing Jake had when it came to Paige. How he should have fought for her when he had felt her pulling away from him all those years ago.

"What the hell happened, John? How did she end up down there? She didn't drink any alcohol at dinner." Jake was pacing frantically.

"So, you were with her tonight?" John asked in surprise.

"Not exactly. We just happened to both be eating at Lorenzo's. Actually, she was on a date with another man." Jake stopped pacing and looked over at the SUV. "Is she alone in the car?" The first responders almost had a door pried open.

"Yeah, it's just her in there. She says as she started crossing the bridge, a dark SUV turned on its headlights and started crossing from the other side. Then it came at her head on. She swerved to go around it, but the driver swerved back towards her and clipped her back end, sending her into a tailspin. She missed the concrete barrier at the other end of the bridge, but the car slid down the embankment and you see where it ended up. I guess there was a big dead branch on the tree and the impact must have jarred it and it broke off and fell on top of her car. Rotten luck."

"Sounds like a drunk driver. Don't get that a lot around here," Jake pondered aloud, still keeping an eye on the progress the firemen below were making on getting Paige out of the wrecked car.

"Yes, it does. We have an APB out looking for any dark SUVs with front passenger side damage. Paige thought it might be an older Chevy Tahoe but couldn't say for sure."

John was also keeping a close eye on the scene at the bottom of the embankment. It was like he knew as soon as they got her out of that car that Jake would be down there wanting to help her himself. *Good luck stopping me,* Jake thought as he looked over at his friend.

Finally, an opening was made, and Jake could see Paige's shaking hands come reaching out. The firefighters grabbed her and pulled her out slowly and gently. He didn't see any blood, but he knew there would be bruises. She looked shaken up and her hair, normally straight, was sticking up all over the place. Thank goodness for airbags. Jake scooted down the embankment, doing his best not to slip. When he got to her, he could see she would have a nasty mark where the seatbelt tightened on her during the crash; an angry red line was already marring her skin. Her thin shirt, while appealing, wouldn't have provided any cushioning.

"Baby, are you okay?" Jake took her hands in his own and looked her up and down. He all but carried her up the hill, not waiting for the stretcher the EMTs were struggling to bring down the slippery slope. He ignored their persistent yelling that he shouldn't be moving her.

"Jake? What are you doing here?" Paige was losing that tenuous sense of coherency she had when she called nine-one-one herself. Jake held her tighter to reassure himself as much as her that she was alright.

"I'm not feeling so good," she barely got out as she started to shake even though it wasn't cold out and Jake's body was definitely putting off heat as he carried her up the steep incline.

"She's going into shock!" Jake yelled and placed her delicately on the stretcher for the EMTs to help her when they got back up to the bridge.

Jake watched worriedly as they loaded her into the ambulance and started to close the doors. He went to climb in, but they wouldn't let him. He felt helpless.

"Where are you going to take her?" Jake yelled up to the young man who would be taking care of Paige in the ambulance.

"MUSC, sir. It's the closest hospital," the EMT said as he closed the door in Jake's worried face.

"I have to finish out my shift, but I'll meet you up there when I get off. I'll go by Faith Brewer's house and let her know what's going on. She'll contact Paige's parents. I'm guessing that's where her kids are tonight," John explained as Jake continued to stare after the ambulance racing away to take his Paige to the hospital.

"Oh, God. I didn't even think about that. Those poor kids. If they lost their mom too..." Jake trailed off. He refused to think of any other outcome than Paige being okay. He felt a protective swelling in his chest picturing the two kids. The same feeling that he had always felt for Paige.

Jake climbed in his truck and headed towards Charleston. It occurred to him that if he had been Paige's husband, they probably would have let him ride to the hospital in the ambulance with her. He felt as if he had let her down again. Different scenarios kept cycling through his mind. Paige having internal damage and needing emergency surgery. Paige being fine and him helping her home to care for any of her minor injuries. And everything in between.

Fifteen minutes later, Jake was parking at the hospital and running into the emergency department doors. "I'm here for Paige Collins," he breathlessly told the twenty-something year old lady working the night shift at the reception desk.

"Are you family?" she asked. Her nametag said "Lauren".

"Not technically, but we've been friends for over twenty years. Doesn't that count for something?" Jake turned on his southern charm and gave her his sweetest smile, hoping it would help him get his way.

"Have a seat, what was your name?"

"Jake Bennett."

"Alright Mr. Bennett, have a seat and I'll see what I can find out for you," Lauren the receptionist said as she gave him a professional placating smile. Maybe he was losing his touch with the ladies or getting too old to charm the ones in their twenties.

Jake watched the receptionist from where he sat. She did some typing on her computer, made a quick call, and then had to help the next person that walked in. It was a very busy emergency department, people moving hurriedly everywhere. He should have expected that, it being Friday night and in Charleston.

A few agonizing minutes later, the double doors that led back to what the sign on the wall indicated was the triage area opened and out walked a tall, dark-skinned female doctor in green surgical scrubs. The confident way she walked in with her head up and shoulders back screamed "in control and badass". The lady had swagger.

"Jake Bennett?" The doctor looked right at him and raised an eyebrow.

"Yes, I'm Jake Bennett. How is Paige? Is she going to be alright? Is she awake? She had gone into shock, and they wouldn't let me in the ambulance," Jake started rambling. He was beyond worried. It felt like he was going to go mad if he didn't lay eyes on Paige soon.

The doctor smiled and let out a little chuckle. "Yes, she is awake. Our girl is tough. They are running some tests, but the initial exam looks promising. I'm Dr. Sadie Jennings," she said as she held out her hand to shake Jake's. "I've heard some interesting things about you, Mr. Bennett."

The doctor was teasing him. Jake figured that he could take that as a good sign. If Paige was on the edge of death her friend wouldn't be out here wasting time with him. As she subtly looked him over, he wondered what she was thinking and what exactly she had heard about him.

"If you don't mind me asking, how did you know Paige was here?" the imposing doctor finally asked when she seemed to be done assessing him.

"I was on my way home when I came upon the scene of the accident. I recognized her car," Jake replied simply. No need to mention he was low-key stalking her.

"Gotcha. Well, wait out here and I'll make sure someone keeps you updated. Or you can leave your number and I can call you later if you'd like to go home," Sadie offered.

Jake had the feeling that she was testing him.

"No, thank you. I'm going to stay." There was no way in hell Jake was leaving there until he knew for sure that Paige was going to be okay.

As Jake went to sit back down to wait and the doctor was turning to go back to triage to check in on Paige, the outer doors to the emergency department opened and in ran a little blond tornado. The air around her seemed to vibrate as she rushed in. She had been crying. Her eyes were red and swollen and she had mascara running down her cheeks.

"Oh Sadie! Is she okay? John Avery came by the house and told me what happened, and I rushed right over," the little blond force of nature exclaimed as she ran over to the doctor.

"They are running tests, but she is awake and coherent." Dr. Jennings gave the woman a quick hug and turned her to face Jake. "Faith, this is Paige's friend, Jake. He came across the scene of the accident and recognized Paige's car and came to check on her. Wasn't that nice of him?"

"But how do you know what her car looks like? Y'all haven't seen each other in years," Faith questioned Jake instead of answering Dr. Jennings' question. The doctor had to turn away to hide her smile at her friend's bluntness.

"I've seen her around Meadow Oaks. Small town you know," Jake replied sheepishly.

"I thought you were from Summerville?" Faith asked confused, her eyes darting back and forth like she was trying to replay something in her head.

Jake chuckled at the little blond woman's lack of filter. He found it oddly refreshing. "I am originally. I moved to Meadow Oaks after trade school," he explained.

Dr. Jennings chose that moment to interrupt. "Alright, I have to get back to work. Y'all keep each other company and I'll come back when I have an update or if my surgery runs late a nurse will come get you." She nodded at Jake and gave Faith a look that Jake took to mean that Sadie expected Faith to be on her best behavior. She turned and walked back through the double doors to the triage area. Jake found it a little ominous that the doctor was shaking her head and laughing as she went.

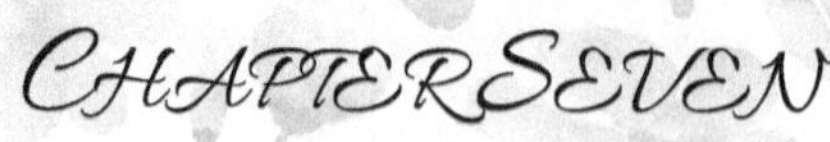

CHAPTER SEVEN

Paige was propped up in the uncomfortable hospital bed hooked up to all sorts of machines monitoring her body's functions. She absently listened to the beeping as she looked at the screens, but only because she had nothing better to do while she waited for the next nurse or doctor to come in.

As she was debating whether or not she should try to take a nap, Sadie softly pushed aside the curtain and entered her semi-private triage bay. Sadie checked that everything with the machines was working properly and sat on the edge of the bed.

"How are you feeling? Meds kicked in yet?"

"Oh yeah, feeling a little better, thanks." Paige winced as she tried to sit up more.

Sadie gently guided her back down. "You need to rest so your body can heal. Faith just got here. She's out there keeping Jake Bennett company." Sadie's right eyebrow raised, knowing there was a juicy story.

"Oh my God. I fainted in his arms. Ugh, that's so embarrassing. We were both at Lorenzo's tonight and he must have driven by the bridge on his way home. I'm surprised he's here though."

Sadie could sense that Paige wasn't really all that surprised, but Paige didn't want to let on how much it meant to her that he came to the hospital.

"I would love to be a fly on the wall for that conversation. Once Faith gets over the shock of your accident, she is no doubt going to be pumping Jake for all sorts of information on the two of you."

"Well, that's just great," Paige mumbled sarcastically.

"It's very obvious that he cares about you. He seemed more like a worried husband than an old friend." Sadie slowly stood up to leave as Paige flinched at her words. "I have to scrub in for surgery in about twenty minutes, but I had to see you one more time to get my head clear. I'll come check on you when I finish in the O.R. Try and get some sleep."

Paige watched as her friend closed the curtain of the little area she was in and shut her eyes. She tried to calm her mind, but she'd be lying if she didn't acknowledge that she was worried about Jake being alone with Faith in the waiting room. Faith would be asking all sorts of personal questions. Paige had not told them much about Jake before their night out at Red's. It's not that she didn't trust them. It was just that if she had told them about him back when they were in college, she would have told them everything. There were things that even Jake didn't know.

***

Back in the waiting room, Faith had taken a seat across from Jake and didn't seem to be trying to hide the fact that she was sizing him up. For a couple of minutes, they just looked at each other in relative silence. Finally, Jake smiled and said, "So, I guess you have some questions for me." It was written all over her face.

Faith took her time considering what to ask him first. "Are you planning on staying until she gets released from here or do you want to head home? I can have Officer Avery call you later. He's heading this way shortly."

So, she was testing him just like Sadie had. Jake knew Paige's two friends were going to be a handful, but he was glad she had such loyal friends looking out for her. And he was up to the challenge.

"I plan on staying." Jake knew more questions were coming. Ones with harder answers.

"I have to say, that surprises me. You guys haven't seen each other in so long. Sadie and I have been her best friends for a long time now and we just know you as her weekend friend Bennett from back when we were in college," Faith said, obviously testing him more and staking her territory at the same time.

"Bennett huh? I never knew she called me that."

Jake felt a stabbing ache in his chest. Had he not meant that much to her? Their history flashed through his mind as he tried to figure it out. No, he knew that Paige had loved him. Unfortunately, it was a fact that he had taken for granted in the past.

"So, she never mentioned what went on between us before she got to college and met you and Sadie?" Jake had to know, even if the answer broke his heart.

"Not until recently, and even then she didn't tell us much. Why do you think that is? I mean, I guess I understand her not telling us in college, we had just become friends and Paige has always guarded her heart, but after all these years of us being like sisters, sharing everything?"

Jake took a moment to process what Faith had told him. He knew that if he wanted any chance at having a future with Paige he would have to acknowledge the wrongs of the past.

"I guess because I hurt her heart too many times and tried to pretend like I didn't realize it. I convinced myself that I wasn't accountable for how she felt. That somehow she had misconstrued my intentions." That was the first time he admitted it out loud to someone else. His younger self had always played it off, but he was a better man. Or at least he tried his best to be.

Faith nodded as she processed his very direct answer. "I can respect someone that owns up to his actions."

"I'm glad," Jake said grinning.

"So, how did you come to be here at the hospital tonight?"

"I saw Paige at Lorenzo's. As I said earlier, I have seen her around town but tonight was the first time we had spoken in years. I realized that I need her to know that I still care about her deeply. When I came across the accident..." Jake started shaking his head. He didn't know how to describe to Faith how he had felt without sounding crazy to her.

"Yes, I can imagine. I drove past the scene of the accident on my way here. A tow truck was pulling her car out of the embankment. That must have been gut-wrenching. Certainly made me bawl my eyes out." Faith gave Jake a reassuring smile and pointed to her ruined mascara.

"So, what was Paige doing at Lorenzo's?" Faith asked with feigned innocence.

"She was on a date. But I have a strong feeling you already knew that." Jake might have respect for the woman as Paige's friend, but he was no push over.

"Fair enough. I'm the one who set her up with him. She deserves to be happy. Are you here to make her happy or break her heart again?" Faith asked, but then seemed to hesitate. "I didn't mean for the conversation to get so serious this fast. It just happened. You don't seem like the kind of man to tiptoe around the hard stuff."

"I won't ever hurt her again. I'll let her decide if she wants me back in her life. If she does though, I plan to be all in." Jake looked at Faith square on as he made the bold declaration. His heart was racing. He hadn't meant to put all his cards on the table to Paige's friend. He had planned on working his way back into her life at whatever pace Paige set. Dire circumstances or whatever you want to call the car accident tended to make big life choices happen faster than they normally would have.

"Fair enough," Faith murmured.

Smiling and obviously needing to lighten the mood after it turned so intense Faith asked him in a playful tone, "So, did Paige tell you about us when she went home on the weekends in college?"

"Oh yes," Jake laughed. "She adored you two. You were right about her guarding her heart, but she had told me that she had a good feeling about y'all. Tonight when I said my condolences about her husband passing, I was happy to hear her say that y'all took care of her."

"Well, that's what best friends are for," Faith simply said.

They sat in silence after that. Faith stared off at nothing in particular, no doubt worried about Paige.

Jake closed his eyes and replayed the night in his head. As he thought about how right it felt holding Paige back in the restaurant hallway, he hoped she let him back in her life. He would love her like she had always deserved. He would be the man she had believed he was long ago.

CHAPTER EIGHT

The doctors handling Paige's case in the emergency department decided to admit her to the hospital for observation until Sunday afternoon. They said the concern of possible internal injuries had them erring on the side of caution. Paige had a strong feeling Sadie had something to do with that. It was good thing that the magazine offered excellent health insurance coverage.

On Sunday, even though the doctors had finally given her the all clear to go home, Sadie insisted on staying in Paige's guest room for a couple of days. "I'm off until Wednesday anyway and this way I can make sure you don't try to sneak into work before you're supposed to. Dr. Meyer said no driving until you are off the pain meds, which will be Wednesday at the earliest."

Sadie settled Paige on the couch in the living room, tucked a soft down blanket around her, and handed her a glass of water. "I'm keeping an eye on you and that's that, so no sense in wasting your precious energy arguing."

"Wouldn't dream of it, Dr. Jennings. You know you are more than welcome to stay. I just don't want you to feel like you have to if you had other plans. I'm sure my parents will be in and out of here over the next few days. They'll keep an eye on me." Paige took a sip of water and settled back into the comfy couch cushions.

"I'm sure they will, but they aren't doctors; I am." Sadie curled up on the loveseat that was caddy corner to the couch and eyed her friend, looking for any signs of distress. "I'll admit you seem fine other than those nasty bruises from the seatbelt. You are definitely one tough lady. Faith said she was going to cook some comfort food and bring it over when she left the hospital this morning."

Almost as soon as Sadie finished saying the words, the front door opened and Faith came barging through with Travis following behind, his arms stacked high with containers of delicious smelling food.

"All of your favorites, Paige. Macaroni and cheese, cornbread made with honey, apple fritters cooked up in cinnamon butter, deviled eggs with paprika and ranch seasoning, and blueberry muffins. Travis got some of those yummy extra thick pork chops from the butcher, so I'll fry those up later if you want," Faith said over her shoulder as she headed to the kitchen.

"You know all that food is every cardiologist's nightmare, right?" Sadie shook her head in mock disgust. "I guess I can let it slide this time since Paige has just been through a trauma, but let's not make this a habit."

"Well, I'm just relieved at finally being able to help *my* good friend Paige in some way that matters. I felt so dang helpless at the hospital," Faith admitted. "Travis, honey, put that stuff on the counter and you can go. We're going to have ourselves some girl talk." Faith shooed her husband out the door.

"Y'all have fun. Glad you are home, Paige," Travis said over his shoulder on his way out.

"He likes girl talk about as much as he likes going to the dentist. He really is relieved you're ok though. He loves me so much and knows I would be absolutely distraught if anything ever happened to you! Losing Matt was hard enough on all of us. Plus, Travis still misses his friend too," Faith said from the kitchen.

Paige eyed Faith warily through the doorway of the kitchen as she flitted between the counter and the fridge putting away all the food she brought. She wondered what kind of "girl talk" they were about to have. They had already discussed the date with Mason and the car accident at length when the doctors let Faith back to her room early Saturday morning.

Jake had been let in as well, to say hi and that he was glad she was okay. He hadn't taken his eyes off of her the whole time. The nurses had kicked him out later that afternoon, and she assumed he went home to check on Caleb. He had gotten Faith's number and supposedly checked in often. Paige tried not to read too much into that. She knew from experience that with Jake that didn't necessarily mean he had romantic feelings for her. She wasn't ready to let her guard down.

Faith finally settled in the extra wide chair across from the couch and folded her legs underneath her and said, "Okay, spill. I want to know everything about Jake. It is obvious from the little I spoke with him that y'all had a serious thing for each other and he keeps checking in to see how you are. Why did you never tell us the whole story about him? He said he hurt your heart many times. So, since you are stuck on that couch for a few days, we have plenty of time to learn every single detail." Faith was not holding back; her curiosity had been boiling over since her conversation with Jake in the hospital waiting room.

"Geez, what did y'all talk about?" Paige asked warily.

"Not as much as I wanted to since I was trying to be respectful of you, but it got serious pretty quick." Faith went on to relay the short, but intense, conversation with Jake to Paige who sat there looking down at her hands twisting on the blanket.

"Huh," was all Paige could think to say when Faith was done. Her head was racing from the implications of Jake saying he would be all in if she let him. Her heart was pounding so hard she was sure her friends could hear it. Jake had said everything she had always hoped he would, but she was scared to death.

"I think you should tell us everything you have left out about Jake so we can help you sort through all the thoughts and feelings I know you are having right now. Only when you get that settled will you be able to take the next step, whether it is with Jake or moving on to someone new like Mason," Sadie said encouragingly to her friend.

Paige was considering how to begin her story when the doorbell rang. Faith hopped up and opened the door to reveal Officer John Avery holding a very cute black Kate Spade clutch.

"That's a good look for you, John. You have great taste," Faith teased as she moved aside to let him in.

John handed over the purse to Faith and nodded at the other two ladies. "Good afternoon, y'all. Paige, you're looking better." He offered Paige a friendly smile.

"Thank you so much for all you have done, John," Paige replied. John had done so much to help keep her family in the loop about what was going on after he came and got her statement about the accident. Above and beyond what she would have expected.

"And thank you for bringing this back, officer. I forgot I let her borrow it," Sadie said as she took the clutch from Faith and hugged it to her chest, making everyone laugh.

Paige was glad too. There was no way with two growing kids that she would be able to afford to replace it anytime soon. Not that Sadie would ever ask her to.

After inquiring after John's parents and a few other pleasantries, the ladies said good-bye to John.

"Well, he could be on a sexy police officer calendar, and I would buy a copy for every room in my condo! He could totally be Shemar Moore's younger brother," Sadie commented after John had left. The other two ladies chuckled and agreed wholeheartedly.

"Sadie, can you grab my phone out of the clutch so I can charge it? I'm sure I've missed some calls and texts. If anyone noticed my demolished car outside of the body shop, then the whole town knows I was in an accident." Paige was trying to delay the Jake talk as much as she could while she tried to organize her thoughts. She was a little fuzzy from the pain meds.

Sadie got up and found a charger for the phone knowing that Paige needed a few minutes. Sure enough, when they got the phone turned back on there were tons of well-wishing texts from people who had seen the car. Only a few missed calls, one being from Mason. Paige called him back and explained what happened.

"He's a really great guy," Paige sighed when she got off the phone with Mason.

"Which is exactly why you need to sort out this Jake thing," Faith and Sadie practically said at the same time.

"I'm not sure where to start," Paige moaned.

"How about you start where you left off at Red's a couple of weeks ago. We know how y'all initially met; that y'all were friends first and then you hooked up and eventually you started referring to him as Bennett to your friends." Faith paused to give Paige the side-eye. "What happened after the first time y'all...you know...*made love*? He said he broke your heart many times. Even though I think one time is one time too many, tell us all about the first time." Faith encouraged Paige with a little pat on the knee and then she settled back into the chair to hear the story.

Paige laid back against the couch cushions and stared up at the ceiling. "I left off at us having slept together for the first time and it had been... amazing," Paige began dreamily.

When Paige woke up the next morning, she couldn't believe what had happened. Their chemistry had been off the charts. Not that she had much experience in that department, it's just that for the first time, everything felt natural but crazy intense at the same time.

Jake was still asleep, so Paige took advantage and drank in every little detail of his chiseled face, his broad shoulders, the lean muscle of his arms and chest. The sprinkling of light blonde chest hair. She even found his soft snore to be cute. So much for not falling for him. She was a goner.

"Good morning, beautiful," he drawled, looking at her from hooded eyes.

"Oh, hey," Paige replied, grinning like the Cheshire Cat, having been caught following that trail of blonde chest hair down to his navel with her fingertip.

After a quick, but completely satisfying round two, Paige had to hurry home before her parents started calling around looking for her. She could hardly wait until the next time she got to see Jake.

They continued to hang out and he took her on a few dates and to a few parties out in the woods. Paige was still a little awkward when they were around other people. Brad had always put her down for trying to join in conversations with his friends, so she was quiet when they were in a group. Jake seemed confused by that, but he never asked why, and she never told him. She had opened up to him a lot in private but not about the physical and emotional abuse at the hands of her supposed "high school sweetheart." She didn't want to seem like a dramatic female, Brad's words of course. And she knew if she ever did tell Jake, he would track Brad down and annihilate him. Brad definitely deserved it, but she didn't want Jake getting into trouble on her behalf. She had gotten out of the relationship and just wanted it behind her.

When they would return to Jake's from the dates or parties, they would sneak off to his room and reignite the hot spark that was between them. Whether in person or on the phone, Jake had a way of making Paige feel like the most special person in the world. He would whisper sweet things in her ear and steal little touches here and there. He would proudly hold her hand or have his arm around her, letting everyone know that she was his girl.

They went on like that for a couple of months. Here and there Paige thought about having the official girlfriend and boyfriend talk. She repeatedly talked herself out of it, convincing herself that they were too mature for that. Jake respected her. They had started out as friends, which was the best foundation for a relationship, right? They had spoken on the phone for hours every night talking about everything and anything.

Until they didn't.

Jake started not showing up to parties she had invited him to when he had said he was coming. Other times he did show up but seemed distant and distracted. He would still say sweet things and kiss her goodbye, but he didn't seem as genuine. He no longer invited her back to his house to stay the night in his bed. Paige had been in a bit of denial at that point but deep down she knew that she had lost his interest. Instead of confronting him like a grown woman would do, teenage Paige had reached out to one of his buddies.

"Charlie, I don't think he's into me anymore," Paige had confided one night over the phone. Charlie had been friends with Jake almost all their lives and was really friendly to Paige when they were all together. He didn't seem to take Paige's shyness the wrong way.

"Naw girl, he's just got a lot going on right now, trying to balance getting into a good trade school and his job. He has told me many times about how great he thinks you are. Just be patient with him," he reassured Paige. That had made her feel much better about the whole thing.

The following weekend a group of girls Paige knew from volleyball invited her to a party out of town at some apartments near the University of South Carolina. One of the girls also knew Jake and said that he and his friends were supposed to be there. They all got dolled up and headed to the college party full of excitement for the possibility of college guys. Paige had only thought of getting to see Jake and hopefully reigniting their connection.

Jake was already at the party when they arrived. He seemed mildly annoyed that she was there, so she stayed close to her friends. She hadn't meant to intrude on his boys' night, if that's what it was supposed to be.

"You should go dance with him," Paige's friend had urged.

"I don't know, he doesn't seem too thrilled that I am here," she had admitted. Honestly, she was ready to protect her pride by leaving. If he didn't want to acknowledge her, that was fine, his loss.

"Girl, you know you want him, and you look hot. Get over there and show him what he's been missing," she insisted as she pushed Paige in Jake's direction.

Jake gave her a knowing smile, and they began dancing. As soon as their bodies touched, that undeniable chemistry took over and they moved together sensually, their bodies fitting together perfectly. She could feel the bulge in his jeans getting bigger. Things were starting to look up. Paige risked a glance at Jake's face, heat flared in his eyes momentarily, but then he swallowed hard, his Adam's apple bobbing, and he looked away.

"Thanks for the dance," he said, hugging her once and walking away.

"Oh my God! Paige, that was so hot!" her friend had exclaimed. "I told you that you had nothing to worry about." Paige wasn't so sure. She knew Jake, and something just wasn't right.

After an hour or so later, the other girls hadn't found any likeable college guys that weren't completely wasted, so they wanted to head home. Paige reluctantly agreed and followed them out to the parking lot. She was shocked to see Jake out there chatting up some blond college girl. He didn't look annoyed with her. Paige was debating whether or not to go and say goodbye to him when she saw him give the college girl his sweet smile and he bent down to kiss her. Paige felt like she had been stabbed in the chest.

"What the hell?" her friend had yelled. The other girls were pissed as well on her behalf.

"Please, let's just get out of here. I don't want to give him the satisfaction of seeing me upset," Paige had begged her friends, turning her back to Jake so she wouldn't have to see him lip locking with the blond.. She convinced them to go to the car and leave. She was supposed to drive home, but her friends knew she was too upset to focus on the road. She spent the ride home staring out the window unsuccessfully trying to hold back tears.

Paige had expected a phone call or something after that where she would get to tell him off. He didn't call. She went back and forth between trying to act tough about it and telling herself that it didn't really matter because they weren't technically dating, and feeling betrayed by someone that was supposed to care about her.

A couple of weeks later, Charlie invited her to a bonfire party in Summerville. "Sorry Charlie, but I don't want to run into Jake right now," Paige declined vehemently.

"I know you don't, which is why I made sure he wasn't coming before I asked you. I got your back, girl," Charlie reassured her.

But Jake was there. "Damn, he really wasn't supposed to be here," Charlie lamented as they walked up and saw him across the bonfire. Paige stayed close to Charlie most of the night and Jake pretended like she didn't exist.

The one time she left Charlie's side was when she had to go find a private spot in the woods to pee. On her way back to the bonfire she saw Charlie and Jake arguing. She walked closer and stood behind a tree so she could hear, but they couldn't see her. Yes, she was snooping. They were arguing about her.

"Why the hell did you bring her here, man?" Jake had yelled at Charlie, waving a beer can around.

"What is your problem? For the past few months all you've talked about is how great she is, and you spent every damn free minute you had with her. Now you are acting like you can't be inconvenienced to say hello to her. To acknowledge that she actually meant something to you?" Charlie argued back.

It wasn't the kiss with the other girl that had completely broken Paige's heart. It was what Jake said to Charlie next, "Look, she's a sweet girl, but I don't like her like that. Never have."

Paige almost crumpled to the ground right then and there. She didn't consider herself to be an overly emotional girl, but she couldn't deny that she was devastated. He was supposed to be her friend at the very least and he had taken advantage of her feelings for him. He had known that she was a good girl and would take sleeping together to mean that he had feelings for her too. She had trusted him, and he betrayed her.

"You're a real piece of shit, you know that Jake?" Charlie said and stomped off with his fists clenched.

Paige couldn't be sure, but it sounded like Jake said, "Yeah, I know," in a voice that sounded like he had lost all the fight in him.

Charlie eventually found her still hiding behind the tree. She hadn't wanted anyone to see that she had been crying. He took her home and she didn't see or talk to Jake for over a year after that.

"That son of a bitch! Now I wish I would have slapped him as soon as I met him!" Faith shrieked. She was sitting straight up in her chair, her face a little red. "He knew exactly what he was doing."

"I have to agree with Faith on this one. It's not like he was just some random guy you hooked up with. It sounds like y'all were close friends, you were into him from the start, and he knew it. I'm surprised he waited that long to take advantage of the situation since you say y'all slept in the same bed on numerous occasions. He was a teenage boy after all." Sadie sighed, "I'm sorry to be blunt, but it seems like his curiosity got the best of him and he acted impulsively. And then tried to do right by you until he... well didn't want to anymore," Sadie stated as gently as she could.

"That's kind of how I've always seen it too. Honestly, I don't regret having sex with him. I only regret trusting him so fully," Paige acknowledged.

Her heart was aching talking about the past. It's funny how unrequited love can still sting so many years later.

"So, when did he end up married?" Faith blurted. When Paige and Sadie stared at her with wide questioning eyes, she said, "What? I did some digging on social media after you told us the story at Red's. So, sue me."

"You have too much free time on your hands lady." Sadie chuckled, shaking her head.

"Well, the next girl he dated or whatever you want to call it got pregnant and they got married." Paige went back to looking at the ceiling as she said that. "I'm really tired. I think I'll take a nap now. And then maybe I'll text Mason when I wake up."

"Both of those things sound like a great idea. I'll head home to have dinner with Travis, and I'll be back first thing in the morning. I'm going to take the day off tomorrow and come hang with you two. We can talk more about Jake and his tom foolery then. It's making Mason look like a shoe in so far!" Faith said as she jumped up and prepared to leave. She stooped down and hugged Paige goodbye and Sadie walked her out.

Sadie came back and gave Paige her pain meds and another glass of water.

"Look, I can tell that story has taken a lot out of you, Paige. You don't trust people easily, and after that story, I can see why. First an abusive boyfriend and then a friend that took advantage of your feelings and didn't even acknowledge that he had hurt you. I hate it when people pull that crap. That's why I focused on my work in high school and college and not on romantic relationships. Try and get some rest." Sadie gently patted Paige's leg before slipping off to check some work emails.

The pain meds helped Paige drift off into a fuzzy sleep. She felt restless in her body and had upsetting dreams. She dreamed that she was trapped in the woods and could see a bonfire not too far away. She could smell the smoke wafting up through the clearing in the trees. As she got closer, she noticed that there was a young handsome man standing in the shadows at the edge of the clearing. She kept trying to reach him to break free of the trees and their troublesome branches. She stretched out her hand to him but no matter how many times she begged him to help her, he stood there staring at her like she was crazy.

J ake returned home from the hospital sometime Saturday afternoon to find Caleb on the couch playing video games and yelling into his headset at his virtual teammates. He made sure his son had enough food to get him through the rest of the night and went to his bedroom to crash. He was pushing forty and pulling an all-nighter was significantly harder than it used to be when he was younger.

Jake quickly showered to get the hospital waiting room smell off of him and practically crawled into his king size bed. For once, the big bed felt like it was too big, like something was missing; more like someone was missing. He had a vision of Paige as he had last seen her, laid up in a hospital bed, looking both beautiful and a bit fragile.

Jake went over his conversation with Faith in his head. The fact that he had hurt Paige in the past was not news to him, but somehow her hiding their relationship from her friends made him realize just how bad he had hurt her. If it had been no big deal, like he had played it off to be, then she would have told them all about him at some point.

Jake sent off another text to Faith to make sure Paige's condition hadn't changed since he left the hospital. Faith quickly answered him back. A curt reply of "no change" with no other details. Jake sighed heavily and placed his phone on his nightstand.

He couldn't say that he regretted all of his actions back when they were teenagers because then he wouldn't have Caleb and lord knows he loves that boy more than life itself; but he did regret causing Paige pain. If he could have gone back to that time, he would have been a better friend to Paige and wouldn't have taken her for granted when they reconnected later. She could have been his wife. They could have had kids together. If only he had been honest with her and explained to her that he loved her too but didn't feel like he was ready to be in a forever type of relationship yet. Especially after everything he went through with Caleb's mom. Jake's mind was heavy with regret, but eventually exhaustion overtook him, and he fell into a deep dreamless sleep.

As soon as Jake woke up Sunday morning, he texted Faith to check on how Paige was doing. He was relieved to hear that the doctors were planning to send her home later in the afternoon and that Sadie was going to go stay with her for a few days. Dr. Jennings was one impressive woman. No doubt about that.

After a cup of coffee and a run through his work emails Jake realized that he hadn't checked the mail the day before. He was expecting some important last-minute tax documents for his surveying business. Owning his own business was a dream come true in some ways, but a lot of paperwork. At the mailbox, he flipped through the envelopes and sure enough there was the one he was waiting for. Weirdly, behind it was a manila envelope with no writing on it. Not his name or address, no return address, no postage. *Strange,* Jake thought.

Jake went inside and sat down at his desk in his home office. He put all the other mail aside and opened the blank envelope, his curiosity getting the best of him. Inside were four black and white photos. The first one was of Paige and him holding onto each other in the back hallway at Lorenzo's. *What the hell?* Jake thought. He turned the picture over to see if there was anything to indicate who or where it was from on the back, but it was blank. He fanned out the other three pictures across his desk. They were all of Paige and her date outside the restaurant by Paige's car looking awfully cozy together. In one they were just smiling at each other, but in the other two photos they were in a passionate embrace, kissing. Jake felt like he was going to be sick. Why would someone send him these pictures? One by one he turned them over to check the backs for writing. There had to be some clue as to who sent them. On the last picture he turned over, written in thick black marker and in all caps was:

SHE DOESN'T WANT YOU

Paige came awake slowly; she didn't feel rested at all. The pain medication had worn off, but it wasn't the physical stuff that was hurting her. She kept her eyes closed as her thoughts took her back to the phone call when she had found out that Jake had gotten his next girlfriend pregnant.

When Paige's cell phone rang and she saw on the caller ID that it was Charlie calling, she went back and forth in her mind about whether or not she should answer. A few months had gone by since that awful night at the bonfire party and she'd been avoiding him. She was so embarrassed about the whole situation. She didn't want to ever talk or hear about Jake again. At the last second, she answered the call. It wasn't Charlie's fault that things worked out the way they had with Jake. Paige also knew that sooner or later she was going to have to talk to Jake and it would be better if Charlie was on her side for that particular conversation.

"Hey girl, where've you been?" Charlie said as soon as Paige picked up the call.

"Oh, you know, just busy with school. Senior year and all," Paige had replied unconvincingly.

"That's bull shit and you know it. You've been avoiding me. I get it though, that mess with Jake was screwed up," Charlie called her out on her lame excuse, but as usual was understanding about the whole ordeal.

"I didn't know what to say. I'm pretty embarrassed about the whole thing. I can't believe I was so stupid and naive," Paige admitted sullenly. After being treated so terribly by Brad, she had vowed to herself to be smarter in the future. Jake had made a fool of her.

"Don't worry about it darling. You're not the first girl to get played by Jake. I was a little surprised by it though. He seemed to really care for you," Charlie said thoughtfully. "But we're still friends though, right? We don't have to have him around to hang out."

"Yes of course." Paige smiled. She did like spending time with Charlie. They both only thought of the other as a friend and not even anything potentially more. It really took the pressure off, but it didn't come close to how comfortable she had felt with Jake before everything got all screwed up.

"Well, since we're friends and all, I should probably get to the why of my call. I have some news and I wanted to make sure you found out from me and didn't get caught off guard by someone else telling you," Charlie hesitated. "I don't know if you've heard or not, but Jake started seeing that Rachel chick that was sometimes at the bonfires with Gunner not too long after that last night you were there."

"Oh really? Well, she's very pretty. I guess it doesn't surprise me that she caught his eye. I had heard that her and Gunner broke up," Paige felt a little ache starting to grow in her chest. She felt nauseated.

"Yeah, well, she's pregnant. Its Jake's baby and they are getting married," Charlie spit out rapidly like the words were a bad taste in his mouth. He knew how much the news was going to hurt Paige.

The bedroom Paige was in started spinning. She felt like she was going to throw up. She closed her eyes and tried to calm her breathing. She started to hyperventilate. The cell phone had dropped to the carpet because she was clutching both of her hands to her aching chest. She felt like her heart was shattering.

"Paige, are you still there? PAIGE!" Charlie yelled into the phone.

Paige took a few deep breaths and picked up the phone, but she kept her eyes shut. "Yeah, I'm still here. Look, I gotta go, but we'll get together soon." She hung up on Charlie without waiting for a response. She could no longer hold in the gut-wrenching sobs. And that is when the unbearable pain started.

***

Jake had spent a few minutes looking over the pictures of Paige and the writing on the last picture. Especially the one where the tall lucky bastard was holding her, kissing her. One of his hands was nestled in the back pocket of Paige's jeans just like Jake used to do when she was his. Jake's initial instinct was that it was Paige's date that had sent the pictures. Maybe as a "stay away, she's mine" type warning.

The more Jake thought about it though, that didn't make any sense. Why would the guy have someone take pictures of him and his date? He seemed normal as far as Jake could tell. He had watched him with Paige almost the whole time. And more importantly, he trusted Paige's judgement. Unfortunately, he had taught her back in her teen years to be cautious with men. She never would have kissed that guy if he had given her the creeps or had seemed ingenuine. The thought of Paige's lips on another man's made Jake's head spin. It had been a while since he had experienced jealousy, and he wasn't liking the bitter taste of it.

Tired of sitting in his desk chair doing nothing, Jake gathered up the pictures, lingering on the one of him holding Paige for a minute, then stuffed them back in the blank manilla envelope. He headed to the living room to tell Caleb that he needed to go stay with his mama for a few days. He wasn't risking Caleb getting caught up in a bad situation.

Once Jake saw his son off in the lifted Jeep that he and Caleb's mom and stepdad had gotten him for his seventeenth birthday, he returned inside the house and tried to figure out what the next step should be. Should he take it to the cops or try to handle it himself? Was he overreacting because it was Paige in those photos? He tried to focus on paperwork to get his mind clear, but by late afternoon he gave up and went to see his buddy Officer John Avery over at the police station.

Jake watched as his longtime friend put on powder-free latex gloves and looked over the pictures and the writing methodically. He appreciated John taking it seriously. His gut was telling him it wasn't some sort of prank. Jake paced the short distance in front of the desk, trying not to rush the process. Finally, John very carefully put the photos back in the envelope and slipped it into an evidence bag. He snapped the gloves off and threw them into the trash and looked up at Jake.

"I think you are right that it wasn't Paige's date that sent them. I'll still get his information from Paige and talk to him to follow procedure. My theory is that whoever this is, was actually following you, and after they saw you with Paige in the hallway at the restaurant, they switched their attention to her. That would indicate that they, most likely a she in this case, got jealous after seeing your exchange in the hallway. Or I guess the same thing could be true for her date. Maybe he is the one with the jealous stalker and they were watching the date and followed Paige to the hallway and then out to the parking lot," John reasoned aloud.

"I don't think it's me. I haven't been anywhere close to a relationship in a long time. Just a few one night stands here and there to take the edge off. Nothing that would make someone go crazy over me." Jake shook his head and looked around thinking. "Either way, it seems Paige might be in danger now."

"I agree. I'll need to go talk to her and find out some information about her date and see if she noticed anything strange that night," John said in his professional police officer tone of voice.

All of a sudden, Jake stopped pacing and blurted, "Jesus, I didn't even connect it until now. Her accident was that night on her way home from the restaurant. Maybe it wasn't a drunk driver after all." Jake was starting to freak out.

"I wouldn't jump to any conclusions just yet, even though I won't rule out the possibility that there's a connection. Whoever it was would have had to know where Paige lives to know which direction she would drive home that night. You say it was the first time you had spoken to her in years, and you were convinced that it was a first date, so that would have been the first time the person behind the camera would have laid eyes on Paige, regardless of which man the photographer was initially following," John said sensibly.

"Yeah, you're probably right. Can you wait until tomorrow to talk to her? I texted Faith on the way over and she's resting. I'll grab something to eat and head over there and keep an eye on her tonight." Jake was eager to lay eyes on her and make sure she was safe. And hopefully get to touch her.

"I guess I can do that. I was over there a little while ago myself. Mitch from the body shop had found her purse in the floorboard when the car was towed in. Two visits in one day from me might be too much. I'll send a squad car by every once in a while. Just to be safe," John said as he stood up to walk Jake out.

"How did she look?" Jake couldn't help but ask, even though he knew he would be seeing her for himself soon.

"Better than at the hospital. She's a tough cookie, that one." John shook hands with Jake at the door and walked back to his desk to finish up the paperwork on the photographs. He hoped it was some kind of sick prank, but fifteen years on the job was giving him that prickle on the back of the neck feeling.

When Jake arrived at Paige's house, Sadie opened the front door before he could knock. "She's sleeping," the doctor said quietly. She stood to the side so Jake could walk past her into the house.

"Can I talk to you about something then?" Jake asked in a whisper, not to disturb Paige who was sleeping soundly on the couch. Sadie led him to the kitchen and made herself a cup of tea. Jake noticed that she was avoiding looking him in the eye. He wondered if Faith had told her about their conversation in the waiting room. Oh well, he'd find out eventually, he was sure.

"So, what can I do for you?" Sadie asked Jake, finally bringing herself to look at him, but she seemed uneasy.

Jake told her about the pictures of Paige that had been put in his mailbox and his conversation with Officer John Avery. Sadie filled him in on what she knew about Mason, and he texted it to John.

"Do you mind if I stay? I'm sure you can handle yourself and you would know just where to cut a person if you needed to take them down, but I really need to be here. I need to keep her safe," Jake asked. He was trying not to sound as desperate as he felt. He failed miserably.

"Let me ask you something first." Sadie took a sip of her tea while she planned out the wording of what she wanted to say. "I get that Paige has left out a lot of details of the dynamic between you two in the past. But what she has told me doesn't sync up with how you seem to feel about her now. Am I reading that wrong? And if I'm not, what's changed in the ten or so years that you've not been a part of her life?"

"No, you're not wrong. I was a young guy that thought being tied down would be the worst thing in the world. Then I got my ex-wife pregnant after only a couple of months of dating and we got married. It didn't go well so that only reinforced the idea that marriage was not something I wanted. It took maturing as a man to realize that it would be completely different with the right person." Jake took a deep breath and ran his hand through his hair. He wasn't used to talking about his feelings so much, but he knew he needed to convince Sadie he was sincere about his intentions with Paige. "I took Paige for granted after we reconnected during her college days. I figured she'd always be around if I ever changed my mind about settling down. She was my best friend...and I loved her. I loved her more than I cared to admit. Then I lost her. I've had over ten years of missing her, of knowing exactly what I was missing. I'm not letting her get away again...if she'll have me."

Sadie brushed her eyes that had begun to water and cleared her throat. "I guess you can stay. At least until Paige wakes up. Then it will be up to her."

"Thank you, Sadie," Jake said relieved.

"Give her these pain meds when she wakes up. I'll be in that back bedroom binge watching *Bridgerton* on Netflix if you need me. It's not too often that I get to enjoy any downtime. You know, your friend Officer Avery reminds me a little of the Duke of Hastings," Sadie smirked.

"Honestly Sadie, I have no idea who that is," Jake quipped.

Sadie chuckled quietly and handed Jake the bottle of pain pills, then headed back to the guest room.

Jake made himself comfortable in the oversized chair across from the couch Paige was sleeping on; so a couple of hours later he was right there when she threw her arm over her face and started sobbing so hard that her whole body was shaking. The sound of utter despair coming from her had his heart plummeting into his stomach.

"Paige, baby what's going on? What's wrong? Talk to me." Jake threw himself down on his knees by the couch frantically looking up and down her body trying to figure out what had caused her to suddenly break down.

Paige took her arm away from her face and tried to see through the tears to see if she had really heard Jake's voice, or if it was a remnant of her devastating dream.

"Jake?" she asked, ashamed that her voice sounded so weak.

"Yeah baby, it's me." He scooped her up and sat on the couch with her in his arms and settled her sideways onto his lap. He reached over to the side table to grab the pain pills and her water. "Here, Sadie said to take these. Are you in a lot of pain?"

"Not really. I uh...I uh had a bad dream," she admitted hoarsely.

Paige took the pills and swallowed them. She was sore from the accident and the crying had not helped. It also gave her a few seconds to separate the dream about the past from the present. *What is he doing here?*

Jake noticed that she wasn't making eye contact with him like Sadie had done in the kitchen. So, the three friends must have been reminiscing about the not so pretty parts of his and Paige's past today. Great.

"Paige, look at me please," he said as he gently tilted her chin up so he could see her eyes.

When she looked up at him with her eyes still shiny with tears his heart nearly broke. Whether those tears were because of him or not, he knew that in the past he had caused her to look like that. To feel like that. He vowed once again to himself that he would never hurt her again.

"Talk to me baby, please. Let me help you. What has you so upset?"

"I'm still a little shook up from the wreck I guess," Paige said as she looked away from him.

Jake knew she wasn't telling him the truth, but he let it go. He knew he had to earn back her trust. He was ready to do whatever it took.

Paige was trying not to think about the close proximity of Jake and was failing miserably. She fit so perfectly in his lap. She could feel the thick, hard muscles of his stomach and chest, and of his arms that were wrapped tightly around her. He smelled so good, like soap and a manly woodsy cologne. Too tired to fight the attraction she felt like she would always have to him, she laid her head on his shoulder and nuzzled into the crook of his neck. He started slowly rubbing her back and running his fingers through her long hair. They stayed like that until her breathing returned to normal and her heart slowed down. When she felt like she had recovered from the outburst of crying the memory had brought on, she looked back up at Jake.

"Better?" Jake whispered softly. He had spent however long they had been sitting there trying to keep his heart from jumping out of his chest. He was sure she could hear it pounding but figured that was better than the blood rushing to a different part of his body. He didn't want to spook her.

"Yeah, much better," Paige whispered back. She stared into his beautiful blue eyes trying to read his mind. He had hurt her more than he could even imagine back then. She was confused because he seemed so different this time, but still felt like he was where she had always belonged. How was that possible?

"What are you thinking? And don't tell me nothing. I can see the wheels turning." Jake smiled as he brushed his thumb across her forehead and then tucked some of her silky raven hair behind her ear so he could see her face better.

"I'm thinking that you seem different. But it feels the same. That doesn't make any sense. I don't know. I'm confused." Paige was trying to organize her thoughts so she could put together the right words to convey what was going through her mind without revealing too much, but either the pain meds or being around Jake was making that extremely challenging.

"I am different, Paige. I grew up. I'm not that dumbass kid that took you for granted. And it feels the same because we belong together. We always have. I messed that up because I was young and thought being in a real relationship meant being tied down and I was scared of that. Instead of just being honest with you I inadvertently pushed you away and because of that I ended up having to live for over ten years without you in my life. I won't be making that mistake again." Jake hadn't meant to get that intense so soon but having her soft body laying up against him and looking into those sad green eyes, it poured out.

Warm tears started rolling out of Paige's eyes again.

"Baby, I didn't mean to make you cry." Jake went to pull her in for a tight hug but instead she kissed him.

It was a timid kiss. A soft peck on the lips. Paige hadn't meant to do it. Her body had betrayed her. She pulled back and looked up at Jake. There was shock in those blue eyes that quickly turned to heat. He leaned back in and rejoined their mouths. He started out gentle, but next thing she knew the kiss had deepened and she went from sitting sideways in his lap to straddling him with her hands gripping his thick biceps.

Jake was running his hands up and down the smooth skin of Paige's back under her shirt. He knew they should stop. She had been in a serious car accident a couple of days before and was still healing. The way she started running her hands through his hair and exploring his mouth with her tongue was driving him wild though and he couldn't find the strength to stop. She didn't seem to be too worried about her injuries and a soft moan escaped her lips, turning him on even more. Paige's hands were moving down to undo the top button of his shirt when they heard someone clear their throat, loudly.

Paige looked up sheepishly at Sadie who was standing in the doorway to the hallway that led back to the guest room. Sadie shook her head and said, "As your doctor, I must recommend that you cease that activity at once. You were just in a car accident for crying out loud."

"Yes, Dr. Jennings." Paige complied with a smirk and crawled off Jake's lap and snuggled next to him on the couch.

Jake looked over his shoulder to make sure Sadie had gone back to her room and then had to do some rearranging. His jeans were fitting a little too tight in the front at the moment.

Paige couldn't help but laugh and blushed thinking about getting caught in a compromising situation by her best friend.

"Well, that was interesting," Jake said as he pulled Paige in to snuggle even closer. "You want to watch a movie? Or do you need something to eat?"

"Let's just relax and watch a movie." Paige settled in the crook of his arm and started scrolling through movie options. She settled on an Adam Sandler comedy. She figured that was the safest genre for the confusing, yet oh so hot, circumstances.

Jake considered trying to continue their conversation from earlier about their relationship, to officially make her his. He didn't want there to be any question about what they were to each other. Paige was so at ease and her eyelids were starting to droop. *The pain meds must be kicking in,* he thought as he looked over her beautiful face. He decided that the conversation could wait. There would be plenty of time to work through the hurts of the past and to plan a future. He wasn't going anywhere and right then he was perfectly content holding her against him.

CHAPTER ELEVEN

Faith allowed herself to sleep in a little later than usual Monday morning since she wasn't going into work. She knew Sadie would have everything under control over at Paige's house. No reason to get out of her cozy bed she shared with her loving husband before the sun came up if she didn't have to.

When she heard Travis's alarm go off around seven a.m. she rolled over and checked her phone. There were no missed texts or calls from Jake. That was weird, she expected to have at least a few. He had been checking up on Paige consistently. Maybe someone had given him Sadie's number. Or maybe his renewed interest in Paige was short-lived. She was secretly hoping that was the case after the upsetting story Paige had told them yesterday. Yeah, the guy had been young, but did people really change that much? She was firmly on Team Mason.

So, imagine Faith's surprise when she walked into Paige's house an hour later and saw Paige on the couch sound asleep in Jake's muscled arms. He was snoring softly, his head snuggled into Paige's dark hair. Faith stood there gaping; it felt like her chin was on her chest. Out of the corner of her eye she saw Sadie waving her over to the kitchen, and after a few more seconds of staring at the scene on the couch, she followed Sadie into the kitchen.

"What the hell is going on with that?" Faith shrieked. "That is the last thing I expected to see when I walked in here after what she told us yesterday."

"Tell me about it. I caught them going at it like teenagers last night and as her doctor, I put a stop to it," Sadie said as she brought her teacup up to her lips.

"Well, thank goodness you did. What is she thinking?" Faith couldn't wrap her head around it.

"We will have to ask her when she wakes up. If he leaves that is," Sadie answered. "I'm not quite as opposed to Jake as you seem to be. I'm just worried about Paige," Sadie added as she watched Faith slam and bang herself around the kitchen to make herself some tea. Sadie knew that Faith preferred Mason over Jake for Paige, but man was she worked up.

"Mornin'," came a masculine southern drawl from the kitchen doorway.

Jake chuckled, entertained by the little jumps the two women gave. They looked like two kids who got caught trying to sneak Halloween candy that their parents had hidden on top of the refrigerator.

"Didn't mean to wake you," Faith said with a little smirk on her face when she regained her composure.

"Uh huh." Jake didn't buy it for a second. "Paige is brushing her teeth. She'll be right in and then I think I need to catch her and you," he pointed at Faith, "up on what I told Sadie last night."

Faith looked over at Sadie with wide eyes in an expression that said, "Oh really?" Sadie shrugged. Faith's imagination started running wild. The three of them stood around in awkward silence with Faith shooting speculative glances at Jake and Sadie.

As soon as Paige stepped into the kitchen, her attention was caught by the expression on Faith's face. She looked like her head was about to explode! Paige started shaking her head and laughed. "Not until I get some caffeine in my system first," she told Faith.

"That's fine. Jake here was just saying that he needs to tell me and you about an important discussion he had with Sadie last night," Faith retorted as she did that hip pop and arm cross thing she does when she's trying to make a point. *Ha! That got Paige's attention,* she thought as her friend whirled around to look between Sadie and Jake.

Sadie let out an exasperated breath while Jake simply remained leaning up against the counter, never breaking his eye contact with Paige. Paige was reassured by what she saw in his eyes. She went back to making her tea and calmly went and sat at the breakfast table when she was done.

"So, what's going on?" she asked as she took her first sip of heaven in a cup. She watched as her two best friends and her past, possibly present, love joined her at the kitchen table.

"I don't want to unnecessarily alarm you," Jake began in a calm level voice, "but someone put pictures of you in my mailbox yesterday. Or maybe the day before. I'm not sure which. I took them to John Avery down at the police station, and he has filed an official police report."

"What do you mean, pictures of me?" Paige exclaimed alarmed and suddenly wide awake.

"I took pictures of them with my phone before I handed them over to John," he said as he took out his phone and brought up the photos. He handed the phone reluctantly over to Paige. "I didn't mention it last night since you already seemed upset about something when you woke up," he added as she took the phone from his hands.

Paige looked over the pictures on Jake's phone slowly. She went through a wide range of emotions as she took in each one. The first picture was a black and white of her and Jake in the hallway at Lorenzo's. They looked as good together as they had felt with their arms wrapped around each other. Paige studied the look on Jake's face in the photo as he held her. She was a bit shocked to see such an obvious expression of deep yearning. She remembered feeling the exact same way. Not to be sidetracked from the matter at hand, she ignored the fluttering of her heart and pushed those thoughts to the back of her mind.

Paige was confused as to why anyone would have taken a picture of them and tried to remember if she noticed anyone else back there in the hallway. Her initial thought was, *did Mason take this?* He didn't seem like the type, but she didn't know him very well. That thought was whisked away when she saw the next picture, which was of her and Mason outside the restaurant, by her car, smiling at each other. She blushed at the next two photos, which showed that the kiss looked as hot as it had felt at the time. She glanced up at Jake, who was looking right back at her gauging her reactions. She quickly looked back down and scrolled to the next photo Jake had taken to see that it was a message handwritten in black marker, probably a Sharpie, in all uppercase letters. A warning.

"That was on the back of the last one," Jake said to answer the unspoken question that was written all over Paige's face.

"Oh my God, the suspense is killing me," Faith exclaimed and held her hand out for the phone. Paige handed it over and as Faith looked over the photos, Jake relayed the rest of his conversation with John Avery and the theories the officer had about the photographer.

"We need to let John talk to this Mason guy and find out about his ex-wife or anyone else the guy has dated that might be responsible for these photos," Jake said to the ladies. He didn't like knowing the guy's name. Made it seem more real that he had competition for Paige's heart. Seeing the pictures of Mason kissing Paige again had jealousy flowing through his veins.

"But that doesn't make any sense," Faith replied. She handed the phone over to Sadie and looked up at Jake. "If whoever is doing this was jealous of Paige because of Mason, why would they send these photos to you with that message? It sounds like they are all for her and Mason being together. Seems to me like they were jealous of her encounter with you in the hallway at Lorenzo's and then they followed her out of the restaurant. So maybe we should be asking about *your* ex-wife and *your* conquests. From what I've heard, you're quite the ladies' man. Mason is a good family man," Faith said accusingly to Jake. Her voice rising to a yell.

Jake knew his face was turning beet red as he clenched his jaw. He was trying to keep his temper down. He didn't appreciate getting screamed at, even if he knew deep down in his heart that Faith was probably right.

Paige knew Jake was getting upset, but Faith was right. She gently put her hand on Jake's forearm and got him to look at her instead of Faith. Softly, she said, "Jake, she's right. Think about it. If they were jealous of me being with Mason, that message would have been on the photo of me and you together instead of the one of me and Mason. And the photos would have been mysteriously left in his mailbox, not in yours."

Jake shook his head. He had already gone over and over in his mind about whether or not the situation could be because of him. He hadn't been able to make it make sense. He was on good terms with Rachel; they both agreed they should never have gotten married just because they had a child together. She was happily married to someone else and had a family. There was one woman he had dated steady for a while, but that was over five years ago, and she had moved to another state and married. The others had been one-night stands in Charleston or wherever he traveled for work. Those were only occasionally when his needs were too loud to ignore. He didn't even know their names. He wasn't proud of that fact, and it was not something he wanted to tell Paige.

"I don't have anyone in my past who would be so crazy about me that they would do something like this," he finally said after a couple of minutes of quiet when he realized all three women were looking at him expectantly.

"Sometimes people don't need much to get them attached," Sadie said in her matter-of-fact doctor tone.

Paige felt bad for Jake. He was in serious denial about what seemed to be going on. He didn't want to be responsible for potentially putting her in danger, even unintentionally.

"Either way, John has to talk to Mason to follow procedure. I had texted his name to John after Sadie told me last night," Jake said.

He stood up and walked to the kitchen sink to look out the window to the backyard. He felt uneasy and restless. He had to do something to prove that what was happening wasn't because of him. "Since it looks like y'all have looking after Paige covered, I'll go run some errands. Is it okay if I come back later?" he asked as he looked back at Paige.

Paige nodded yes. She knew that he was jumping around on the inside. He was going to be frustrated until he figured everything out. He was a problem-solving kind of guy. He leaned down to kiss her on the top of the head and gave her shoulder an affectionate little squeeze. Paige watched as he headed out of the kitchen and waited until she heard the front door close behind him before she looked over at her friends.

"I need to call Mason and give him a heads up," she said.

"I think this is an in-person conversation. He's about to have the cops questioning him about his personal life," Faith replied. "The issue of Team Mason versus Team Jake doesn't matter anymore. Well, maybe just a little, but I am more worried about your safety. Whoever sent those photos is sick in the head." Faith paced around a bit. "I feel bad for yelling at Jake. It isn't entirely his fault."

"I didn't realize that there are teams. But you are right about one thing. I'll call Mason and ask him to come over here. I doubt my doctor will let me go anywhere." Paige smiled at Sadie. She was trying to ease the tension in the room, but it wasn't working. They were all worried about the situation. Who knew how crazy the person behind those photos could be.

Paige sent a quick text to her parents asking them to keep the kids at their house. That at least would be one less thing for her to worry about while she tried to sort the whole mess out. Then she texted Mason as she walked up the stairs to get dressed. *What does one wear to tell a man you barely know, but like, that the cops are going to want to talk to him about pictures of y'all kissing that were left in the mailbox of another man?* Paige wondered.

***

She sat in the storage room she had converted into a dark room in the basement of her little house on the outskirts of Charleston, on the opposite side of Meadow Oaks, looking at the photos of her handiwork. *How did that bitch survive that crash?* she asked herself as she looked over the photographs of the wreckage she had caused. It was beautiful, like a work of art. The white SUV had spun and spun until it slid off the embankment to smash into a giant tree. The only way it would have been better is if the bitch's car had flipped over the concrete barrier of the bridge and sank in the creek, drowning that horrid woman. Who did she think she was touching her man like that?

She was getting angry just thinking about it. That dark-haired slut. How lucky was it she guessed right on which direction the whore lived and that there was a bridge! If only she had died like she was supposed to! *Oh well, I'll just have to step it up. Get more hands on as it were,* she thought to herself. She knew that no one had noticed her at the restaurant that night so it would be easy to get close to her target again. As she shoved the pictures of the car wreck into a blank manilla envelope, having made sure to wear gloves throughout the process, she planned her next move and thought about where to leave the next set of photos for her lover to find.

It was one of her favorite parts of the game she liked to play. The game she had started playing at the ripe age of twenty-two, when her betrothed had abandoned her at the alter for another woman. *Another whore, exactly like this one.* Visions of the church filled with flowers, friends, and family invaded her sight. She couldn't stand the thought of the looks of pity as she stood there in her ballgown style wedding dress with tears ruining her special make-up. She shook her head side to side hard to push the thoughts of her dream wedding gone wrong from her mind.

Usually, she went after the man for being disloyal to her, but he was different. She would get her dream wedding and happily ever after with him. Her true love only hugged that pathetic woman out of pity. But she was going to make sure he knew that she wasn't happy about it.

CHAPTER TWELVE

After Paige called Mason and asked him to come over, she spent some time dawdling in her walk-in closet so she could think by herself for a little while. He wasn't coming over until lunchtime, so she had a little time to think of what to say to him. How was she going to explain Jake to him? She wasn't even sure herself what was going on between them.

She felt a little silly about giving in to her physical urges the night before and blushed at the memory. Paige promised herself to use more reason in the future. They weren't teenagers anymore and there was a lot more at stake. She had to think of what was best for her children. Mason seemed like a great steadfast guy, and she would be stupid to throw him aside because Jake was finally giving her the time of day. Yes, they had history; but maybe history shouldn't repeat itself. The inner conflict continued to rage as she pulled on her best pair of skin tight jeans and a V-neck tee that showed just a hint of her ample cleavage. The giant bruise from where her seatbelt secured her in place during the accident ruined the look and she had to settle for a less flattering top. After checking herself out from every angle in the floor length mirror she headed to the kitchen to tell Faith and Sadie that they were going to have a lunch guest.

Faith, of course, was thrilled. "I'll make those pork chops I never got around to yesterday! You know, my mama always said that the way to a man's heart is through his stomach, and it is as true today as it was then."

"Well, I guess that means he is going to fall madly in love with you, Faith," Paige teased, getting a chuckle out of Sadie.

"Hardy har-har," Faith smirked.

Faith started going through cabinets and the pantry in the kitchen to make sure Paige had all the necessary seasonings and such to make her famous, to her friends and family that was, fried pork chops. When she was satisfied that Paige did indeed have what she needed, she came and joined the other two ladies back at the breakfast table.

"Since we have a couple hours until Mason will be here, why don't you tell us the rest of the Jake story," Faith said, not wasting anytime on small talk.

"Do I really have to? I was trying to stay clear headed today since there might be a deranged stalker after me." Paige poked out her bottom lip and fluttered her eyelashes at her friend.

"You know that's not going to work on me and the deranged stalker is exactly why I need to know the rest of the story. What makes Jake so special that he is worth all this dadgum drama?" Faith was not going to back down.

"I would like to know too. If he is in your life, then that means he's in ours as well. Tell us what happened," Sadie added reasonably.

Paige couldn't bring herself to talk about the phone call with Charlie and the aftermath. They would never forgive Jake and since Jake didn't even know about that phone call, it didn't seem right to tell them.

"Nothing happened."

"Do not try to play this off. He said he broke your heart too many times. So, if I'm going to have to possibly open a can of whoop ass on some crazy chick for you because of him, I want to know why," Faith insisted, looking over at Sadie for backup. Sadie simply sat there patiently, which infuriated Faith more.

"Isn't one time too many times to have your heart broken?" Paige asked, repeating Faith's words from the day before, but quickly held up her hands in surrender and relented. "Fine. Fine. Technically, he didn't do anything wrong."

Faith let out some sort of snort that might have been a "yeah right" in human language, but Paige decided to ignore it.

"After his brief marriage to his wife Rachel ended, he started hanging out with some of his old friends again. I had become friends with a couple of them during the time he was off being married and a new dad, so we were thrown into spending time together again," Paige shrugged.

"Ok, continue," Faith said when Paige didn't say anything else after a few seconds.

"I don't remember exactly what happened back then. I just know that I had been determined not to fall for him again, but the problem was I had never really stopped having feelings for him. I tried to pretend like I had and did my best to never be alone with him. I dated other guys as y'all well know, and lord knows he dated other girls. But eventually we fell into old habits and became super close friends again. It became harder for me to deny my feelings and to not get hurt." Paige stopped to take a sip of water and shrugged her shoulders again, hoping her friends accepted that watered down version of the story.

"Ok, but exactly how close that time?" Sadie asked. She was leaning in on one elbow, eager for more details. "I know you are leaving a bunch out. You are too level-headed to be so into a guy you haven't seen in years without some *serious* history. And from what I walked in on last night, you are definitely into Jake. Y'all were making me blush! If I didn't know you as well as I do then maybe, just maybe, I could have brushed it off as only physical attraction, but I know better. You haven't been with anyone in that way since Matt. You wouldn't jump into bed, or couch as it were, with just anyone."

"We didn't sleep together if that's what you're getting at. He would occasionally hold my hand and *stuff*, but I knew better than to think it meant anything, so I never let it go too far. We would both be really affectionate towards each other if we both found ourselves single at the same time. I guess we were both really comfortable with each other. Sometimes he would say things that implied there was a future for us, but I wouldn't let myself put too much stock in it; I knew better," Paige said in what she thought of as her most convincing voice.

"I'm not buying it." Faith was shaking her head vigorously. "I know you. There *has* to be more you are leaving out or you wouldn't have felt the need to downplay y'all's relationship or friendship or whatever you want to call it to us back when we were in college. What about his kid? You never even mentioned that *Bennett* had a kid. Were you around him any?"

"I was around Caleb plenty. He was a very cute kid. What has that got to do with anything?" Paige was not liking where the conversation was going.

"Girl, we are your best friends. Stop bullshitting us. I'm not trying to upset you, but we really need to figure out the whole Jake situation fast. I would also like to understand the hold Jake seems to have over my *best* friend who is normally level-headed and no-nonsense," Faith pushed.

"Fine." Knowing Faith was not going to back down, Paige took a deep breath and as she released it, blurted out, "Even though I tried to act like I didn't have feelings for him anymore, it felt like a brutal rejection every time I had to hear about him with someone else. A knife to the heart every single time. And considering we were around each other for years this go round instead of just months like before, that was a whole lot of hurt. Any time he held my hand or put his arm around me or showed me any kind of affection, the pressure in my chest from all of the feelings I was holding back made my heart feel like it would implode."

Paige swallowed around the lump in her throat and continued, "Watching Jake be such a great daddy to his son made me ache for things I had no right to. And I loved Caleb so damn much. I tried my hardest not to because I knew that one day he would have a stepmom and that it wouldn't be me… and that it was going to shatter my heart. And I never told you about Caleb because I knew y'all would pick up on how much that little boy meant to me and there would be questions and that would mean I would have to face how I really felt about the whole messed up situation with Jake."

Paige could feel the tears pooling in her eyes as she poured her heart out. She blinked really fast a few times to try to push them back. One traitorous tear had slipped out and she brushed it away with her hand.

Faith and Sadie had teared up as well. Other than big life changing events like when Matt died or her kids had been born, it was rare to see Paige get so outwardly emotional.

"Sweetie, if it was that hard for you to be around Jake, why do it at all?" Faith asked, reaching out to hold Paige's hand.

"I guess because he really was a great friend when you put all the romantic stuff aside. He was so encouraging when it came to school and my goals. He was protective and sweet. The deepest conversations I have ever had have been with Jake. And I can admit now that a part of me was hoping it would be like a romantic comedy movie or that Usher song and he would come to realize that I was the one for him. I was hoping for the big dramatic gesture when that finally happened." Paige shrugged and rubbed her hands over her watery eyes. "I didn't know that he knew how I felt the entire time though. I thought I had hidden it better. Whoops."

Paige laughed at the absurdity of it all. She was sitting in her house talking about things she thought she had put behind her years ago, and there was some crazy person taking pictures of her. *Stop lying to yourself. You've never forgotten the connection you had with Jake,* her mind reminded her.

"So, how did y'all end things that time?" Sadie questioned.

"I got busy after graduating from college, and he had Caleb to take care of and his job. I started to feel like I was at a point where I needed to make some decisions about what direction I wanted my life to take. I knew I wanted to get married someday and have children. I took some time away from him to sort through how I felt. When the feelings didn't fade I decided one day, when I was feeling bold, to call him up and find out if there were any feelings on his side of things." Paige paused in her story and got up to find a snack.

"Come on! You're killing me, and you know it. What happened?" Faith exclaimed.

Paige rooted around for a minute in the pantry and came back with some chips. She was stress eating, but it could've been worse.

"Jake said that he missed me. I asked him if he was seeing anybody, and it turned out he was hooking up with my friend that I had gone to that college party with back in high school. The one where he kissed that random girl. At that point I realized that if he had felt the same way about me, he wouldn't be sleeping with my friends. He said they weren't dating or anything, just friends, that he had needed someone to talk to since I wasn't around. I made some comment about being replaced, to which he replied that I could never be replaced. Part of me wanted to believe him, but I knew how it felt to be on the other end of the *technically just friends but sleeping together* situation, so I decided right then to move on. It was kind of a relief in a way. I had thought that he was the one I was going to end up marrying and having children with. Turns out, he wasn't. I met Matt shortly after and the rest was history. If he hadn't slept with her, I might not have been open to giving someone else a real chance and would have been waiting around even longer than I already had for that elusive grand gesture." Paige gave a one shoulder shrug as she shoveled the salty chips into her mouth.

"Hmm. It kind of sounds like history is repeating itself a bit. Matt. Mason." Faith smiled at Paige while wiggling her finger at her.

"Uh huh. Right. Shouldn't you be getting some pork chops ready or something?" Paige threw a chip at Faith. Faith laughed and got up to prep lunch.

Paige knew why Faith was letting her change the subject. Faith was hoping that everything Paige had relived telling the history with Jake would help push the odds over to favor Mason.

Faith was taking the pork chops out of the skillet when Paige's doorbell rang. Paige patted her hair and straightened her clothes on her way to answer the door. She may have also glanced in the mirror in the foyer on the way, but what woman wouldn't when she was expecting a handsome man?

"Hey, Mason. Thank you for coming on such short notice." Paige welcomed him in and got those little butterflies in her stomach. He was wearing another Henley with jeans. The man certainly knew what worked for him.

"I'm so glad you called. How are you feeling today?" Mason had brought her a bouquet of wildflowers and handed them to her as he looked sweetly into her eyes. He gave her a shy smile and leaned in to give her a quick kiss.

"Thank you, these are gorgeous. I'm sore but feeling better every day," Paige said as they pulled away. It had been an extremely long time since she felt the rush of early attraction.

"Dang it smells good in here," Mason said appreciatively.

"That would be Faith's famous pork chops. She's a great cook."

Paige led him into the kitchen where Faith and Sadie were trying to pretend like they hadn't been peeking around the corner. She rolled her eyes at them and introduced Mason to Sadie. Once all the pleasantries had been exchanged and plates were fixed, Paige had to tell Mason why she had asked him over.

"Let me make sure I have this right. Someone took pictures of us on our date and put them in an old friend of yours's mailbox? The one you ran into on the way back from the ladies' room? Doesn't really make much sense," Mason said around a bite of macaroni and cheese.

"We think they are jealous of Paige because she hugged him in the hallway at Lorenzo's. We think it is a woman and that she had been watching Jake and then switched to Paige after she saw them together," Faith summarized. She watched as Mason nodded his head thinking it over carefully.

"But this Officer John Avery wants to talk to me about my past love life," Mason said matter-of-factly.

"Just to follow procedure," Sadie reassured him. She could see why Faith was so eager for Paige to date Mason. He was polite, handsome, and she liked how he looked at Paige. It wasn't as intense as Jake looked at her. It was a sweeter, almost hopeful expression.

"Well, there is not much to tell him. My wife left me about a year and a half ago for some rich stockbroker or finance guy. Still not sure exactly what he does. I have full custody of Anna-Grace because her mom would rather travel around the world vacationing than stay put for her daughter. Paige here is the first date I've had since the divorce." Mason looked sideways at Paige gauging her reaction to that little piece of news.

"Well, isn't that nice," Faith said giving both Paige and Mason googly eyes.

Paige looked over at Mason and it looked like he might be blushing, but it was hard to tell with that dark sexy beard. She closed her eyes and shook her head. She really shouldn't be thinking about that sort of stuff with the more pressing matter of a psycho stalker to be worried about. *Get your head out of the gutter, Paige.*

Mason cleared his throat and asked, "What are the police going to do to keep you safe until they figure out if this is a real threat or not?"

"Um, I think a squad car goes by every so often. Sadie is staying here with me, and my kids are with my parents," Paige replied.

"I feel like I should do something, but I have Anna-Grace to think about." Mason was clenching his fist. "Honestly, I feel helpless. I don't know you well enough to insist that you come stay with me so I can keep you safe, but that's exactly what I want to do."

"That is so sweet, Mason. We'll keep her safe. Don't you worry," Faith reassured him.

They changed to small talk and Mason had them cracking up with hilarious stories about Anna-Grace and her shenanigans. It was obvious to the ladies that his daughter was the center of his world. It felt like it was too soon that he had to head back to work. All three women were walking Mason to the front door, still laughing, and chatting, when it opened and in walked Jake.

CHAPTER THIRTEEN

Jake froze in the front doorway to Paige's house as he realized there was a small crowd of people walking towards the door. Mason was there, in Paige's home. Not only that, Paige and her two best friends were hanging on the tall bastard's every word. They were giggling like school girls. *Well, isn't this cozy,* Jake thought. He gathered his wits and headed over to the bench in the foyer to put down the box of security cameras he had brought, then went over to shake Mason's hand and introduce himself.

Jake felt like he had been punched in the stomach and bile was threatening to rise up his throat. He thought that after last night he and Paige had an understanding about where their relationship stood. *I wonder if this was how Paige felt all those years ago,* he thought guiltily to himself. Back then he had convinced himself he wasn't doing anything wrong because he hadn't actually made any promises. He had been an ass.

"So, Jake, why do you think whoever this crazy mystery person is left pictures of us in your mailbox?" Mason asked.

Mason put his arm around Paige as he said, "us". Jake watched the movement and tried not to let it show on his face how much it bothered him. Bile was churning angrily in his stomach. He looked over at Paige who seemed to not know where to look. The other two ladies were watching the show with interest. All that was missing was a tub of popcorn between them.

"We are still trying to figure that out. That's why I brought some security cameras to install, and Paige can monitor them with an app on her phone. I just got done putting some up at my house. It would have been nice to have had footage of my mailbox to see if

I recognized whoever put those pictures in there. None of my neighbors are close enough to have seen anything," Jake explained.

Jake knew it was ridiculous, but he felt like a caveman whose territory had been invaded. He attempted to reign in his emotions. Paige would not appreciate him going all possessive on her and he technically had no right to. *Bullshit, she's mine,* he couldn't help but think.

"That's a great idea. I wish I could stay and help you install them, but I have to get back to work." Mason turned and gave Paige a kiss on the cheek and whispered, "Call you later," in her ear. As he walked out, he nodded at Faith and Sadie, and they gave little swoony waves back.

"It was nice to meet you, Jake," Mason said as he passed by Jake to get out of the front door. It was hard not to notice the two men sizing each other up.

Paige thought she might have a heart attack, she was so overwhelmed by having both men in her house at the same time. Why did it feel like her house had suddenly shrunk? She had assumed Jake would be gone all day working. She knew logically that she hadn't done anything wrong by inviting Mason over for lunch, but her heart felt heavy with guilt anyway.

"Thank you for bringing the security cameras, Jake. That was very thoughtful of you. I'll feel a lot safer with them around the house." When Jake nodded and looked at the ground without saying anything, Paige took a step towards him. "I invited Mason over to explain to him why the police are going to be contacting him and asking him questions about his past love life. I felt like I owed him a heads up."

Faith and Sadie took that as their cue to return to the kitchen.

"It's okay, Paige. You don't have to explain anything. I'll just go out and put these up...if you are sure it's okay? I don't want to overstep." Jake picked up the box and when Paige nodded her assent, he headed outside.

I don't deserve her, he thought sullenly. Jake knew that she was possibly in danger because of him. He had spent the entire time he was installing cameras at his house racking his brain as to who could be responsible for the photos. He could vaguely picture a few faces of his past one-night stands, but no names came to mind. John had stopped by while he was out on patrol, and they had tried to talk through it to no avail.

Paige stood motionless in her foyer for a few minutes trying to process everything that had just happened. She could hear Jake moving around in the garage getting the ladder and tools. When it became clear that she wasn't going to figure anything out standing there like a statue, she went into the kitchen to find her friends.

"Well, that was awkward," she said sitting at the table, putting her head in her hands.

"It could have been much worse," Sadie responded. She walked over and put her hand on Paige's shoulder. "And as your doctor I am recommending that you go upstairs and get some rest. You've had a lot of excitement today. You're still healing."

"Yeah, and I'll head home and check in later," Faith said as she finished cleaning the last dish in the sink. She wiped down the counter and started gathering her things.

"Thank you so much for everything Faith. Lunch was delicious." Paige stood and hugged her friend goodbye. She gave a little nod to Sadie and headed up to her bed to snuggle in for what she hoped was a long, restful nap. As she lay in bed, she could hear Jake moving around outside, the clanging of the ladder as he set it in place against the eave of the roof and the whirring of the drill. Concentrating on the comforting sounds of him working to keep her and her children safe, she drifted off to sleep.

When Paige woke up, the sky had darkened outside, and the house was quiet. She made her way downstairs and found Sadie curled up on the couch reading a medical journal.

"Well, that looks interesting," she said, plopping down on the opposite side of the couch.

"It is. It's about a new technique to do a double bypass.... you were being sarcastic, weren't you?" Sadie gave Paige a dirty look and then couldn't help but laugh as her friend starting giggling.

"Jake went home a while ago. You left your phone down here, and since I know your PIN, I had him install the app for the cameras on your phone and show me how to use it. I'm glad he put those in. I was worried about leaving you alone when I have to be back at the hospital on Wednesday," Sadie said as she handed over the phone to Paige.

"It was very sweet of him to think of it," Paige said quietly.

"Yes, it was," Sadie admitted. "It seems you have two great men who care a great deal about you. You are going to have to make a choice soon. Love triangles are so played out," Sadie teased to lighten the mood. "For what it's worth, I don't think you could go wrong with either. I know Faith is not a Jake fan, but I got to spend some time with him, and he seems steadfast in his feelings for you."

Paige sighed heavily and pulled her legs up under her. "I have no idea what I'm going to do, Sadie. Mason is a wonderful man and I get butterflies in my stomach when I am around him. But Jake...when I'm around him, the whole world shifts. I'm not even sure I could explain it. It is so intense, but at the same time so comfortable. It's a complete oxymoron. But I'm so scared that things with Jake will fall apart again, and it will ruin me."

"I think you have your mind made up, you just have to make peace with it," Sadie replied. "But for tonight, why don't we relax and watch a movie. We can save the difficult decisions for another time."

"Sounds perfect," Paige said. She relaxed into the cushions pondering what Sadie had said. She knew that her friend was right, as usual.

CHAPTER FOURTEEN

On Wednesday, Paige returned to work at the magazine. She was determined to resume her normal life. Tuesday had been uneventful. Jake and Mason had both called to check on her, but no one came by. She had hung around the house with Sadie all day, and even though spending time with her friend was great, she was ready to be productive. She was also hoping that working would make it harder for her to spend all her time thinking about Jake. And Mason. Everyone at work was fussing over her all day long. Normally, the attention would have driven her crazy, but it was a welcome distraction from her present predicament.

Paige called her parents to let them know that she was more than ready for the kids to come home after school on Wednesday. The kids, however, begged her to let them stay one more night. They convinced their grandma to rent a superhero movie they were dying to see and hadn't watched it yet. Paige missed them so much, but she eventually gave in. *It might not be a bad thing to have one night alone at the house to see if the stalker person tries anything,* she thought to herself.

The security camera app was straight forward, and she got an alert anytime anything came into the yard. She was aware of every squirrel, cat, dog, and possum that wandered onto her property. Even though it was a bit of a nuisance, it did give her a sense of control in an unnerving situation. *Jake did that for you,* she thought.

When Paige got home from work, she put on her comfy clothes and poured herself a big glass of wine. She figured she could indulge a little since she was off the pain pills. She was warming up some of Faith's scrumptious leftovers in the microwave when her doorbell chimed.

Under normal circumstances, Paige would not have given a second thought to answering her door. She lived in a very safe small town after all. But things were definitely far from normal. She grabbed a kitchen knife and creeped silently towards the front door. She felt like one of those silly women in the horror flicks from her youth, but she wasn't taking any chances. *I'm Sarah Michelle Gellar as Buffy, not as Helen in I know What You Did Last Summer,* Paige told herself, trying to give her body a little pep talk.

Halfway to the door she remembered that she could check the app on her phone to see who was at the door. Why hadn't she heard the notification? Lord knows she had heard the ping enough while she had been at work. She realized then that she had left her phone upstairs in her bedroom when she changed into sweats and a t-shirt after arriving home. *Brilliant job Paige,* she chastised herself for not being more careful and decided to chance looking through the peephole. It was Jake. Her heart fluttered.

Jake couldn't help but smile when Paige opened the door. She was standing there in gray sweats, an old Shania Twain t-shirt, holding up a butcher knife. She looked adorable. He was sure she was going for badass, so he put up his hands in fake surrender. "Don't stab me, please. I just wanted to check on you."

"Ha-ha. You're so funny," Paige mumbled and turned to walk back into the kitchen.

Jake took that as a cue to follow her. He closed the door and made sure he locked it. "Where is your phone? I thought I had installed a handy app on it, so you wouldn't have to answer the door armed to the teeth."

"What makes you think I didn't know it was you?" Paige asked, grinning ear to ear.

"Now who's being funny?" Jake smirked. "Where's everybody at anyways?"

"The kids wanted to stay at mom and dad's one more night, and Sadie went back to work. I'm heating up some leftovers. I wasn't about to cook for just me. You want some?" Paige asked Jake when he came into the kitchen. She really wanted him to say yes. She wanted more time with him.

"Yes, please. It smells mouthwatering." Jake helped her get the plates ready. They moved around the kitchen together like a couple that had been doing it for years.

"I can't take credit for the food. Faith cooked it," Paige admitted.

They ate in comfortable silence for a few minutes, enjoying the meal. Paige was still thinking over what Sadie had said about Paige making peace with the decision she couldn't seem to admit that she had made about Jake and Mason. However, there was a different problem that needed to be solved first.

"Have you heard anything more from your buddy Officer John about our case?"

Jake took a few seconds to chew and wiped his face with his napkin. He hated thinking about her being in danger, especially when seconds before he was thinking about how at home he felt sharing a meal with her.

"Nothing new to report. I called him late this afternoon, but since I couldn't come up with a list of potential suspects when he asked me Monday morning, there is not much he can do. There weren't any prints on the photos other than mine. Or on the envelope."

Paige could sense that Jake was feeling guilty about the situation. His shoulders had tensed up and his hands were tightly fisted. She reached over and gave his hand a reassuring squeeze, loosening his fingers. He held onto her hand, running his thumb back and forth over her knuckles. Tingles of electricity flowing between them. After a few minutes he let go and they went back to eating.

Jake wanted to know everything about what was going on in Paige's life, so he asked her endless questions about the kids and her work while they ate. His genuine interest in even the minute details of her life touched her heart deeply. They fell into an easy rhythm and the wall Paige tried to put up came crumbling down piece by piece.

"I would like to stay the night and make sure you're safe. I'll sleep on the couch," Jake said while they were clearing the dishes. He had debated on whether he would bring it up, but with Sadie back at the hospital he couldn't bear the thought of Paige being home alone. The worrying was driving him crazy.

"What about Caleb? Doesn't he need you at home?" Paige asked.

She wondered what Caleb looked like as a teenager. She hadn't seen him since he was six or seven years old. In the few pictures of him on Jake's social media, Caleb always held something silly in front of his face like a car part covered in grease, or a fish he had caught. She'd have to ask Jake about that bit of quirkiness later.

"He's staying at his mama's this week," he answered simply.

Jake didn't want to pressure Paige into letting him stay. He let her think about his request to spend the night in quiet while he dried their dinner plates. He could feel her eyes on him. *I'm not going to push if she says no. I will park my truck on the street and sit in it all night and watch over the house if I have to. Anything to keep her safe,* Jake thought.

"I probably would sleep better knowing someone else is here. Not very Buffy of me, but it's the truth." Paige shrugged nonchalantly, but on the inside was spazzing out at the idea of having Jake in her home with no one else there to keep her from giving in to temptation.

"Buffy huh? Still a fan I see." Jake chuckled. "Well since you are still healing from your accident, how about I slay any monsters that try to attack us tonight."

Paige looked over Jake's hard muscled body, picturing the damage it could do to anyone who tried to cause her harm. She felt heat flushing her cheeks, so she turned away before he could notice. She wasn't sure if she could deny him if he acted on her attraction to him.

Jake followed Paige into the living room. She made up a bed on the couch with a thick blanket and two fluffy pillows. She liked the house cold at night while she slept snuggled up in her bed. When she was satisfied with the makeshift bed she plopped down in the oversized chair, not quite ready for their time together to end. When she looked up at him, he seemed happy that she hadn't immediately went upstairs.

"Paige, I've had a wonderful time catching up talking about our lives and our children, but I think it's time we talk about us," Jake said nervously. "I know us running into each other the other night has brought up memories. Hopefully not too many of them unpleasant, but maybe it would be good if we worked some things out so that we can have a future together. That's what I want Paige. A future with you."

Paige gulped. She knew that it was a talk they needed to have, but she wasn't sure she was ready. They were either going to end the conversation trying to have a life together or possibly going their separate ways again.

"Can we skip over the time before you had Caleb and focus on when we were a little older?" Paige asked warily.

"For now," Jake complied.

"Ok, so I don't doubt that you care about me Jake. I haven't forgotten that we were really close friends. Best friends in fact. The issue is that I always had feelings for you, and you didn't feel the same way. Which is fine, I'm not mad about that or anything. You can't make yourself feel something you don't," Paige explained. "But now you are saying that you do feel that way about me and I guess my biggest concern is that maybe it's not real."

"What do you mean by *not real*?" Jake asked.

"You didn't want me in the way I wanted you back then Jake. I was right there in front of you the whole time and you didn't want me. I'm scared that this is some kind of...I don't know...you love the idea of me or something since we used to be so close and maybe that's all you miss. Does that make any sense?"

"Yeah, it does. I get what you are trying to say. But it wasn't like that Paige. I did have feelings for you too. I tried not to because I had it in my head that I was too young to settle down, that maybe I wasn't even capable of that type of relationship, and I had thought you wouldn't understand. I took our friendship and your love for me for granted. I assumed you would always be in my life and that if I ever decided I was ready for a serious relationship that you would be there. That makes me sound like an asshole, but that's the truth." Jake looked at Paige, then down at his hands, scared of what she would say next.

Paige tilted her head, thinking over what he said. "I called you once, to see if there was any chance for us to end up together. I was willing to keep waiting if there was. But when I asked you if you were dating anyone, you said you were sleeping with one of my friends. So, I didn't even ask. I made up my mind that it was time to move on," Paige said, knowing that this was going to be where the conversation took them down the path to their future, whether it be together or apart.

"Ah, I remember that conversation well. I heard the change in your voice after I said it and knew I had messed up big time. I tried to explain it was just a casual thing, but I knew I was digging a deeper hole for myself."

"Why would you sleep with my friend when you knew how I felt about you if you really had feelings for me too? You had to realize how that would hurt me. Picturing you two together..." Paige shook her head trying to get the images out of her mind.

"I didn't really think about it like that. Y'all hadn't seen each other in a long time, and I was lonely I guess. She was too. We both needed the companionship. You were dating other guys, not seriously, I know. It wasn't that big of a deal at the time. It really was just two people filling a need."

"But what if she did have feelings for you too and you were conveniently ignoring them like you did with me?"

"She didn't, Paige. I promise."

"It's just that I know how you are Jake...." Paige began.

"No, Paige. You know how I *was*," Jake interrupted. He sighed heavily and came over to kneel on the floor by Paige's knees.

"Look Paige, I can't change the past. Lord knows I wish I could sometimes. I should have fought for you after that phone call. I knew you were pulling away from me, but I didn't know what to do about it. And then you were with Matt. I thought that he was a better man than me and you deserved all the happiness in the world. I've missed you so much. I know that I am going to have to prove myself and I will," Jake said as he looked pleadingly into her eyes.

Paige couldn't deny the connection she felt to him. Even if her brain was able to talk her out of it, her body's response to him would betray her. It had been so long since she felt such longing. Only Jake could make her feel the overwhelming burning need to be touched. She had missed having him in her life. But still, she had to be careful.

"Jake, if it was only me I had to consider I would be with you. But my kids have already lost their dad. I can't risk them getting hurt by losing you too if we get together just for you to realize that you don't want me."

"That's never going to happen, Paige. You don't have to make any decisions right now. All I ask is that you promise me you'll think about giving me a chance," Jake said, taking her hand in his.

"Ok, I'll think about it," Paige agreed.

She didn't want the night to end, but she knew that she needed her rest and that the longer she stayed up talking so intimately with him, the more likely something more intimate than talking would happen. "I'm gonna head up to bed. The couch is comfortable, but if you can't sleep the guest room is down the hall," Paige said as she pointed the way. "I keep the house kind of cold at night, so if you want to turn the heat up down here the thermostat is in the hallway."

Jake stood from where he was kneeling and hugged her goodnight. She wrapped her arms around him and nuzzled into his chest. *I could spend the rest of my life like this,* he thought as he kissed the top of her head softly.

Upstairs, Paige did her nighttime routine in a daze. Jake was in her house, and they were alone, and they were reconnecting. She was proud of herself for coming upstairs solo, even though if she was honest with herself, she had wanted to grab him by the hand and bring him to bed with her. She doubted that she would be able to fall asleep knowing that he was so near. Her body felt heated, and it wasn't from the wine.

Jake stretched out on the couch looking up at the ceiling. He could hear Paige moving around upstairs. He was more determined than ever to prove to her that he was the one for her. They would get through whatever the situation was with the stalker and then they could settle down as a family.

There was no way that she and Mason had the connection they had. Sure, he seemed like a nice guy, but they were soulmates. The thought of bringing their families together reminded him that he hadn't texted Caleb goodnight yet. Yes, the kid was almost grown, but Jake wanted to make sure his son knew that his dad would always be there for him. He wondered what Caleb would think about his dad settling down again after so many years of bachelorhood.

Jake hit send on the text and was putting his phone on the coffee table when he heard a loud crash from upstairs. It sounded like glass breaking. Jake threw off the blanket and ran up the stairs two at a time. He busted through the door to Paige's room ready to take on anything. It took him a minute to convince his body that the broken coffee mug on the floor was not attacking Paige.

"I'm so clumsy. I wasn't paying attention and turned around to get something and knocked it right off the dresser. I must have left it there this morning when I was rushing to get ready for work," Paige explained as she bent down to pick up the broken mug.

Jake lifted her up from the floor and moved her aside and picked up the jagged pieces. He took them in the bathroom and when he came out, he pulled her into a tight embrace.

"I need to hold you for a minute. I'm having trouble getting the adrenaline rush to go away," Jake said into her hair.

Jake started rubbing his hands up and down her back. She wasn't wearing a bra. She had gotten rid of the sweats and was just in the t-shirt. *Lord, have mercy,* he thought. The thought of all that bare skin was driving him wild. He plunged one hand into her hair and pulled firmly so that she was looking up at him. Jake brought his mouth down on Paige's and kissed her with everything he had. All of the pent-up passion he felt for her pouring into the kiss.

Paige responded with the same intensity. She jumped up and wrapped her legs around his hips, rubbing her body up against his. Her t-shirt bunched up around her waist. Gripping her thighs, he carried her over to the bed and sat down on the edge with her still wrapped around him.

"Wait. Wait," Paige said, breathing hard, but trying to regain some self-control. "We can't do this. We know we are physically attracted to each other. That never was a problem. It means more to me than it does to you, and I can't go through that again, Jake."

Paige climbed off of Jake's lap, and the impressive erection he was sporting, and sat down on the bed next to him. She ran her hands through her hair and rubbed her face. She looked over at Jake, who looked as flustered as she felt. He took her hand in his and brought it up to his lips for a gentle kiss.

"I know I hurt you before. I was a stupid kid that wasn't ready for an amazing woman like you. I'm a different man now. Before, I was careful not to make promises with my words so that I didn't have to take responsibility for my actions. That's not what is going on this time. I want to wake up next to you every day, as your husband. I want to be a father to Chloe and Henry, and I want you to be a mom to Caleb. I'll give you another baby if that's what you want. I would love to have a child with you. I want us to be end game. I know I don't deserve another chance. I took you for granted and it took me way too long to realize that what I had with you was the real deal. I know you have options. Mason seems like a great guy, and I'll admit I thought about stepping aside because you deserve the best. But I have already done that once and it was the biggest mistake of my life. I'm not doing that again. I know what I'd be missing. I love you, Paige." Jake laid his heart bare. Everything he had wanted to say downstairs but held back came spilling out of him.

Jake searched Paige's eyes for a clue as to what she was thinking. He feared rejection for the first time in his life. It was his first time ever feeling so vulnerable.

Paige wasn't sure what to think. On one hand, Jake had said everything she had always dreamed he would. On the other, it was scary to take that leap of faith. And that's exactly what it would be. To trust this man that had at one time denied feeling anything for her. Would getting everything she had always wanted be worth the risk of getting her heart broken again? Of putting her kids through the heartbreak of losing another father? Or would she risk letting him go and then spend the rest of her life comparing every man that she dated to him? Her mind turned these questions over repeatedly.

Finally, she decided to tell Jake exactly how she felt. "I love you too, Jake. Truthfully, I always have. I'm scared though."

"I understand, baby. It kills me that I caused that doubt. I'm going to spend the rest of my life making it up to you," Jake promised. *I'm never going to cause this woman pain ever again.*

Jake reached over to Paige and brushed her hair from her face. She leaned into his warm hand and closed her eyes. After a few breaths, she opened her eyes and leaned towards him. She placed a gentle kiss on his mouth before pulling back and looking up questioningly at him. After a brief moment, she seemed to have come to some sort of decision. She leaned back in and deepened the kiss. Her tongue sweeping across his. He kissed her back and laid her down on the bed, covering her body with his own.

Much, much later, as they lay next to each other breathing heavily from their exertions, Paige thought to herself, *and I thought teenage Jake had skills. Grown man Jake is mind-blowingly phenomenal.* She smiled to herself, snuggled up to Jake, and fell blissfully asleep, a little sore and wrapped up safely in his strong arms.

CHAPTER FIFTEEN

To say Jake was on cloud nine would be a massive understatement. He had woken up that morning with Paige, the woman of his dreams, safe and naked in his arms. Paige was his. Finally. He was going to marry that woman and they were all going to be one big happy blended family. He strolled into his office with extra pep in his step, whistling a joyful tune. Unfortunately, his jubilation was abruptly cut short. As he walked up to his desk, he noticed an ominous plain manilla envelope laying on his desk.

Jake sat down heavily in his chair behind the desk and took a deep breath before lifting the tabs to open the envelope. He silently prayed that it was paperwork a client had dropped off for him. He wasn't that lucky. Sliding the contents out onto his desk, he eyed the black and white photos of Paige's SUV from the night of the crash that would haunt him for the rest of his days. Her car down the embankment, smashed into the giant oak tree with the dead branch. The images matched the horrible memory that was seared into his brain. And now someone was using his nightmares to threaten Paige.

Jake went through the pictures slowly, dreading what the message would say this time. *No doubt now that this is all my fault somehow.* He felt like he was going to throw up as the thought crossed his mind. The bile was burning his throat. Before he flipped over the third and final photograph, he took another deep breath to help shore up his nerves. As he exhaled, Jake slowly turned the photo over and on the back was written:

SO CLOSE.

GUESS I'LL HAVE TO TRY AGAIN.

SOON.
AND THEN WE WILL BE TOGETHER MY LOVE.

"MARIE GET IN HERE!" Jake hollered still looking at the threatening message. When his secretary came running in with a very confused look on her face, he asked, "How did this envelope get on my desk? Where did this come from?" he demanded pointing where it lay empty on his desk.

"A messenger service dropped it off yesterday morning. I didn't think you were expecting anything important, and it wasn't marked urgent, so I put it on your desk for when you came back into the office. You seemed stressed on the phone yesterday when you said the job over in Charleston was taking longer than it was supposed to, so I decided it wasn't worth mentioning it. I'm sorry, did I do something wrong?" Marie had never heard Jake raise his voice. She had never seen him that frantic looking either in the seven years they had been working together.

"No Marie, you didn't do anything wrong. I am so sorry for yelling. It wasn't directed towards you. I've found myself in a really messed up situation." Jake rubbed his hands over his face trying to calm down. Jake gave Marie the watered-down version of what was going on and asked her to call Officer John Avery at the Meadow Oaks Police Station.

Before Marie left his office, she went around his desk and gave his shoulder a squeeze. "I am so happy that you've finally found someone to spend your life with. And I'm sorry that you are going through something so scary. I'll do everything I can to help you find out who is doing this. You're a good man, Jake," Marie said before leaving his office and shutting the door to give him a few minutes of privacy.

When John arrived at Jake's office, Marie had the security footage from the day before when the messenger came already pulled up on her desktop computer. The messenger was a lanky young man driving a plain white delivery van. John played around with the recording and was able to zoom in for a closer look at the guy.

"He's just a kid. He's got peach fuzz on his upper lip," Marie commented.

"Yeah, I would say late teens, maybe early twenties. The logo on his vest says C.M.S.," John said absently as he watched the rest of the footage of the delivery. "He didn't have you sign anything when he dropped it off?"

"Come to think of it, no he didn't. That's unusual, right?" Marie looked up from googling on her phone. "Found it. Charleston Messenger Service. I probably should have guessed that. Pretty straight forward name."

"I'll go talk to them, see if I can figure out who paid for that envelope to be delivered," John said as he stood up and grabbed the evidence bag he had put the photos in. "Marie, can you make me a copy of that footage, please?"

"Of course." Marie got to work making the copy, while John walked into Jake's office where Jake was frantically pacing the floor.

"Jesus Christ, John. Paige is in danger because of me, and I don't have the slightest idea who could be doing this. What does that say about me? I've been trying to remember every single woman I have talked to, flirted with, slept with, and nothing. Most of them don't even know my name," Jake confessed. "I thought by living my life that way I was keeping it simple. How did things get so out of control?" At that point Jake was trying to figure things out by talking out loud to himself rather than to John.

"This isn't your fault Jake," John answered anyway. "This is someone that is mentally unstable. Even if you had led them on or whatever you're worried you've done, them threatening Paige's life is beyond irrational."

"I want to go with you to talk to the messenger service. It's in Charleston and I need to drive out there anyways to tell Paige what's going on. She's back at work," Jake said as calmly as he could in hopes that his friend would not deny him.

"If I let you come you *must* let me do the talking. This is an official police investigation. You were right that Paige's wreck and those first set of pictures were related, but it's *my* job to figure this out," John said sternly.

When Jake nodded, signaling that he would behave himself, the two men headed out. John climbed into his police cruiser, while Jake followed in his pick-up truck.

About twenty minutes later, at the office of Charleston Messenger Service, Jake was going crazy waiting while the old guy at the front desk looked up the log for the previous day's scheduled deliveries. He was moving slower than molasses on a cold winter day.

Finally, without even looking up from his screen, the old man said, "Nope, nothing on here about a delivery to Bennett Survey Company, or Jake Bennett, or that address in Meadow Oaks at all this week. Sorry I couldn't be more help fellas." At last, the old man tilted his head up to look at the men he was talking to. "Uh, what was in the package that has y'all so worked up?" the man asked as he took in Jake's worried expression.

"I'm still going to need to talk to the young man that made the delivery." John said in his professional tone, politely ignoring the man's question, and went on to describe the skinny young man.

"That sounds like Will Carter. He's out making deliveries, but I can…" the old man started to say.

"He's pulling into the lot," Jake cut the man off and started to walk outside with John tight on his heels. At the last second, Jake stood aside and let John step up. He didn't want to overstep and then John not let him be involved in finding out who was threatening his Paige.

"Excuse me, son? I'm Officer John Avery with the Meadow Oaks Police Department. I have a few questions about a delivery you made yesterday," John began.

"I think I know which one you are talking about," the kid, Will Carter, said shaking his head. "Man, I knew it was sketchy and was gonna land me in trouble, but the lady offered me two-hundred bucks cash. I found out last week that I got my girlfriend pregnant. I'm only nineteen and my parents are freaking out. I couldn't turn down the money. I'll tell you as much as I can, just please don't tell my boss. I really need this job," he pleaded, his eyes wide with fear.

"Can you tell me exactly what the lady said and what she looked like?" John asked the flustered young man calmly. "You're not in any trouble, we need to know the details of your interaction with her."

"I can't really tell you much about what she looked like. She was white and average height, about five feet six inches, I guess. She was wearing big sunglasses, had a ton of make-up on and had her hair tucked in a ballcap, like she didn't want me to know what she really looked like. She approached me on the street downtown Tuesday afternoon. I'm not exactly sure where; I think it was somewhere in the more rundown section. It happened fast and I was kinda in the zone. She showed me the cash and said it would be mine if I would make the delivery without logging it, an on-the-side type deal. Couldn't get her to write down the address for me; she said for that much cash I should be able to remember it. I'm so sorry. I didn't mean to cause any problems," Will finished nervously.

"I believe you, son. Don't worry about that part. I am going to need you to go down to Charleston P.D. and give a statement as soon as you can. I'll let them know to expect you and to follow up if they don't hear from you by the end of the day today." John gave his card to the messenger and walked with Jake back over to their vehicles.

"You're going to pull in Charleston P.D. That's good," Jake said. "Maybe we can get Paige some protection at work too."

"I have to involve them after this new development. They can look at traffic cams and talk to the businesses downtown and see if they can get any footage of this kid talking to a mysterious lady trying to be incognito," John replied. "I'm going to head over to see a fellow officer friend of mine and get the ball rolling. Unless you want me to come with you to talk to Paige first."

"No, that's okay. I'll take her out to lunch and let her know what's going on. Call me when you get done with Charleston P.D. or I'll call you if I get done with Paige before I hear from you."

Jake shook hands with his friend and went to surprise Paige at work. Too bad it wasn't for romantic reasons. He hoped that the new photos and the message with them wouldn't make Paige change her mind about being with him and run screaming for the hills.

CHAPTER SIXTEEN

Paige was slowly pacing the floor in her office reading over an article about the best Airbnb in South Carolina when Jake knocked on her door. "Well, this is a lovely surprise," she said as she gave him a shy smile and blushed slightly. "I could get used to this."

Paige set the article down on her desk and closed the door to her office. She went into Jake's open arms and looked up at him for a kiss. After a few moments, they pulled away breathless and smiling.

"I was hoping that you are free for lunch today," Jake said as he leaned back against the door.

"Yeah, I am actually. And I'm starving, so we can go now!" Paige said excitedly.

Jake felt a twinge of guilt knowing that what he had to tell her was going to ruin her happy mood. *This woman deserves so much better.* He helped her up into his truck using some creative hand placements and headed to a little hole in the wall place that served great food and also provided a bit of privacy.

"I can tell something is up Jake, you barely said a word the whole way here. So...spill," Paige said once the waiter walked away to put in their order.

Paige was steeling herself up for whatever Jake had to say. Maybe he had changed his mind about wanting a romantic relationship with her. Maybe the night before hadn't been as great for him as it had been for her. *Great is an understatement*, but she didn't want to think about that at the moment.

Jake reached across the table and took her hand in his and started tracing the lines on her palm softly with his fingertip. "I see those wheels turning in that beautiful head of yours. It's not about last night, darling. I'm thrilled that we finally found our way to each other. I love you. That will never change, so please don't worry about me breaking my word." Jake took a few seconds to gather his wits. "I got more photos. This time they were sent by messenger service, well kind of, to my office. They arrived yesterday, but Marie didn't know what they were and left them on my desk without letting me know they were there."

Jake went on to show her the pictures he had taken with his phone and the message on the back of the last one. He relayed to her what John said about involving Charleston P.D. When he was done, he waited quietly while she processed everything he had told her.

Paige was numb. Someone wanted her dead. Because of her relationship with Jake. How crazy was that? Her kids would be orphans. Would giving up Jake be the best thing to do? Would that stop whoever it was from wanting to kill her? And that was the question that put things into perspective for her. No, the person was crazy and had her sights set on Paige because of some irrational jealousy. If she broke things off with Jake, she would lose him and still be in danger.

"Okay. So, we work with the police in Charleston and Meadow Oaks to make sure me and the kids are kept safe until we find this psycho," Paige finally said. She looked up at Jake with fierce determination in her luminous green eyes.

Jake let out the breath he had been holding and felt sweet relief flooding through him when she didn't tell him to get the hell out of her life. God, he loved her so much. She was a warrior. He nodded his head and called John to let him know that Paige was up to speed with the situation and on board for police protection. John agreed to meet Jake and Paige back at Paige's office with a police officer from the Charleston department. He was waiting for them in front of Paige's office building thirty minutes later.

"Paige, this is Officer Ernie Sanders. He's heading up the team in charge of your protection detail when you are at work," John introduced Paige and Jake to the other officer.

"Mrs. Collins, we are going to do everything in our power to keep you safe," Officer Sanders said as he shook Paige's hand. "You might want to let your staff know what's going on, or at least that we will be seen around the office. We are not going to be subtle. John here says we can't use you for bait," the man shrugged like it was no big deal that he had considered using Paige to draw out a mentally unstable murderous person that had already tried to kill her once.

"Umm…okay sure." Paige wasn't too thrilled about her co-workers knowing about this particular detail of her personal life, but the other option was to dangle herself as bait. Even if that was something she was up for, John and Jake would never allow it.

Paige turned to Jake and hugged him goodbye. "Be careful baby, and I'll be here when you get off work to take you home," Jake promised as he held her tight.

Paige waved goodbye to John and thanked him for all he was doing and led Officer Sanders to the elevators to go up to the fourth floor where the magazine's offices were located. Paige asked her Executive Assistant, Brenda, to call an emergency staff meeting and met everyone in the conference room. They rarely called a meeting with everyone employed by the magazine at the same time, so they were packed in like a can of sardines.

"Everyone, this is Officer Ernie Sanders from the Charleston Police Department. There has been a threat on my life. I don't want to go into too much detail, but I will say that I don't believe the person will be so bold as to do anything here. Regardless, we will be taking every precaution to make sure our offices and staff are safe. I will turn the rest of the meeting over to Officer Sanders to go over new safety protocols."

Paige took a seat and put her hands under the table. She clenched them together as tight as she could to keep her coworkers from seeing how badly they were shaking. She had put on a brave face when she addressed the room, but the truth was that she was on edge. Just because she had decided to stay in a relationship with Jake and not let the stalker win did not mean that she was blasé about someone wanting to kill her. Having to say it out loud to people outside of her inner circle made it feel more real and serious somehow.

Once Officer Sanders finished his talk about what to expect in the coming days from his fellow officers in terms of their presence and bag searches, etc., staff members slowly filed out of the room whispering amongst themselves. Paige having a stalker was definitely some hot office gossip fodder.

Paige stayed where she was, giving herself time to regain her composure knowing everyone was going to be watching her every move out of curiosity. Cora Rae and Stacey hung back and waited until everyone else was gone before approaching her.

"I'm so sorry to hear about what's going on Paige. How are you doing with all this?" Cora Rae asked sympathetically.

"I'm hanging in there. Thank you for asking. I'm sorry that this situation is causing a commotion at work. I don't want anyone to feel unsafe here," Paige answered levelly.

"Oh honey, we are just concerned for you. Do they have any suspects? Does it have anything to do with that handsome man that came and took you to lunch today? Why would anyone threaten you? I don't understand it," Cora Rae went on and on.

"I'm not really sure, Cora Rae. I'd rather not talk about it right now. If anything comes up that affects this office, I will let you know." Paige hoped that would be the end of the questions. Thankfully, it was. Cora Rae nodded and gave Paige a quick hug and walked out of the conference room.

Paige looked over to Stacey, who had been taking in the conversation but not adding to it, and raised an eyebrow. Spending all that time with Sadie had rubbed off on her at last.

"I was wondering if you finished looking over my article about the Airbnb," Stacey asked. "I was hoping to leave a little early today. I'm meeting a guy for drinks after work and wanted to have time to run home and freshen up. I know that sounds silly, but I'm tired of the single life if you know what I mean." Stacey blushed and tucked her brown hair behind her ear, looking down at the ground.

"Ah. I gotcha. I'm almost done going over your article. I'm loving the detailed descriptions you gave. Your words paint quite the picture. Come to my office in half an hour and it will be ready for you." Paige stood and headed to her office to get back to work. It was good to have something else to focus on besides her stalker. She was not going to let some psycho control her life.

***

She pulled the rental car into her driveway and couldn't help but do a little happy dance when she got out. The pictures she had couriered over to her lover's office had gotten an even bigger reaction than she could have ever hoped for! She had been bummed when nothing happened Wednesday. She thought that moron messenger boy had ripped her off. Her lover must not have gone into the office yesterday. Oh well, all of the excitement had totally been worth the wait.

She entered her garage and walked past her dented up Chevy SUV. She missed driving it, but it was too soon to try to get it over to her cousin Jimmy to fix. The little sedan she was stuck with didn't have the same kind of power under the hood. Wasn't as intimidating out on the road. She patted the hood of the wrecked vehicle lovingly and went inside and fixed herself a celebratory vodka tonic. *I deserve a little treat,* she thought smugly.

The police were going to be all over that pathetic slut, so she might have to take a little break from her game. Let them get comfortable and let their guard down. The anticipation would add to the fun and make the grand finale even more satisfying. It wouldn't be the first time she had to bide her time with an enemy. When she had decided that her unfaithful fiancé had to die all those years ago, she waited a full six months. She even moved away from her hometown, pretended to move on with her life. Then she snuck back and made him suffer horribly for being untrue to her.

Maybe that bitch would be driven crazy by the mere thought of her and leave her lover alone. She'd still have to die, of course, for putting her old filthy hands on her true love; but her lover needed to be punished too. He was spending too much time with the other woman. It's not that she thought he was like those other men, her ex-fiancé and the men that came after. She knew he was acting out of pity because he has such a pure heart, but it's the principle of it all. Losing the ugly witch might hurt his feelings for a little while and then she would swoop in, and he would realize that the woman had meant nothing to him compared to his one true love. He would forget all about that woman. They were going to be so happy together! She danced around her kitchen to Rhianna's "Love on the Brain," drinking her cocktail and planning her happily ever after with her lover.

CHAPTER SEVENTEEN

Paige knew she had to tell her parents and the kids about the threat made against her, but she was dreading it immensely. After much thought and deliberation, she decided that being direct about it was the best way to go. She would save her emotional reaction to the situation for when she was alone. She preferred to freak out in private.

Sadie and Faith also needed to be updated as soon as possible. *Maybe a group dinner where I could tell everyone at the same time. I could tell the adults first and then give the kids a watered-down version to explain the police presence and why I will be super overprotective for a little while.* Yes, that was what she would do. That way she would only have to say it one time, well make that one and a half times.

Paige texted her idea to Jake, and he agreed. Jake vowed to be by her side for the difficult conversation. He would have Caleb join them too if Rachel could spare him for a little while. He said it was time his son met his future bonus mom and siblings, even if Caleb wasn't going to realize that was what was going on yet.

Jake returned to Paige's work around five o'clock, and after a few minutes of speaking with Officer Sanders, they headed home to Meadow Oaks together in his truck.

"I think you should let me do most of the talking tonight." Paige looked over at Jake and then down to the console where their hands were joined. She loved how he always seemed to want to touch her.

"You're probably right. Your parents aren't going to like me much for putting you in this mess," Jake worried. He absent-mindedly brought their joined hands up to place a kiss on the back of Paige's as he kept his eyes on the road, navigating through traffic.

"They are reasonable people who will understand that this person is clearly mentally unstable. You haven't done anything wrong Jake," Paige insisted.

"Doesn't change the fact that you're in this messed up situation because of something I did," Jake replied stubbornly.

Jake was caught up in his thoughts for a few minutes, until those thoughts took a sudden detour in a different direction. "You think your kids are going to like me? I hope to be their dad in the near future. Are they going to be okay with that?" Jake was really excited about the prospect of being a father to Paige's two children. If he was honest with himself, he had always been envious of Matt for having that honor. What he wouldn't give to watch Paige's belly grow round with his child inside.

"Henry is going to be thrilled. Right now, he's outnumbered by females, and Chloe has been giving him a little bit of a hard time. Honestly, I'm not sure how she'll take it at first, but she'll come around. She's a smart girl. I think maybe we should wait to tell them about us. It might be too much for them...you know? Police hanging around the house and a new dad all at once."

"I completely understand, Paige. I respect however you want to handle the kids. Just don't wait too long, okay?"

"Don't worry, I don't think we are going to be able to hide how we feel about each other very well. How is Caleb going to feel about all of this?" Paige was nervous and excited about getting to see Caleb again. She'd loved him since he was little, but more than likely he wouldn't remember her.

"I think he'll be happy for me and will love having more younger siblings. Rachel gave him a little sister with her second husband. They are really close. He's good with kids." Jake paused for a few seconds and then turned to Paige with a big grin on his face as he pulled to a stop at a red light. "He knows who you are by the way. There are some pictures in a photo album from when he was little of you holding him on your hip and playing with him on the floor. He asked me when he was looking through it a while back who the pretty lady was."

Jake turned his gaze back to the road in front of him and smiled at the memory. He was looking forward to them all being a family. He promised himself to make whoever was delaying their happy ending suffer.

"So, what did you tell him when he asked you that?" Paige had to know, her heart rate sped up.

"Oh, that the pretty lady used to be my best friend in the whole world and that I missed her terribly," Jake answered honestly.

"I don't want to make you feel bad or anything, but it kind of broke my heart to miss out on his childhood. I got pretty attached to him back in the day," Paige said carefully.

"I know you did, baby. I always knew that you would be an amazing mom. I'm so excited for him to have you in his life again," Jake said, bringing her hand up for another kiss.

Paige couldn't help but grin the rest of the way home. She was so happy. Even with the death threat looming over her, she couldn't help but to be hopeful of the future.

When they pulled up to her house, her happiness faltered. Her parents were already there with the kids, as were Faith and Travis. Sadie would be along in an hour after the post-op exam of her last surgery patient of the day was done. Paige hoped that no one would question the reason for the get together until Sadie got there. She didn't want to have to repeat herself when it came to the adult version of what was going on and she needed the emotional support Sadie's calming presence would provide. Her friend helped her be strong simply by being in the same room.

"Paige, what's with the cameras all around the outside of your house?" her dad asked as soon as she and Jake walked through the door.

Well, that didn't take long, Paige thought to herself. "That has to do with why I invited everyone over tonight. If you don't mind Dad, I want to wait until Sadie gets here to talk about it. That way I only have to say it once."

Paige's dad nodded, but the worried look on his face didn't go away. He looked down at his wife to see if she had any idea what was going on, but she looked clueless as well. Luckily, they didn't push the subject.

Paige re-introduced Jake to her parents. They had met him once before, but that was when he and Paige were teenagers. Her mom gave her a little eyebrow wiggle when Jake's back was turned. Sherry Hawkins could appreciate a good-looking man.

Surprisingly, Faith was very friendly to Jake when Paige brought him over to introduce him to Travis. Paige would have to ask her about that later. Not that she wasn't thankful, but something was up.

Then came the tricky introduction. Chloe looked at them suspiciously as they walked over to the couch where her and Henry were trying to decide what they wanted to watch on tv. "Chloe, Henry, this is my good friend, Jake. We've known each other a very long time and you guys are going to be seeing him around here a lot," Paige said to her children. She had to admit that she was more than a little nervous.

Chloe gave Jake a half-hearted wave and went back to focusing on her movie selection. Paige didn't miss that her daughter's shoulders remained tense as she pretended to ignore her mom and Jake.

Henry took a liking to Jake right away, asking a million questions about trucks and fishing. Paige kept an eye on them while mingling with the others. The warm look in Jake's eyes as he discussed the best type of fish bait with Henry made her heart swell with joy. Chloe was watching her brother protectively like a hawk.

There was a knock on the front door and when Sherry opened it up, Caleb was standing on the other side. Paige would have thought a rock star walked in by the look on Henry's face. It was adorable. Caleb was tall and blond like his dad. He charmed Sherry right away with his, "Nice to meet you, ma'am," and the same easy smile his dad used to disarm people. He nodded to the others around the room as he went over to greet his dad. Henry never took his wide-eyed stare off of the teenage boy. When Caleb noticed, he got down to Henry's level and started up a conversation about dinosaurs. Instant best friends. It brought tears to Paige's eyes to see them together.

Paige noticed that Chloe was watching the whole scene with interest, but she didn't say anything. She was a very observant and intuitive young girl. Since her dad died, she tended to keep her emotions concealed as much as she could.

With Henry occupied by Caleb, Jake went around the room finding out what everyone wanted on their pizza and ordered while they waited on Sadie. It worked out perfectly because she practically walked in with the pizza delivery guy.

"Now that's what I call service," Sadie jokingly said as she came in and went around to greet everyone.

Paige noticed Sadie and Faith whispering between themselves and looking at her with what her dad would call "shit-eating grins". She was sure they would tell her what that was about later; they never kept stuff from each other. Plus, she had enough on her plate to worry about at the moment.

"Okay kids, I need you guys to go eat your pizza at the table outside on the patio please while the grown-ups have a talk. Y'all can take those cinnamon sticks out there with you," Paige added as extra incentive.

Chloe and Henry didn't need to be told twice. They grabbed a slice of pizza each and the box of the cinnamon pastries covered in sweet icing that were supposed to be for dessert and ran out the door. Paige saw Caleb give Jake a questioning look and when his dad nodded his head towards the door for him to follow the other kids, he got up without complaint and took his pizza outside. Caleb was at that tricky age where he wasn't quite an adult, but definitely was not a little kid either.

The adults got themselves some pizza and chairs were brought in from the kitchen so they could all eat together. As they got settled, Paige went over and turned the tv off and gathered her strength to tell her nearest and dearest that someone wanted to kill her. She stuck to the facts trying not to let on to any of the fear, worry, and anxiety she was experiencing. She told them about the police protection and that she was sure they would catch the person soon and that everything would be fine.

Paige had chosen a spot right above Faith's head to focus her gaze on while she spoke; so it wasn't until she finished her story and looked around that she noticed everyone had put their pizza down, barely touched, on their plates. They were all looking back and forth between her and Jake.

Jake could feel the others' eyes on him, but he kept his focus on Paige, looking for any hint that he needed to step in or that she was getting overwhelmed. He sensed that she was holding her emotions in check. Paige was so strong and brave. His warrior. He hoped that one day soon, she would let him shoulder some of the hard stuff and let her guard down.

"What are you going to tell the kids?" Paige's mom, Sherry, asked.

"A watered-down version. I have to tell them something because there will be a police officer here at the house. I'm also going to be acting like a crazy mama bear and be overprotective, so I need them to understand the seriousness of the situation and listen to me. I'll need yours and dad's help with that too," Paige said looking back and forth between her parents.

"Of course, sweetheart," Sherry responded, while Paige's dad nodded his head in agreement.

"We'll help too in any way we can," Faith chimed in, her gaze taking in Travis and Sadie as she said it.

For a moment the adults were quiet. Everyone seemed to be processing the giant bomb Paige had dropped on them. Even Faith and Sadie, who knew everything up until the new set of photos were really feeling the gravity of the situation. A jealous former lover was one thing, but an outright death threat was another level of crazy.

"How long has this thing with you two been going on?" Sherry asked as she waved her finger back and forth between Paige and Jake, breaking the silence.

Paige started to answer her mother, but Jake beat her to it. "I've been in love with your daughter for almost twenty years, ma'am. I lost her because I took her for granted. I'm never going to do that again. You have my word."

"So, this is pretty serious then, huh?" Sherry asked.

"Yes mama, it is," Paige answered as she looked lovingly over at Jake.

Sherry nodded, tears glistening in her eyes. She was thrilled that her daughter had found happiness again after so much heartbreak.

"Not to burst this happy bubble, but someone wants to hurt my daughter. I'm glad that you are happy with your love life Paige, but I think we need to keep our focus on the more pressing matter here," her dad said. He was angry and frustrated.

"You're absolutely right and I'm so sorry Mr. Hawkins that Paige is in this situation because of me. I promise I will do everything I can to keep her safe," Jake insisted. Jake could understand how Paige's dad was feeling. He was going to have to work extra hard to get on her dad's good side.

"Dad, we are not going to let this psycho win by living our lives in fear. However, we will be taking precautions. I will need your help with the kids sometimes. I'm going to talk to the afterschool programs and make sure they are extra diligent about who picks the kids up. We'll be safe, I promise," Paige reassured her father.

As Paige said the words, she felt her resolve strengthening. She would protect her family.

"Okay, let's tell the kids," Paige declared, going to the back door to call the kids inside.

Paige simply told the kids that someone was bothering her and that there would be a police officer at the house to make sure they were all safe. The other adults reassured the kids that they would also be looking out for them. Paige explained to her kids that since they were the most precious things in the world to her, she might be overbearing, and it was really important that they listen to her.

"Are you going to be alright?" Henry asked, sounding a little bit scared.

"Yes sweetie, don't you worry about me. I'm tough, but more than that I am going to be careful until the police can figure this thing out which I'm sure will be soon," Paige reassured Henry, hugging him tight.

"Chloe, what are you thinking over there?" Paige asked her daughter when she noticed that it looked like Chloe wanted to say something but was staying quiet instead.

"I guess I'm wondering why this person is bothering you," Chloe answered softly.

"Unfortunately honey, this person seems to not be thinking clearly. She is mentally unstable," Paige tried to find the simplest way to explain it without getting into specifics.

"You mean like she is sick?" Chloe asked.

"Yeah, maybe."

"Can she go to the doctor and get better?" Henry questioned.

"That is a great question Henry, and maybe she can. But first the police have to find her so they can get her the help she needs. But I need to make sure you understand that is a job for the police and not for you. Okay, buddy?" Paige could imagine her sweet-hearted son trying to take the stalker to the doctor to get better.

"Yes mommy, I understand," Henry replied.

Paige looked around at all of her loved ones and let out a deep breath. The situation she was in was so bizarre, but she knew that she was blessed to have these wonderful people to support her.

When the dinner party, if one could call it that, came to an end, Paige and Jake walked everyone out to say goodnight. Paige was squeezed over and over as she was hugged tightly by her friends and family. The last one to leave was Caleb, so Paige and Jake walked him over to his Jeep.

"I didn't want to ask this in front of the younger kids, but is the lady who is bothering Paige the reason you sent me to mom's house the other day and asked me to stay over there when it's supposed to be your week?" Caleb asked his dad.

"Yeah son, it is. This woman thinks she is in love with me and is jealous because she saw me hug Paige at a restaurant. It's the craziest thing and we didn't think it best to get into that much detail with the younger ones," Jake answered honestly.

"I figured as much when Paige was telling them what was going on." Caleb turned his attention to Paige. "I'm sorry this is happening to you. I can help out with Chloe and Henry anytime you need me to."

"That is so sweet, Caleb. I'm sure they would love that," Paige said, her heart full of love seeing what a thoughtful young man he grew up to be.

After another round of hugs with Caleb, Paige and Jake went back inside to get the younger kids to bed. Caleb went back to his mom's house, promising to text Jake when he got there safely.

"I'd like to stay if that's okay with y'all. I'll sleep on the couch. I'll be like an extra protector," Jake said to Chloe and Henry.

Jake smiled as Henry jumped up and hugged him. Chloe shrugged her shoulders, not saying anything, and headed upstairs. Jake looked questioningly over at Paige, but she simply smiled, shrugged, and followed Chloe up the staircase. Jake had no idea how to handle a pre-teen girl. He guessed he would figure it out eventually.

"Will you tuck me in, please, please, please?" Henry pleaded to Jake.

Henry gave Jake the puppy dog look that always worked on his mom. It worked on Jake too. Jake chuckled and followed Henry up to his room. Upon entering Henry's room, Jake looked around at all the Hot Wheels and Legos scattered all over the bedroom floor and was taken back to when Caleb was a little boy. After Henry put on his pajamas and brushed his teeth, Jake tucked him in and read a quick story about a dinosaur that was scared to go to school. Henry drifted off to sleep as Jake whispered the words of the last couple of pages. Jake brushed the hair out of Henry's little face, turned off the superhero lamp and went back downstairs.

Jake thoroughly checked all of the locks on the doors and windows, then settled in on the couch to protect his new precious family. His phone let out a ding. Caleb texted that he had made it safely to his mother's house. *Love you son. G'night,* Jake answered.

About an hour later, Paige snuck back downstairs to snuggle under the blanket on the couch with Jake. His body heat was a comfort to her after the long emotional day.

"Chloe going to be okay with me staying here tonight?" Jake asked her as he pulled Paige into the crook of his arm.

"Yes, she is. She doesn't know you, so she asked a lot of questions about you. I explained that we have a lot of history as friends and that the years just kind of melted away when we saw each other again. And being the good friend that you are, you want to make sure that we are all safe," Paige assured him as she nuzzled his neck, inhaling his woodsy scent.

"That's a good way of putting it," Jake said thoughtfully.

"Mmhmm," Paige said as she pulled Jake's mouth down to hers hungrily.

Jake's body heat warmed Paige up in more ways than one. They made love quietly on the couch, as they would every night for the next couple of weeks. Despite all of the outside drama, Paige felt that right there in that moment, life was just about perfect.

CHAPTER EIGHTEEN

Paige called Faith over the Bluetooth as she was driving her dad's truck to work the next morning. It was a blessing that Paige's dad preferred to drive his old Chevy that he had restored over the new one that her mom had convinced him to buy last year. She didn't have to worry about what she was going to drive until she found the time and energy to go car shopping. She wasn't sure about the newer concept of buying a car online without seeing it in person and test-driving it before getting saddled with a loan payment. She figured maybe she was a little old-school like her father in that regard.

"Okay, let me have it," Paige said as soon as Faith answered the call.

"What are you talking about?" Faith thought she'd give Paige a little taste of her own medicine in the avoidance department.

"What were you and Sadie whispering about last night when she first got to my house? And it's not that I'm not appreciative, but you were really sweet to Jake. So, what gives?"

Faith waited a few heartbeats before answering her. "Aren't I always sweet?" Faith scoffed.

"To me, yes. To others, most of the time. But come on, you know what I mean," Paige replied with faux impatience. She knew darn well that Faith was toying with her.

Faith giggled and finally relented, "Girl, I knew as soon as I saw y'all walk in the house together that it was a done deal. You two just seem to fit together, like two puzzle pieces or something. I can't explain it, but I accept it, and I am very happy for you. I was filling Sadie in on my epiphany about that. I'm worried about you because of the murderous stalker lurking about, but we'll handle it one day at a time. I'll admit that Jake won me over last night. But I swear if he hurts you again, I'll castrate him." Faith added for good measure.

"Fair enough," Paige acquiesced.

Paige was so relieved Faith was on board. Her two friends meant the world to her. She would never want anything or anybody to come between them. She had been worried that Faith wouldn't be able to see past Jake's earlier behavior and acknowledge his personal growth. It's not that she thought her friend was petty or unreasonable. She knew how loyal and protective Faith was over her. It was the same for Paige when it came to Faith and Sadie.

"You know you have to tell Mason that you're off the singles market. He's going to be disappointed, but I have a feeling he'll be just fine. You should see all the thirsty moms eyeing him at evening pick up. These women used to come in here looking tired and run-down at the end of the day, but now their hair is neat as a pin and their make-up looks fresh. It's a hoot," Faith chuckled.

Paige giggled picturing it in her head. "I can totally see that. He's such a good man. I hope he finds the right woman for him. Doesn't sound like him and his ex-wife were a very good fit."

"Not at all," Faith agreed. The friends spoke a few minutes longer about the daycare moms, both glad to be back on the same page.

Paige pulled into her designated parking spot at the magazine's office building and one of Charleston's finest came to open her truck door for her.

"Good morning, Mrs. Collins. I'm Officer Eliza Romero with Charleston P.D. I've been assigned to be your personal shadow until we figure out who is behind the threatening messages your friend received about you."

Paige shook the officer's hand and looked over the tall, lean-muscled woman. She gave off the same kind of hard-core competent energy that Sadie did. Paige was instantly put at ease by it.

"Nice to meet you, Officer Romero, and thank you so much. I hope you don't get too bored following me around. Well actually, I guess I hope you do since the alternative would mean someone was trying to kill me, again." Paige shook her head. "Life is a crazy thing sometimes."

"Yes, it is ma'am," Officer Romero replied in a business-like tone and followed her new charge into the bustling Charleston office building and up to the fourth floor. Her watchful dark brown eyes taking in everything around them.

Besides the addition of the police presence, the day passed by like any other workday. Paige spent her day reading articles, assigning stories, and approving photographs. She caught herself comparing the professional photos to what she could remember of the ones sent to Jake. *Is the person a professional photographer?* She didn't think so, but it's not like the person would have had time to adjust the lighting and change lenses when taking the quick candid shots at Lorenzo's and at the crash site.

Cora Rae stopped by Paige's office to let her know that the Mackenzie's had loved their feature in last month's issue. "That's because you're the best at weddings," Paige complimented. "The Walters' wedding is this weekend, right? Where are they having the ceremony again?" Paige asked, already planning next month's layout in her head.

"The ceremony and reception will be held at Hotel Bennett," Cora Rae answered excitedly.

"Oooh, snazzy. It should be a good one."

"The bride has nine bridesmaids, so it will be big, that's for sure." Cora Rae laughed and shook her head in awe. "The food is always superb there, so I'm looking forward to it. Speaking of food, you never answered me yesterday about that man who took you to lunch before we had to have that big meeting. Who is he?" Cora Rae inquired.

"That was an old friend of mine, Jake," Paige answered simply.

"He's mighty handsome. Just a friend, huh?" Cora Rae waggled her perfectly arched dark eyebrows.

Paige debated on playing their relationship down since it was her personal life, and she usually didn't share those details at work. Since Jake would be seen around the office when he had business in Charleston anyway, she decided to go with the truth instead.

"Well, not just friends anymore. It's pretty serious actually," Paige admitted.

It looked like Cora Rae was going to say something else, but there was a knock at Paige's open office door. Paige looked over to see Stacey and the staff photographer, Mike, standing in the doorway.

"Hey, we didn't mean to interrupt y'all, but I have the shots of the Hideaway Cottage for the next issue and wanted to see what you thought in case you were wanting something different," Mike said as he came in, spreading photos over Paige's neat desk.

Paige looked over the photos slowly. Mike was extremely talented at catching light and getting the most out of a shot. Paige had never seen the Airbnb cottage in person, but the pictures made her want to.

"I personally like this one for the outer shot. It makes it seem like a magical fairy cottage deep in the woods even though it's technically a waterfront property on the inlet. You just walk through the trees behind it to get to the water, according to Stacey's article," Paige said as she glanced over to Stacey for confirmation. Stacey gave a slight nod.

"And this one with the fireplace blazing for the interior, it looks like a cozy romantic getaway," Paige contemplated out loud.

"That it is," Stacey said absent-mindedly.

"Oh, you've stayed there before? It's beautiful." Paige looked over the photos, thinking it might be a good weekend getaway spot for her and Jake when everything settled down.

"Yes, once. I was doing some remodeling at my house and needed a break from all of the noise and people stomping around in work boots." Stacey was also looking over the pictures carefully. She took her work very seriously.

"What is your opinion on the photographs, Stacey? Are there different ones in this bunch you would pick to go with your article? Any you think portray the actual vibe of the cottage better?" Paige asked. She liked to empower her writers to be a part of the decisions made regarding their work.

"I absolutely agree with the ones you picked out. You were spot on with your descriptions, inside and outside." Stacey went on to tell them more about the cottage's history. "It was built in the early nineteen-hundreds and has stayed in the Calhoun family ever since. They have since moved on to grander residences and vacation homes, so one of the younger adult Calhoun's started renting out the cabin through Airbnb.

Paige already knew the history of the little place from when she edited Stacey's article, but it was interesting hearing Stacey speak it aloud. She was a passionate and bright woman, and when she spoke so animatedly like that, it was easier to understand how she had become such good friends lately with the bubbly Cora Rae. The two women seemed like complete opposites on the surface. Paige was starting to like the young woman the more she got to know her. Stacey had been working at the magazine for a little over a year, but she only recently started coming out of her shell.

They spoke for a few more minutes about Mike's magical photographs, making him blush from all of the ladies gushing over his work. As the three staff members filed out of Paige's office, Cora Rae took another shot at getting Paige to come out to lunch with her and Stacey. Paige politely declined, again.

"Hoping your hot stud will come whisk you away to lunch again, huh?" Cora Rae teased, doing a little shimmy out the door.

"Something like that," Paige chuckled as she waved Cora Rae off.

At lunchtime, Paige sat at her desk and ate the meal Jake had thoughtfully packed for her that morning. He had even packed the kids' lunches for school. She could get used to having someone to take care of stuff like that for her. She had spent the past two years throwing herself into taking care of others to fill the void losing Matt had left. It was a joy to have a partner to take care of her for a change and help with Chloe and Henry.

Thinking of how she and Jake pretty much made things official the night before in front of her parents and best friends reminded her that she had a phone call to make. She dreaded having to let anyone down, but she put on her theoretical big girl panties and pulled up Mason's number.

"Hey, pretty lady! I was just about to text you. I spoke with Officer Avery a little while ago and I'm sure we've ruled out anyone from my limited romantic past," Mason said cheerfully.

"Thank you so much for being so gracious about all this. I know its inconvenient and intrusive," Paige replied.

"It really wasn't a big deal. He was very straight to the point and professional. I was wondering though, what are you doing tonight? Want to grab some dinner?" The eagerness in Mason's voice sparked a twinge of guilt.

"That's kind of why I was calling you. I think you are a wonderful man Mason, so I don't want you to be interested in me when you could be with someone else." Paige shook her head side to side, that hadn't come out right.

"I'm not sure what you mean, Paige," Mason wondered.

"I want to be completely honest with you. When we went on our date, I was completely unattached. Since then, however, some old feelings between Jake and I have been rekindled. I didn't mean for it to happen. I hadn't seen him in years. It is what it is I guess," Paige rambled.

"Ah, I see. I could tell when he walked in your house the other day with the cameras that he cared about you in more than a friendly way. I guess I had been hoping it was one-sided. You're a special lady Paige. I'd be lying if I said I wasn't disappointed. Thank you for being up front with me. I wish you all the best," Mason conceded.

Paige sighed. "I hope you find the perfect woman for you, Mason. I really do. And I know you are still kind of new in town, so if you need anything, please don't hesitate to ask. That seems like a lame thing to say, but I do mean it," Paige insisted.

"Thanks, Paige. Listen, can I ask you one favor though? I know I don't know you all that well, but please be careful. I'm sure Jake is a great guy. You seem like a very smart lady who can handle her business, but this stuff with the stalker worries me. From what Officer Avery said, there have been more threats. Take care of yourself is all I'm trying to say I guess," Mason finished a little awkwardly.

Paige thought it was sweet that he was concerned more about her safety than his male pride. He really was a class act.

After she got off the phone with Mason, she wandered over to the window and looked down at all the people hurrying around on the street below. Was her stalker down there at that very moment, watching her? The suspense kept her on her toes, but she refused to let herself get too worked up over it. She had a feeling that was exactly what the psycho wanted. Paige knew it was eventually going to come down to her and the homicidal stranger. She was going to make sure that she was the one to come out on top. Keeping herself mentally level and sharp was going to be key. Feeling confident, she turned back to her desk to finish out her workday.

Later that evening, Paige arrived at her home hoping for a much simpler night than the one before. A night off from dramatic revelations would be bliss. Jake's truck was already parked in her driveway, as well as Caleb's monster Jeep. She had been expecting her parents to be there with the kids, but maybe they had taken Chloe and Henry to their house instead. They had been helping out with the kids even more than usual because of the car accident and the stalker who they now knew caused the wreck. Paige greeted the officer sitting in his patrol car in front of her house and walked inside.

The scene she walked in on stopped her in the doorway. Jake, Caleb, Chloe, and Henry were all sitting on the floor around the coffee table playing Monopoly. They looked like they were having the absolute best time together. Paige felt her heart swell and tears pooled in her eyes. She noted to herself that she seemed to be getting weepy every time she was around Jake and the kids lately. It was so wonderful to feel like a happy family again.

Jake looked up at Paige standing in the doorway and smiled. He could tell how she was feeling because he felt the exact same way. They were a family. His heart was so full of love. He got up from the floor, teased the kids about not cheating, and walked over to welcome Paige home. He put his arms around her and kissed her forehead. They turned, still holding onto each other, to look at the kids playing together. Even Chloe was openly smiling and laughing. It had been so long since Paige had seen her daughter so carefree.

"Your parents thought the kids and I should have some time together to get used to each other. They left shortly after I got here. Your kids are wonderful," Jake whispered the last part in her ear.

"They're your kids too now," Paige answered back too low to be overheard.

"Yes, they are. And I promise to be the best daddy to them Paige," Jake vowed quietly.

While the kids were distracted with their game, Jake and Paige gave each other a quick passionate kiss and went to play Monopoly with their children. Jake immediately resumed teasing the kids. Chloe and Henry were rolling with laughter. Paige couldn't have asked for a better Friday night.

CHAPTER NINETEEN

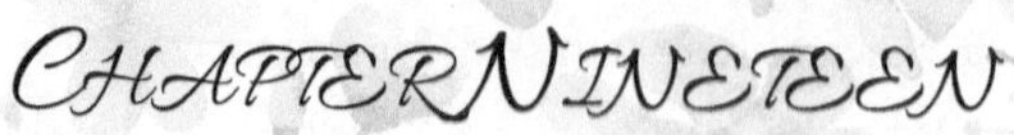

Two weeks later, on another Friday, Jake sat in his office lost in his thoughts. Nothing life threatening had happened to Paige since Charleston P.D. started watching over her. He had not received any new mysterious manila envelopes with unsettling pictures and death threats. Life was moving along like it should, plus police protection, of course. Jake, Paige, and the kids fell into an easy rhythm at home. It was like Jake and Caleb had been there the whole time.

Jake was still sleeping downstairs on the couch. He didn't want to make the kids uncomfortable or set a bad example for them. Even though he and Paige were planning on getting married in the near future, he technically hadn't been in Chloe and Henry's lives for very long. Plus, they hadn't had the official "we're together and we are all going to be a family" talk with the kids yet. Caleb figured it out and thought it was cool that his dad had finally decided to give up the bachelor life. Jake didn't mind sleeping on the couch. Paige snuck down the stairs every night after the kids fell asleep and they spent hours wrapped up in each other. He was thinking that he should go ring shopping soon, make things official.

"Hey Jake, Officer Avery is here to see you." Marie poked her head in his office, interrupting his daydreaming about domestic bliss.

When Jake nodded, Marie stepped aside to make room for the officer to walk in. She offered refreshments and when both men declined, she closed the door quietly behind her.

The two men shook hands and made small talk for a few minutes, but Jake had a pretty good idea as to why John was there. "I'm always happy to see you John, but I know you didn't come down here to talk about the high school's new automotive program; even though I am happy to hear about it," Jake said.

"I wanted to tell you in person that my buddy over at Charleston P.D. says they are going to have to pull their officers off of Paige's protection detail. I convinced them to keep Officer Romero with her next week because Paige said she will be working late a few nights next week to get her next issue out, but that's it. Nothing has happened and there are no new developments in the case. Traffic cams didn't get a good look at the lady talking to that messenger kid. She knew to pick a spot in front of a store without security cameras and stood behind a tall SUV. Then she just disappears. They couldn't track her. She's a clever fox, this one." John rubbed the back of his neck as he ran through the case in his head.

Jake nodded his head and stood up to pace around. The movement helped him keep his mind from feeling overwhelmed. "I was afraid that was going to be the case. Part of me is relieved nothing else has happened, but at the same time, I would rather have this over with. Paige feels the same way. Obviously, our biggest concern is the kids' safety," replied Jake.

"Well, we are going to stay on her and the kids when she's in Meadow Oaks a while longer. My boys are taking it real personal that someone is trying to hurt one of their own. We take pride in being a safe town. It doesn't hurt either that we don't have the case load Charleston P.D. has. To be honest, I was shocked they were able to keep officers on her this long."

"We appreciate that y'all are going to keep an eye on her and the kids John. Tell the crew we say thank you," Jake answered in relief. At least the kids should be safe enough, that would give Paige peace of mind. Jake was glad too, but he would still worry about Paige during the work week while she was in Charleston.

John had said what he came to say in an official capacity and switched back to friendly chit-chat. "What do y'all have planned for this weekend?" John asked.

"I was actually going to text you about that. Tomorrow is Henry's seventh birthday, and he wants to have a bonfire tomorrow night and smores. You are invited on behalf of the birthday boy himself. He thinks you are *so* cool and tough. He's been asking your officer that's at the house at night, Officer Denton, all sorts of questions about being a cop and catching the bad guys." Jake laughed remembering the boy's enthusiasm. Man, he loved that little guy.

"Sounds like a good time, I'll be there." John stood to leave. "Call me if anything comes up. Even if it seems minor. You never know what will break a case," he added.

"Will do. See you tomorrow night, John."

Jake walked his friend out to the front lobby and decided to leave too. He headed down the road to check on his house. It had been a few days since he or Caleb had gone by there. Nothing other than the normal wildlife had shown up on the cameras, but he liked to make sure everything was still fresh inside. The last thing he needed was his house smelling like roadkill. He was debating whether or not to rent it out or sell it when he officially moved into Paige's house. They hadn't discussed which house they would live in yet, but he thought less change for the younger kids might be better. He was kind of amazed at how natural it came to put their needs first after only a few weeks. He thought it was probably because he has cared about them from a distance their whole lives due to his love for their mother.

Everything was as he had left it at his house. Caleb had remembered to take out the trash last time he stopped by. Jake wandered around expecting something or someone to pop out at him. He was kind of hoping for it. To face whoever the stalker was by himself and get it over with was his ideal scenario. He knew deep down that he wouldn't get that lucky.

"The Psycho," as him and Paige started calling the woman, had her sights set on Paige. His plan was to make it impossible for her to get Paige alone. He had yet to come up with any possible suspects and it angered him.

Jake gathered up a few clothes and personal items, then went outside to load up the back of his truck with wood for Henry's bonfire and headed back to Paige's house.

***

Henry's birthday bonfire was a major success. Jake and Caleb built the fire bigger than any Henry had ever seen before and the look of absolute hero worship on his face was priceless. The birthday boy had a few friends come over and they roasted hotdogs for dinner and made smores for dessert. Henry had never been big on traditional birthday cake. Chloe invited one of her friends over too, and they were giggling, having a great time roasting marshmallows, even though most of them ended up falling off of their sticks into the fire. Faith and Travis were sitting on a wooden bench Matt had made years ago, snuggling by the bright fire. A pleasant surprise for Paige was that John and Sadie seemed to really be hitting it off. How great would it be for her friend and Jake's friend to get together!

Paige looked at all of the people around her and smiled. *How was it possible to be so happy?* She thought after Matt died that she would never feel true happiness again. She was relieved to have been wrong.

Jake came over and put his arms around Paige's waist from behind and held her close. Her hair smelled of the smoke from the bonfire and it reminded him of when they were younger. A big group of teenagers sneaking off into the woods on Old Man Phillips's property over in Summerville, having bonfires, drinking Natty Lights, flirting, and sneaking off into the trees to make out and do some "heavy petting" as Paige used to call it. Paige always looked beautiful by fire light. He turned her around, pulled her into the shadows, and kissed her deep.

"Thank you," he said to her when they came up for air.

"For what?" Paige asked breathlessly.

"For giving me a chance at this wonderful life with you and the kids," he said, looking around at their family and friends.

"I should be thanking you. It feels like you brought us all back to life," Paige replied softly, nuzzling his neck.

Jake kissed the top of her head and chuckled.

"What's so funny?" Paige questioned, peering back up at him.

"Oh, just that you might not feel like thanking me after I tell you what I promised Henry for his birthday," Jake admitted sheepishly.

"Oh yeah? And what was that exactly?"

"I told him that me and Caleb would take him to ride dirt bikes, but only if you said it was okay, of course."

"Good lord, Jake! The boy is only seven years old!" Paige shook her head. She knew that Jake would keep him safe, but it was a mom's right to worry.

"Oh, I won't let him do any big jumps his first time out," Jake joked.

"Fine, but only if you wrap him in bubble wrap first." Paige giggled as she pictured it in her head. Henry would have a fit.

"Promise," Jake said as he hugged her tight to him and felt all was right in the world.

Too bad someone else had different plans for them.

***

She was being so patient. She was extremely proud of herself, but it was getting harder and harder. The urge to lash out was growing with each passing day that bitch got to breathe. *Just a few more days and the game can recommence,* she told herself. There was no way the police would play babysitter to a nobody for much longer. Didn't they have bigger fish to fry?

She trudged out to her back yard and took up the axe that was sticking out of a tree stump and started whacking at a dead tree that had fallen in the last big storm. Swinging the axe had become her release when the urges to commit violence grew too great to ignore. She would just picture that dark hair and chop, chop, chop. She couldn't afford to make a move at the wrong time. She'd never lost a game before and certainly wouldn't start now.

Her lover was the prize, and she would not lose him to some sad old hag just because he clearly felt sorry for her. He was such a sweetheart, and he was being taken advantage of. Not for much longer. *Just be patient. Just be patient. Just be patient.* Chop. Chop. Chop.

CHAPTER TWENTY

Since Paige's remaining protection detail was about to end, she spent Monday and Tuesday getting as much work done as possible to get the next issue done before she was left to fend for herself. She worked until nine p.m. both nights and would have stayed longer, but she felt a little guilty for keeping Officer Romero there so late. Officer Romero was the strong silent type and she never complained about anything. Paige was going to miss her reassuring presence around the office.

But even with the late hours, Paige still had a couple of writers dragging their feet on finalizing their stories. Tuesday night, she sent one more email insisting that everything be turned in by lunchtime Wednesday so she could finalize the layout, and then shut down the office with Officer Romero watching her back.

Paige came home to find Jake watching the local news on the couch and the kids already put to bed. Paige had to admit she was impressed. It's not that she had doubted Jake as a parent, she just hadn't imagined that the transition into full-time co-parenthood was going to be so smooth for them. She threw off her shoes, went over and snuggled with him on the couch.

"Hi honey. How was your day?" Paige said playfully.

"I know you are joking, but I like the sound of it nonetheless," Jake said pulling her on top of him for a kiss. "You hungry?" he asked when they finally took a break from making out like horny teenagers. "I made grilled catfish, slaw, and hush puppies. The kids gobbled it up. I was amazed."

"They are good eaters. I think it's from all the activities they do. Makes them ravenous. I might eat some later. Thank you for holding down the fort by yourself the past couple of nights," Paige said.

"We're a family now. You know I got your back," Jake assured her.

As Paige sat on top of Jake looking into his mesmerizing blue eyes, she thought about the unusual predicament they found themselves in. They needed to figure out who was behind the photos and threats, but she knew he didn't want to discuss his past one-night stands with her. Up to that point he had only discussed them with his buddy, Officer John Avery. He wouldn't like her bringing it up. However, she was tired of being left out of the loop on that part of the investigation. She also felt like she could give Jake some reassurance that she wasn't judging him for his choices as a single man.

"I've been thinking, and I know my time with Officer Romero is running out." She hesitated for a moment, and when Jake sat there quietly, she continued. "Maybe if we went over possible suspects together, something new might come up."

"Baby, I have been over and over it with John. I don't know what us talking about it could accomplish except possibly upset you or make you think less of me. It's not that I'm trying to hide anything. I just don't see the point."

Jake did not want to go down that road with Paige. He was worried that she would start to doubt him again and he loved her so damn much, he didn't want anything to disrupt their relationship. Spending everyday taking care of their children and every night holding each other, he couldn't lose that.

"I understand sweetie, but John has never been on the receiving end of your charm. I feel like I'd bring a different perspective. The female perspective," Paige pushed gently but firmly.

"If you insist," Jake conceded reluctantly.

"Ok, well how many were there?" Paige couldn't help but ask.

"Not as many as you're imagining, I'm sure." Jake shrugged. "Maybe a handful."

"Where would you go to find these women."

"Usually a bar. I would go for a drink after work when I was feeling lonely. Nowhere too sleazy. I wouldn't drink too much, only enough to sleep with someone I didn't know. Baby, do we really have to do this?" Jake pleaded.

"Yes. Would they approach you or the other way around?"

"They approached me."

"Always?" Paige accidently blurted.

"Yes," Jake smirked, "not to sound cocky or anything, but I would sit there, they would make eye contact and that was that. They would come over and start talking, and I would buy them a drink, then tune out and nod and smile in the right places."

Paige nodded. She knew how good Jake was at making a woman feel like she had his undivided attention, even when she didn't. She knew him well enough after a while that she could tell when he had done it to her in the past.

These women wouldn't have had the chance to get to know him like that, but she was curious to know his take on it, so she asked, "Could the women not tell that you weren't really paying attention?"

"Paige, they didn't care. They were there for the same thing I was. Temporary companionship. I was always really clear on my expectations before I went home with them."

Jake hated having to explain his choice to have casual sex with strangers to Paige. That part of his life was over the moment he saw her walk into Lorenzo's. He didn't want her to get the wrong idea about him.

"So, you always went back to their place? Maybe we could retrace your steps," Paige suggested.

"I already thought about that, but I don't remember any specific addresses. I would follow them, so I never put anything in my phone or GPS. I didn't want to remember. I might be able to think of a neighborhood or something, but nothing specific."

"Do you ever worry that you might have gotten any of them pregnant?" Paige was trying her best to not sound judgmental, but these were questions she wanted answered.

"No. I always used protection with them. I paid more attention in health class than my teen years proved, okay Paige? I promise." Jake looked her straight in her eyes. It was so important to him that she knew he was telling her the absolute truth. He would never let her down again.

"Can we please not talk about this anymore? I really wish I could remember something useful, that I had paid more attention to the women I went home with, only so that I could get you out of danger now. More than that, I wish I had never done it at all. I was trying to make life simple, but instead I have put the person I love most in the world in harm's way, and it is killing me."

Paige nodded and curled up on his lap and laid her head on his chest. Her mind was wandering, picturing Jake at bars and the women that would approach him. "I'm not jealous of those women, Jake, and I don't judge you for being with them. I know what it feels like to get lonely."

If none of the women stood out to him, it was going to be impossible to figure out who it was before they made their move on Paige. She would have to be ready for anything. There was no way she was going to let some psycho ruin her happy ending with Jake.

Paige got lucky and Officer Romero was able to stay with her through Friday. She was able to get the magazine's next issue out without a hitch. Meadow Oaks officers were still on watch over the weekend. Paige, Jake, and the kids took it easy and relaxed around the house. They were all due a little rest from drama.

On the following Monday, Paige had to admit that she was a ball of nerves without the backup of Officer Romero. She dressed in business slacks and flats instead of her usual pencil skirt and heels. She felt silly while she was getting ready, picturing herself having to fight some crazy chick and dressing accordingly. It didn't help that Jake was texting her every five minutes either. He was working over in Seabrook all day and was stressed out about not being near Paige for her first day alone.

The staff writers were in and out of Paige's office all day, getting approvals for expenses on their next assignments. While the constant interruptions didn't allow Paige to get much of her own work done, it sure helped the day pass by quickly. Cora Rae was going to be traveling to Myrtle Beach to cover a beach wedding and Stacey wanted to go with her to check out Airbnb's in that area.

"Where's your shadow today?" Cora Rae asked after all the work-related topics were covered.

"Well, since nothing new has happened, Charleston P.D. had to pull the protection detail. It's not a big deal. I can handle myself just fine," Paige assured her. No need for others to know that she was indeed more than a little worried about being on her own.

"I noticed she was the only officer left last week. Sweetie, aren't you even a little scared without her?" Cora Rae kept on. "Do you think the person that made the death threats against you has all of a sudden forgotten about you?"

"No, I don't, Cora Rae. I can't and won't live my life in constant fear. I will be cautious and at this point that's about all I can do. The rest is out of my control," Paige said levelly.

"Well, me and Stacey are going to go grab some lunch at the deli in a bit, you wanna come?" Cora Rae asked. Persistence should have been her middle name.

"Thank you for the offer, but I brought my lunch today."

"Honey, don't you think you'd be safer out in public? The office is practically empty at lunch time," Cora Rae exclaimed in her sweet, southern belle drawl.

"Cora Rae, I'm sure Paige has everything in hand. We should get back to work. The articles aren't going to write themselves." Stacey started guiding Cora Rae out the door and turned and winked at Paige behind her back.

Paige mouthed a silent thank you to Stacey and sat down to eat lunch at her desk. After a moment, she got up and closed and locked her office door. No need to tempt fate, right?

On Tuesday, Paige dressed in slacks and flats again, but thanks to some extra-curricular activities in the closet with Jake while she was trying to get her clothes on, he didn't have time to pack her a lunch as he had been doing almost every day. She was seriously debating whether or not to skip lunch that day when her assistant Brenda came in and invited her to lunch with a bunch of the other staff.

"That actually sounds great, Brenda. I'll finish this email to the jewelers about advertising space and meet you downstairs." Paige usually avoided big group lunches, but "safety in numbers" was a common saying for a reason she reckoned.

Paige sent off the email, gathered her purse, and headed towards the elevator. "Geez, what happened, Larry?" Paige asked the building janitor as she took in the giant mess on the elevator floor he was carefully mopping up.

"I guess somebody dropped a giant soda. Smells like root beer. Extra sticky. I'm sorry, Mrs. Collins, but I gotta get this mess cleaned up before it attracts ants. You're gonna have to take the stairs," Larry said, never looking up from his mop.

"That's okay, Larry. Thank you for taking such good care of the building."

Paige headed toward the door for the stairs. She hesitated with her hand on the knob, debating her options. With perfect timing, her stomach rumbled, and she remembered that her fun in the closet with Jake also made her miss breakfast. *It is daytime. Would "The Psycho" really attack me in a busy office building in broad daylight?* she reasoned to herself. With her mind made up, she went into the concrete stairwell. She peeked down over the cold metal railing and could see that the stairwell was completely empty. She wasn't sure if that was a good or a bad thing. Her office was on the fourth floor, so not too bad of a trip going down. It was lucky that she was wearing flats. She held her purse close and started down the stairs as fast as she could.

As soon as Paige passed the door to the third floor and started down the next set of stairs, the door swung open, and somebody rushed her from behind. They pushed her down the stairs and into the cold cement wall of the next landing. Paige's breath was knocked out of her, and she banged her head against the unforgiving concrete. She felt a brief flash of despair, but then the self-defense training her dad made her take before she left home for college kicked in. With blood steadily dripping down her face, she turned to see that her attacker had also been thrown off balance by their trip down the stairs. She noted that her attacker was wearing loose, plain black athletic clothing with a black ski mask.

Paige decided to channel her inner Buffy Summers and rolled her eyes at her assailant and said, "Cliché much?"

Her taunting enraged the attacker, who screamed and rushed at Paige again. With the element of surprise being lost, Paige was ready for the next assault and crouched in a defensive posture. As her assailant got closer, Paige moved her body to the side so the person was going past her, unable to stop their momentum. Paige was sure by the angry screams coming from her attacker, that it was undoubtedly a woman. When the woman in black turned around to face Paige again, Paige was already moving in closer to elbow her in the throat. Paige heard a crunch as her elbow made contact with the woman's windpipe. As the woman struggled for breath, Paige kicked her legs out from under her sending her flying up and back. As the mysterious woman fell back, her head hit the handrail for the next set of steps. She crumpled to the ground, unconscious at Paige's feet.

Paige's brain warred with itself as to what to do next. Should she unmask the woman and find out who she was? Should she rush for help? Her head wound was gushing blood, and she was starting to feel faint as the adrenaline that kept her upright wore off. *I'm going to pass out.* She realized that she wouldn't last much longer, and the woman might wake up sooner rather than later. Making what she thought was the responsible decision, Paige stumbled past the unmoving body of her stalker and ran down the remaining stairs, using the handrail to keep herself upright, to get to the security guard on the first floor.

As Paige stumbled into the lobby through the stairwell door, she saw a small group of her coworkers start moving towards her with looks of horror on their faces. The security guard noticed the commotion and ran over, yelling something to someone behind him. Paige couldn't understand what he was saying, her ears were ringing too loudly.

"She's in the stairwell. Second or third level, I can't...I don't know. She's unconscious," Paige managed to get out before the room started to spin. *I really should have eaten something this morning*, was the last thought Paige had before her world turned black.

CHAPTER TWENTY-ONE

Sadie completed her second heart bypass of the day and was in her office debating on whether or not to get a protein bowl from the cafeteria when her cell phone rang. She didn't recognize the number, so she sent it to voicemail. The number called again, and she rejected the call once more. On the third try, Sadie answered, already annoyed with whoever was on the other end of the call. "Dr. Jennings," she huffed impatiently.

"Dr. Jennings, this is Brenda Mathis, Paige Collins's assistant over at the magazine. She was attacked in the stairwell here and is on the way to MUSC in an ambulance right now. She has you down as her emergency medical contact," Brenda was struggling to get the words out between gasping sobs.

Sadie didn't even say anything to Brenda, she ended the call and took off running at full speed through the hallways to the emergency department doors. By the time she got there after having to bob and weave around patients and other hospital staff, the paramedics were already wheeling Paige in through the automatic doors and rushing her towards the triage area.

"Thirty-five-year-old female, attacked in a stairwell, apparent head laceration, other injuries unknown." As the paramedics continued to relay STATS to the emergency department doctor and nurses, Sadie followed along with the stretcher, filling in any holes to Paige's medical history that the other doctor might need to know.

Sadie did not usually worry about emergency department patients unless they were brought to her operating room, but Paige was her dearest friend in the entire world and there was no way she was leaving Paige's side.

The nurses were hustling around the cramped triage space getting Paige hooked up to IVs and machines while the doctor was yelling out orders as he assessed her. Head wounds always bleed a lot, but her being unconscious for so long was a bit concerning. Once they finished her initial examination and got her stabilized, blood was drawn for the standard tests, and they rolled her away from triage for a CT scan.

Satisfied that Paige wasn't going to take a turn for the worse in the next few minutes, Sadie went into the hallway and called Faith to let her know what was going on.

"Is she going to be okay, Sadie?" Faith was crying on the other end of the phone after hearing the news.

Sadie could hear the typical daycare noises in the background. Innocent children in a world that could be so cruel. The thought of innocent children made Sadie's heart hurt for Chloe and Henry. There would be no hiding what happened to their mom from them, and they would lose some more of their innocence. Their dad dying had been the first time they'd had to face something beyond their young years.

"I think so, Faith. Right now, we just have to wait and see. She hit her head pretty hard. They are doing a CT scan now. I'll know more after that. Can you call her folks and Jake? I haven't had a chance and I really want to go watch them do the scans. They are about to start them now."

"Yes, of course. I'll be up there soon. Love you, Sadie," Faith said sniffling.

"Love you too. See you when you get here."

Sadie got off the phone with Faith and quickly made arrangements for her other scheduled surgeries to be covered. She was in no shape to operate on anyone at the moment. Luckily, she had banked a couple of favors with one of the other surgeons and he happened to be available since it was one of his days off.

Sadie went into the room with the computer monitors for the CT scan and looked over the scans of Paige's brain with the neurologist on duty. Everything looked normal to her trained eye, and the other doctor confirmed it.

"Well, then why isn't she waking up?" Sadie questioned, worried as she looked through the glass to her friend who was still unconscious on the gurney. She wasn't used to seeing Paige so helpless.

"The mind protects itself, Dr. Jennings. I can't tell you when she'll wake up, but I have a feeling it won't be long now." Her colleague gave her a reassuring squeeze of the shoulder and left Sadie alone in the room.

Sadie let out a deep breath and went to help roll Paige to a room in the Intensive Care Unit and patiently waited for her friend to wake up. *You better wake up before Faith gets here or you'll never hear the end of it,* Sadie thought as she looked down at Paige.

***

By the time Jake got the call from Faith about Paige being assaulted at her office, all of the school buses were out on the road running their afternoon routes, making his trip to the hospital even more nerve-wracking than it already would have been. He did his best to not start cussing at the big yellow monstrosities. As it was, his steering wheel took the brunt of his anxiousness.

When Jake finally got to the hospital, he pulled his truck up on a curb, not even in a parking spot and ran in. The same receptionist, Lauren, was working at the reception desk again.

"I'm here to see Paige Collins. I'm her fiancé, Jake Bennett, and Dr. Sadie Jennings is expecting me," he said as quick as he could. Hopefully she wouldn't make him wait to find out how Paige was doing and where exactly in the hospital she was being treated.

Lauren smiled her professional smile at him and said, "Yes, Mr. Bennett, she is in a recovery room in the east wing on the third floor. Room E seven. Dr. Jennings is waiting for you there."

Jake took off for the elevators, following the signs and asking nurses for help until he found her room. When he went in, Paige was sitting up in the hospital bed, getting stitches sewed into a big cut on her forehead, right below her hairline.

"I can't seem to get enough of this place," Paige mumbled, trying not to move while the doctor worked on closing her up.

"Hi, I'm Dr. Harris. Plastic surgeon," the doctor doing the sewing introduced himself to Jake, never stopping his graceful hands weaving the stitches into Paige's forehead.

"Yes, one of the perks of working here is that I can ask the doctor who does the best stitches to sew up my friends. You won't even be able to tell where the cut was once it heals," Sadie said to Jake as she got up to offer him her seat next to Paige. "I'm going to go check on my patients from this morning. I'll be back in a jiffy."

Jake sat in the hard chair next to where Paige rested on the hospital bed and held her hand as the doctor finished his delicate stitching. They stayed quiet looking at each other, but knowing what the other was thinking, until the doctor left.

Once they were alone in the room, Paige rushed to talk first. "I'm fine, Jake. Really. My CT scan came back normal. I have some big ol' ugly bruises, but I kicked that psycho's ass." Paige squeezed his hand trying to reassure him. She could see that he was barely holding it together.

"Faith said you were unconscious for a really long-time, baby. I actually expected you to still be in the ICU when I got here," Jake said worriedly.

"I did pass out, it's true, but once I woke up after the CT scans were normal, they moved me from the ICU to a recovery room. Plus, I have a feeling that I only passed out because you wouldn't let me out of the closet to eat this morning," Paige teased suggestively.

Before Jake could even say anything in his defense, another doctor came into the room holding a laptop with Paige's medical chart pulled up. He scrolled a little bit before saying, "Well Mrs. Collins, you already know that your CT scan was normal. Your bloodwork came back, and your blood sugar was very low. Had you eaten today?"

"No, actually I hadn't. I was on my way to lunch when I was attacked," Paige answered.

"Okay, well that would explain those numbers. Obviously, I have to suggest that you eat a balanced breakfast to keep your blood glucose levels from getting so low. Between that and the blood loss from the nasty head wound would explain why you lost consciousness," the doctor explained.

"I understand," Paige replied, ready to have all of the commotion over with so she could get some rest.

"Oh, and you're pregnant."

CHAPTER TWENTY-TWO

"I'm sorry, what do you mean I'm pregnant?" Paige questioned disbelievingly.

Paige sat up straighter in the bed, looking at the doctor like he was a crazy person when he didn't immediately answer. There was absolutely no way she was pregnant. And then it hit her like a lightening strike that she hadn't bothered getting her usual birth control shot at her annual check-up appointment a couple of months before. She hadn't seen the point; it's not like she had been getting any male companionship since her husband passed. *Oh, shit! Shit! Shit! Shit!* she thought, freaking out.

The doctor laughed a little awkwardly and said, "Well, according to your hCG level, it's really early, probably too early to hear a heartbeat, but the standard pregnancy test when we did your bloodwork came back positive. Have you missed your period yet?"

Paige took a minute to think about his question. With all of the drama going on, she hadn't noticed that she was indeed a few days late, which actually wasn't unheard of for her. Nervously, she glanced over at Jake to see his reaction to the unexpected news. He was beaming. He was smiling so big with tears in his eyes. He came and sat gently on the bed next to her and pulled her into a soft hug and kissed her forehead.

"You're not mad?" Paige whispered nervously.

"No, baby, of course I'm not mad. I'm the happiest man alive," Jake replied gently. "I didn't even think to ask about birth control with you, probably because I knew that I would have no regrets having a child with you. I love you so much Paige. This is the best news ever."

Then Jake kissed her mouth and held her up against his chest, resting his chin on top of her head. The doctor snuck out of the room, letting the happy couple have some privacy.

Jake could not believe how lucky he was. He had the woman of his dreams, she was finally safe, and she was carrying his child. He couldn't imagine a better feeling.

A short while later, Sadie came back into the room clapping her hands in excitement. "I saw your chart! Y'all work fast! But this means no pain meds for you this time. Only regular Tylenol. You'll just have to suck it up, buttercup."

"Yes, Dr. Jennings," Paige said as her friend gave her a gentler hug than she normally would have. Paige was tired of being banged up, it was happening too often for her liking. At least it was all over.

"Where's Faith? She'll hate to miss this hot gossip," Paige asked.

"She's in the waiting room on the phone with the yummy Officer John Avery, trying to get information out of him on the identity of your attacker," Sadie answered.

"I'm so happy that this is all behind us now and we can just focus on our family. I don't want to tell the kids about the baby yet. We still haven't officially told them that we are a couple. Let's wait a few weeks at least," Paige said to Jake and Sadie both.

"As a doctor, I agree. You'll need to follow-up with your OB/GYN next week too. You'll need to be monitored closely after all this excitement," Sadie reminded Paige. "You should be fine, but better safe than sorry when it comes to my new niece or nephew."

"Who am I to argue with two smart ladies?" Jake grinned as the two ladies in question gave him identical smirks. "I do want to say however, that we should tell the kids about us sooner rather than later. They might notice your belly getting round with my baby in there and that could be awkward if they don't know we are planning on getting hitched."

Jake was beyond relieved that Paige was going to be alright. He hated she had been hurt, but he was so proud of her for taking down her attacker. His warrior. Honestly, he was a bit disappointed he didn't get to do it himself; not that hurting a woman was something he ever thought he would consider doing. At least it was all over. They would all be able to relax and enjoy the new life they were building, together.

As usual, Faith entered the room like a little blond tornado, fussing over Paige and asking tons of questions about her injuries and why she hadn't eaten anything that day.

After answering a few of her friend's mother hen questions, Paige decided to have some fun with Faith and nonchalantly threw in, "At least the baby wasn't hurt."

Paige got the reaction she hoped for. Faith immediately stopped talking and her mouth kept gaping open and closed like a fish. Then she squealed so loud, everyone had to cover their ears before their eardrums burst. Faith ran over to Paige and pulled her in for a tight hug, the complete opposite of Sadie's delicate embrace.

"Um Faith...watch the bruises," was all Paige managed to get out since her air supply felt like it was being cut off.

"Oh my gosh! I'm so sorry, I got over excited." Faith got up and backed off from Paige. "A baby! How wonderful! Did you know?"

Jake was the one who answered her question. He couldn't help it; he was so excited. He couldn't wait to see Paige's belly swollen with his child. Just imagining how she would look had his eyes tearing up a little again. "No, neither of us had any idea. It's really early. I mean, we've only been together about a month or so, this go round anyway, but I couldn't be happier. Thank goodness all this mess with the stalker is over with and we can finally breathe easy," Jake said as he looked lovingly over at Paige.

Turning his attention to Faith, he asked, "By the way, did John give you any information on the woman? I'm dying to know who it was so I can try to make sense of this mess I got Paige into. I hate to say it, but I doubt I'll recognize a name, but maybe if the police got the woman to tell them how or where she met me, I might be able to remember something."

Paige, Jake, and Sadie watched as the smile disappeared from Faith's face. She looked around the room with wide eyes, moving from one face to another, finally settling on Paige. "They didn't get her." Faith shook her head and walked over to hold Paige's hand. "I'm not supposed to tell you that. John wasn't supposed to tell anyone. Charleston P.D. is on their way to come talk to you. When the security guard went up the stairs, she was already gone. They could tell where the altercation was. Your blood was on the wall and on the floor. I'm so sorry sweetie, she must have woken up and fled the building."

The joyful energy from only a moment before drained away and a dark cloud seemed to settle over them. Jake went and sat back down on the bed with Paige and put his arm around her to provide comfort. It was definitely not the news they had been expecting to hear.

"I should have pulled the mask off," Paige whispered, her voice heavy with despair.

All three of her loved ones immediately started talking over one another, trying to reassure her that she did the right thing by going for help. Paige didn't hear any of them. She kept shaking her head disbelievingly. Her ears were ringing, and it felt like her world was falling away.

Finally, Sadie was the one who managed to get through to her. "Paige, look at me. *Look* at me. Between the blood loss, low blood sugar, and the pregnancy, you would have passed out in that stairwell, and she would have woken up first. It wouldn't matter if you had found out who she was, you wouldn't have lived to tell anyone. That also means we wouldn't be here right now celebrating this joyous news of yours. You did the right thing."

Paige nodded at her friend and the tears started pouring out of her. She hated that she was crying. She was so angry, and fearful for her unborn child and Chloe and Henry, and so unbelievably tired. She knew that she would have to stay strong to face her stalker again, but right then she was letting the tears flow freely while she was being held by Jake and watched over by her two best friends.

***

That bitch. I didn't think she had it in her, she thought to herself. She popped a couple of Percocet she bought off a sketchy guy on a street corner in downtown Charleston and slinked home with her tail between her legs. She was holding an ice pack to the back of her head, laying on her couch, fuming.

In the past, she had successfully taken out five grown men and never been seriously hurt. But she had let herself get upset when that slut teased her. She needed to stay level-headed. She just hated the dark-haired bitch so much. *A couple days to heal and then I'll come up with another plan,* she decided as she drifted off into a drug induced sleep.

CHAPTER TWENTY-THREE

Once again, the doctors insisted Paige spend the night in the hospital for observation. The difference was that as her fiancé, Jake was allowed to stay in the room with her overnight. He guessed they had gone from being unofficially engaged to officially engaged. He really needed to get her a ring. He knew Paige wouldn't mind not having one, but he wanted her to have something she could always look at that was a symbol of how much he loved her. What she probably would have preferred at that moment in time was a pair of brass knuckles to take down "The Psycho" with.

Charleston P.D. came by the hospital to get Paige's statement shortly after Faith broke the bad news of The Psycho's escape. They had nothing new to tell Paige or Jake about her assailant. They had closed off the building, since it was an official crime scene, and gotten statements from everyone present. No one had noticed anything unusual until Paige staggered into the lobby covered in blood. About half of her staff had been in the lobby and the other half on the way to the restaurant they were meeting at. It was a giant mess for authorities as they tried to make sure everyone else was accounted for.

A few of the magazine staff called the hospital to check on Paige and Jake spoke to them on her behalf while she rested. It was obvious to him which ones had seen her after the attack because they cried when they asked about Paige. He could picture it all too well in his head and it broke his heart. His Paige attacked and bleeding, then collapsing on the floor. He looked over to where she was asleep on the hospital bed. He took her hand in his, kissed it, and did something he hadn't done in a long time. He prayed out loud until his voice was hoarse.

***

On Wednesday afternoon, the doctors let Paige go home on the condition that she come back at the first sign of distress. She had a feeling that was really Sadie's condition for her release since she wasn't available to come stay with Paige again. Jake did not leave her side and waited on her hand and foot. He wouldn't let her do anything. Paige found it cute and unnecessary.

"I'm not going to break, Jake. I can walk by myself to and from the bathroom," Paige teased as he guided her to the couch. He had been waiting for her right outside the bathroom door and was upset with her that she hadn't called him from the kitchen to help her walk *to* the bathroom.

"Just because you can doesn't mean you have to," Jake insisted stubbornly.

Jake planted a kiss on her forehead, tucked a blanket around her on the couch, and dropped another snack in her lap, a protein bar to follow up the fruit he made her eat earlier. "Eat up. You're growing my baby in there." He winked and went into the kitchen to finish getting dinner ready.

That evening, Paige's parents came over to her house to check on her and drop the kids off. They had picked the kids up early from school the day before when Faith called them with the news that their daughter had been attacked at work.

"This is becoming a common occurrence sweetheart. I'm worried," her dad said after the kids went upstairs to unpack their overnight bags. He settled himself on the couch next to her and patted her knee.

"I know, Dad, but you don't need to worry; I'm going to be fine. Those self-defense classes you made me take came in awfully handy," Paige tried to reassure her dad. She knew she wasn't doing a great job of it.

Paige looked up to see Jake watching them from the kitchen doorway. The guilt he was feeling was written all over his handsome face. She knew it was eating him up that she was in danger. Paige looked back over at her dad and changed the subject to the kids. There was nothing her parents loved more than their grandchildren. Her mom sat down across from her in the big chair and started telling her about something funny Henry said the night before at dinner. The story had them all laughing in no time.

"Henry was so worried about you, and he could tell that we were too, so he started telling jokes to cheer everyone up. He's such a sweetie pie," Paige's mom gushed.

Paige smiled outwardly, but inside she was worried about her children. She wanted the whole mess to be over with so they could have a sense of normalcy again.

Jake tried his best to convince Paige to take the rest of the week off to recuperate. He even got Faith and Sadie on his side. She wasn't having it. She returned to work on Friday with Officer Romero back as her shadow. Two days off stuck on the couch with her thoughts was more than enough.

"I'm very sorry that you were hurt, Mrs. Collins," Officer Romero said when she met Paige at her parking spot like she had done the times before. "I heard you got a few strong hits in. Good for you."

"Thank you. I am glad to have you back. I doubt she's going to give up. Whoever she is," Paige replied wearily.

When Paige stepped off the elevator and entered the office, all hell broke loose. People came rushing up to her asking all sorts of questions. Paige decided to go ahead and address the group and get it over with so she wouldn't have to keep repeating herself. Plus, Officer Romero looked flustered having so many people coming at Paige like they were.

"Okay, everyone settle down please," Paige boomed as loud as she could. "Yes, I was attacked in the stairwell Tuesday, but I am fine now. No, they do not have any suspects at this time. Charleston P.D. does not believe that anyone else is in danger and has, as you can see, reinstated the police protection. That is all I have to say about it at this time. Thank you all for your concern."

Paige went into her office and closed the door, something she didn't usually do. Her head started to throb after raising her voice. Maybe Jake had been right about staying home. She spent the rest of the day basically hiding in her office.

Paige arrived home that evening to an empty house, except for the police officer parked outside. It was a relief to get some quiet alone time, so she kicked off her shoes and settled in on the couch for a nap. She awoke a couple of hours later to Jake rubbing her feet.

"Hmmm…. I could get used to this," Paige moaned appreciatively.

"Faith wanted the kids to have a sleepover at her house tonight, so we have this house all to ourselves," Jake said, waggling his eyebrows. "So, how was your day? Not too exciting I hope?"

"No, it was pretty boring. I think Officer Romero was disappointed. I could tell that she was itching for a fight."

"Ahh. I personally hope she gets one and not you. You have proven you can handle yourself, but now that we know you have that precious cargo in your belly, can't be too careful," he said rubbing her middle. Her stomach hadn't changed any yet; he just liked to imagine.

"Oh, speaking of our precious cargo, I have an appointment with my OB/GYN next Wednesday afternoon."

"Can I come to it?" Jake asked shyly.

"Of course you can. I don't think much is going to happen. Just confirm I'm pregnant, get some prenatal vitamins, and talk about what to expect. I'm definitely pregnant. My boobs are sore and huge, and I'm exhausted. I had forgotten how tired pregnancy makes me." Paige sank back into the couch pillows.

"I'll be there. And I think I need to make my own judgement on the boobs. Don't worry, I'll be gentle."

Jake pounced on Paige, causing her to squeal and giggle like a teenager. They both laughed and held each other tight. When they caught their breath, Jake slid to the ground next to the couch and pulled a red velvet jewelry box out of his pocket. He opened it to reveal a beautiful princess cut diamond ring.

It took a few seconds for Paige to realize exactly what was happening. Even though they had already decided to get married soon, to see Jake down on one knee made it even more special to her. Her heart warmed in her chest at the romantic gesture.

"Paige Collins, I swear to love you for the rest of my life. To love your wonderful children as my own. I promise to be the best daddy to this baby. I'll change diapers, get up in the middle of the night for feedings, and take the best care of its beautiful mama. It would make me the happiest man on earth to be your husband. Will you marry me?"

Jake was nervous. Even with it being a sure thing, his future happiness was in someone else's hands. He didn't think he could live without her knowing how wonderful life was being with her.

"These hormones have me crying over everything. And yes, I will marry you, Jake. I love you so much," Paige said through her happy tears.

Paige jumped onto Jake's lap on the floor, and he slid the ring on her finger. Paige felt like she had waited her whole life for him. "I guess this means you don't have to sleep on the couch anymore, well once we tell the kids," she teased Jake.

Jake took that as his cue and carried his fiancé up to their bedroom to once again claim what was his. He made sure to give the pregnancy boobs some extra special attention.

Over the weekend, John stopped by on behalf of Charleston P.D. to give an update on Paige's case. "They are leaning towards the theory that your attacker works in your building. The building only has cameras on the entrances and exits, none in the interior. That will probably change after this incident, at least in the stairwell. It took some time, but they were able to identify everyone who came in that day. Visitors and messengers are signed in at the front desk and everyone was accounted for on the login sheet. None were present in the building at the time of the attack, all had signed out with the front desk and could be seen on the cameras exiting the building. The tricky part is that we can't tell which employees were unaccounted for after the attack because nobody was let back inside, and it was lunchtime, so a lot of people had gone out. The only people we can weed out are the ones that were in the lobby when you came out of the stairwell. On Monday, Charleston P.D. will start talking to the different offices seeing who can vouch for who and go from there. It's going to take some time. Jake, they might ask you to come look at the footage to see if you recognize anyone."

"How many people work in the building?" Jake asked, turning to Paige who was snuggled up on the couch resting.

"Three hundred give or take," Paige replied. "There's the magazine, a huge law practice, a small book publisher, and a few financial advisors."

Paige shrugged and wrapped the blanket she was snuggling in tighter around her. It was a difficult pill to swallow that someone she might pass by everyday wants her dead. Or even worse, someone in her own office. *Could someone I work with everyday be trying to kill me?*

"I wish I had better news for y'all. We'll figure this out. In the meantime, be as careful as you can." John got up to leave and Jake walked with him.

John turned around at the last minute and pointed his finger at Paige, "And no more stairwells."

"Yes Officer," Paige answered sheepishly.

"I'm going to walk John out, honey. I'll be right back," Jake said as he closed the front door behind him.

Jake figured by the expectant look on John's face that he was probably hoping Jake had something he needed to say about his past conquests that could help them break the case, something he didn't want to mention in front of Paige. Unfortunately, nothing helpful had come to mind yet.

"John, Paige is pregnant," Jake said, getting straight to the point.

John opened and shut his mouth a few times. "Well, that wasn't what I had expected you to say," he mused.

"We're officially engaged too, but Paige doesn't want to tell the kids until we get this all figured out. One thing at a time...you know."

"Congratulations man. That's great news! Horrible timing, no offense, but great news nonetheless," John said when he finally got over the initial shock. He patted his friend on the back and pulled him in for a quick guy hug.

"Thanks. You'll understand that I am freaking out even more than I was before. I hadn't thought that was possible, but here we are. Paige has proved that she can handle herself against whoever this is hand to hand, but she'll come after Paige again and next time she might have a knife or a gun. How are we supposed to live like this?" Jake asked his friend.

"Jake, I don't have a good answer for you. This woman is proving to be tricky to find and then we have to figure out if she's working alone. According to Paige, her attacker was wearing all black, but no one left the building dressed like that when we watched the footage. We will find her though, Jake. We'll keep up our patrol here and Charleston P.D. will do the same. Hang in there man."

John shook hands with Jake, got in his patrol car and drove away. He felt bad for his friends and wished there was something more he could do. He had complete faith that his guys would do everything on their end to keep Paige and the kids safe in Meadow Oaks. He just hoped it was enough.

CHAPTER TWENTY-FOUR

On Monday, as Paige entered her office building with Officer Romero, she couldn't help but look at every woman she walked by and wonder if she was the one who wished Paige dead. She gauged their build, height, and tried to see if they had a bruise on their throat or looked like they were recovering from a head injury. If only she had known when she returned to work last Friday, she would have paid more attention to the other women in her building then. She was going to drive herself crazy with paranoia.

Paige's oversized purse had extra weight due to the twenty-two-caliber magnum pistol Jake insisted she carry until they caught "The Psycho." It was her gun, bought by Matt for her to have on the nights she worked late in Charleston.

"It's probably not going to kill anybody, but it'll slow 'em down," Matt had said when he gave it to her and insisted that she take a concealed carry course.

Paige had never actually carried it with her to work before. It stayed locked in the fireproof safe except for when she took it to the shooting range to practice, which she hadn't done since the last time Matt made her. "I can't live without you," he had said. *The irony,* she thought unhappily.

Paige was uneasy every time she interacted with a female coworker. She caught herself paying extra attention to their mannerisms. Cora Rae without heels on would probably be the same height as the attacker and she did wear her make-up a little on the heavy side. Stacey and Brenda both wore clothes a little loose on them, so it was hard to tell, but it seemed like they could have the same build as "The Psycho." Their make-up was a little more natural than Cora Rae's, but that didn't necessarily mean anything. From what Jake had told her the young messenger said, the mysterious lady looked like she was trying to be in disguise when she arranged for him to deliver those photos of her wreck to Jake's office. Paige felt like she was going crazy overwhelming herself with trying to keep all of the details straight.

Paige had not thought to ask John which of her colleagues were in the lobby the day of her attack, and she couldn't remember who had run up to her when she came out of the stairwell. She was almost sure that Brenda was slightly too old; for Jake's taste and to have attacked her with such vigor. When asked, Officer Romero confirmed that Brenda had been ruled out as a suspect in the attack, but not Cora Rae or Stacey. At least Paige could trust her assistant. Well, unless she was an accomplice. Yep, Paige was going to go crazy.

During the times she was alone in her office, Paige let her mind wander to happier thoughts. Her and Jake were engaged and going to have a baby. Her heart felt like it was going to burst, it was so full of love. Chloe and Henry absolutely adored Jake and Caleb. Paige never thought the day would come when her kids would have a father again. She hoped this whole mess would be over soon so she could tell them that they were all going to officially be a family and a new baby brother or sister was on the way.

Paige still missed Matt terribly. Jake let her talk about her late husband whenever she felt like it, and there was never a hint of jealousy or annoyance. Just acceptance. He even understood when she admitted that sometimes she felt a little guilty about moving on and being happy again. It was an amazingly freeing thing, to be so honest with someone. It reminded her why she had stayed friends with him, even when he had broken her heart.

Of course, Faith and Sadie were not surprised when Paige face-timed them to announce the news of their engagement. They fully expected to be bridesmaids in the wedding and were fighting over who got to be maid or matron of honor.

"What makes you think I'm doing a ceremony with bridesmaids?" Paige asked her friends. The thought honestly hadn't crossed her mind. She was simply looking forward to being Jake's wife and Caleb's bonus mom.

"Because you've been in love with the man forever. And because it's for the kids as much as it is for you. An official celebration of the joining of your families. It doesn't have to be fancy, but it does need to happen," Faith explained.

Paige caved and Faith went straight into planning mode.

"Show us the ring! I'm dying to see it," Sadie chimed in.

"Oh, it's in the safe at home. I can't wear it around people until I tell the kids. But it is gorgeous. I'll text you a pic later," Paige promised.

"Are you going to have Cora Rae cover it for the magazine?" Faith asked, already making notes to put in the wedding planning notebook she would pick up at Target later.

"I doubt the wedding will have any of the grandeur required to be featured in the magazine, which is how I would want it. And there is the little hiccup of Cora Rae hasn't been ruled out as a suspect. For all I know, she might be trying to kill me." Paige shrugged, even though it bothered her to think that her long-time work colleague might want her dead.

"Well dang. Wouldn't that be something?" Faith pondered, trying to picture the woman she had met a few times at Paige's work functions. Cora Rae had seemed sort of simple, but really sweet. *Guess you never know,* Faith thought to herself.

"I gotta run. Call me if you want me to come over and protect you." Faith was dead serious. She would fight like a banshee for her friend and those kids.

"I appreciate that. See ya later."

Paige waved at the screen to an excited Faith and a suddenly silent, since she was in the doctors' lounge and some colleagues were walking in, and thrilled Sadie. She hung up and smiled picturing her little blond friend throwing down. She pitied the fool that underestimated Faith's fierceness.

***

Jake had been eager for the appointment to confirm Paige's pregnancy all week. Once the time approached, however, he turned into a giant ball of nerves. He was so scared that the hospital's pregnancy test had been wrong. He wanted a baby with Paige so badly.

Jake also knew that Paige would be absolutely crushed if she wasn't pregnant. He had caught her a few times rubbing her stomach and talking to it after she got home from the hospital. It was the sweetest thing he had ever seen. *She's already been through so much; it wouldn't be fair for this to be taken from her too.* When the doctor came in with her lab results, he stood up and went over to the exam table and put his arm around Paige for support. For both of them.

"Yup, you're definitely pregnant. Going from the date of your last period, I would say about four to five weeks. Still very early. Congratulations!" Dr. Joseph Woodard announced.

Jake kissed Paige on the mouth and then started bombarding the doctor with questions. "Last week she had a bad fall with a head injury. Will that affect the baby at all?" Jake asked anxiously.

As the doctor went into the risks associated with pregnancy and precautions to take, Jake listened adamantly. He had practically been a kid when Caleb's mom was pregnant, and it was so long ago that he felt like a newbie. So many of the guidelines had changed since then. He knew Paige had more experience in this department, but she was not going through the pregnancy alone. He was determined to take great care of her.

"The most important thing is to eat healthy, drink lots of water, get plenty of rest, and avoid anything too stressful or strenuous," Dr. Woodard summarized.

When Paige and Jake gave each other sideways glances, the doctor added, "I know that can be tricky when you already have children, so just do the best you can."

Jake quickly explained "The Psycho" situation to the doctor so that there was complete transparency with the doctor who was responsible for the medical care of his unborn child and the love of his life.

"Hmm, well, that does change things a bit," Dr. Woodard pondered. "I'm going to send you home with a blood pressure cuff. I want you to check your blood pressure twice a day, and anytime you are starting to feel overwhelmed. Call my office immediately if it gets out of control or if there is another incident. Because of your age and this being your third child, with this added stress we'll need to monitor things closely. And Dad, you'll need to do everything you can to keep her relaxed."

"I'll take great care of her, Doc," Jake said and shook the doctor's hand.

Paige giggled when the doctor left the room and beamed up at Jake with eyes full of love.

"What?" Jake questioned.

"Oh nothing. You are just so cute, that's all." Paige was overjoyed by how involved Jake was.

Pregnancy itself was hard. Add in everything they had going on and it was a recipe for exhaustion. Paige was relieved to know that he wasn't going to pull any ignorant macho crap on her while she was trying to grow a human being.

They scheduled the next appointment at a time when they could both come again and walked out of the office hand in hand. They couldn't help smiling lovingly at each other and stealing a steamy kiss once outside on the sidewalk. It hadn't fazed them at all that people were chuckling at them as they passed. They were so caught up in their own little bubble that they did not notice the extremely irate woman death-gripping her steering wheel in the blue sedan across the street. If looks could kill, Jake and Paige would have been vaporized.

***

That bitch was trying to trap her man. That had to be it. He didn't really want the dark-haired slut. She and her lover were soulmates. She went outside to her dead tree in the woods and went wild with the axe. When that didn't have its usual therapeutic effect, she let out a primal scream. Birds that were resting in the pine trees shrieked and took flight. Squirrels hid in their burrows of the oak trees. Her world felt like it was spinning out of control.

She tried to calm herself by taking deep breaths and repeating, "He loves me. He loves me. He loves me."

Finally, she felt a little better. But what was she going to do about her current obstacle? She laughed aloud at the thought. "This is not an obstacle," she said to her axe. "This is an opportunity. An opportunity to wreak some havoc on that stupid bitch before I kill her."

Feeling much better, she retreated to her house to start the next phase of her plan to get her lover out of the horrible woman's clutches.

CHAPTER TWENTY-FIVE

Every day following her doctor's appointment, Paige went back and forth between feeling completely blissful in her pregnancy glow one minute, and on high alert for another attack on her life the next. It was a very strange way to live. Normally, she would have attributed the extreme mood swings to pregnancy hormones, but there were extenuating circumstances at play.

"The Psycho" was biding her time. Paige wanted to get whatever was going to happen next over with before her belly started affecting her range of motion. The thought of trying to swing her arms around with a big swollen belly made her giggle nervously aloud.

"Everything okay, Mrs. Collins?" Officer Romero glanced up from her case notes to look at Paige.

Officer Romero had decided it was best to be as close to Paige as possible. She allowed a rare grin as Paige shook her head, feeling silly. Officer Romero hopped up from her chair as two of the staff writers knocked on the door. Nobody was going to get the jump on her while Paige was under her protection.

"Cora Rae, Stacey, come on in. What's up?" Paige waved them into her office.

"Hey hon, we're about to take off to head up to Myrtle Beach. I have that beach wedding tomorrow and Stacey here has vacation rental properties to check out. Unless she changes her mind about going as my plus one to the wedding." Cora Rae nudged Stacey with her elbow.

"I would love to be your plus one, but there are two places I can't decide between for next month's issue, so I'll be busy all day," Stacey replied.

"Since you are seeing both anyway why don't you pick one for the next issue and put the other one in your back pocket for a slow month. Or, if they are both amazing, we could do a double feature for summer," Paige suggested.

"Great! I'll get the local photographer I found down there to take shots of both. Mike requested off this weekend, so I need you to sign off on the extra expense for the accounting department. They don't trust me yet, even though I agreed to share a hotel room with this one to save the magazine some money." Stacey nudged Cora Rae back playfully and shrugged.

Paige filled out the necessary expense form and sent the ladies on their way. She noticed Officer Romero eyeing them closely the whole time they were in her office. At least Paige wasn't the only one eyeballing everyone that interacted with her. She had a feeling Officer Romero would fit in well with her, Faith, and Sadie once she opened up a little bit. First things first though, find "The Psycho."

The next morning, Jake woke everyone up early to take them to the Folly Beach Pier to do some fishing. The pier was pretty crowded with locals on that warm Saturday morning. Henry had the best time talking about sharks and the different types of fish that could be found off the coast of South Carolina. The kid was like a mini encyclopedia. Caleb was so patient with him. The soon-to-be older stepbrother was setting a great example for Chloe. She was doing her best to match Caleb's relaxed demeanor. They spent hours on the pier casting lines and reeling in seaweed along with the occasional fish.

Shortly after noon, they were all famished. Jake stowed the fishing gear in the back of his truck and took out the cooler with the picnic lunch Paige had packed. She was always hungry these days and had come prepared. She figured the hunger was a good sign that the pregnancy was progressing well. They laid out blankets on the sandy beach and ate, talked, and laughed. At one point, Paige looked over to see Henry had fallen asleep. His ham and cheese sandwich lay next to him, half eaten on the blanket.

Paige and Chloe decided to take a walk along the edge of the salty water, barefoot so their toes could squish in the gritty sand, staying in sight of Jake and Caleb for safety. Paige asked Chloe how she felt about everything that was going on and they had the best discussion. It was the most open Chloe had been with her mom in a long time. She missed her dad, and they both cried sharing funny stories about Matt's corny dad jokes. Chloe admitted she hadn't been feeling as sad with Jake and Caleb hanging around and was worried it meant she was betraying her dad's memory. Paige explained that sometimes she felt the same way, but she was one-hundred percent sure Chloe's dad would have wanted them all to be happy again.

When they returned to their blankets, Jake and Caleb gave up throwing the football around and laid down to nap next to Henry. Luckily, they had the forethought to open up the beach umbrella to avoid sunburn. Paige could understand why Jake was so exhausted; always being on guard duty around her and the kids had to be physically and mentally draining. She took out her phone and snapped some pictures of her boys resting side by side. Chloe rolled her eyes, but smiled, and grabbed the magazines her mom brought for her. Paige opened up a historical romance novel about a devilishly handsome Scottish laird and a busty milkmaid she'd been looking forward to reading for the longest time. She kept catching herself staring over at her family instead. *How did I get so darn lucky?*

In the truck on the way home to Meadow Oaks, Paige and Jake held hands in the front seat while the kids talked quietly in the backseat. Jake kept looking over at her grinning from ear to ear. She didn't even have to ask what he was thinking; it was written all over his face. It was their first family outing and it had been a perfect day. The notification ping repeatedly chiming on her phone was the only thing interrupting their peaceful ride home.

"Seems like you better check that," Jake suggested.

"I don't want to go back to the real world yet," Paige faux whined, poking her bottom lip out and batting her eyelashes at him.

"But this is real life, baby," he said, kissing her hand and winking at her.

Convinced, but still not happy about it, Paige let go of Jake's hand to take her phone out of her bag. She had ten new emails in her work email marked important. They were all from Stacey.

"Oh wow. The freelance photographer in Myrtle Beach took some gorgeous shots for next month's travel feature," she exclaimed, flashing the phone at Jake so he could see the pictures.

"Uh-huh. I'll take your word for it. I need to pay attention to the road. Too much precious cargo in this vehicle to get distracted," he insisted.

Paige chuckled and stuck her head out of the truck window. The wind flowed through her hair and made her eyes water, but she felt so alive and joyous that she embraced the sensations.

When they pulled in the driveway and parked, a red sedan pulled in behind them and Paige freaked out. Jake quickly grabbed her shoulders and said, "It's just Officer Denton, baby. I asked him to follow us today in plain clothes. I wanted to give you and the kids one day of normal but wasn't risking y'all's safety."

"That was very thoughtful of you, Jake," Paige replied as she willed her heart to slow down. She gave Jake a small smile and focused on breathing evenly.

Officer Denton, a young burly man, went inside and made sure the house was clear and then helped Jake get all of the fishing gear back into the garage.

Paige whipped up a quick dinner of fried chicken and sauteed vegetables for everyone. They gathered around the table to eat as a family like they had been doing for the past few weeks.

"Are you like our new dad?" Chloe asked all of a sudden, looking over at Jake.

It took Jake a few seconds to answer as he had choked on the bite of food that was in his mouth. She had caught him completely off guard. "I want to be Chloe. Would that be ok with you?" Jake asked nervously. Who knew a preteen girl could be so scary.

"Does that mean y'all are going to get married?" Chloe asked, not answering Jake's question yet.

Jake looked to Paige for guidance. When she nodded and smiled, he turned back to face Chloe. "Well, as it just so happens, I asked your mother to marry me, and she said yes. But it has to be okay with you and your brother too," Jake said, looking over at Henry, who was smiling ear to ear, and then back to Chloe. "I want you to understand that I'm not expecting you to forget your dad. He was a good man. I met him once, a long time ago, when I ran into them when he and your mom were dating. You can talk about him as much as you want. I want you to. I just want to be your dad now, in my own right. Is that okay?"

Chloe took a minute to think about it and during that time both Jake and Paige were sitting on pins and needles. Finally, she looked at Jake and smiled brightly, her eyes shining with tears. "Yes, that would be okay," Chloe said. She got up and walked around the table to hug Jake tightly and started crying earnestly. Jake wrapped one arm around Chloe and the other reached out to Paige who had tears pouring down her cheeks. She took his hand and they held onto each other through the emotional onslaught from Chloe showing such affection.

To Henry, his sister was in charge, so when she said yes, that was all he needed to hear. "Did you hear that? We are going to be brothers!" he said excitedly, running over to Caleb and jumping up and down.

"Yeah, buddy. I heard the awesome news," Caleb said with a smile and brought his new little brother in for a bear hug. The two boys went over to Paige and wrapped her up in their arms.

"This is just so wonderful," Paige whispered as she held on to her family.

"Wait a second," Chloe sniffled, wiped her eyes, and pulled back from Jake to look him in the eyes. "Did you get my mom a ring?" she questioned. The preteen attitude was starting to work its way back front and center.

"Yes, I did. She has it upstairs. And I got down on one knee and professed my undying love for her," Jake vowed as he tried to keep from chuckling.

"You better have," Chloe said seriously. Then she laughed and hugged Jake quickly before going back to her seat and taking a bite of dinner.

Everyone else laughed happily at Chloe's good spirits and returned to their seats as well. They started planning their future together as a family. The kids had big ideas for family vacations. Hawaii was mentioned quite a few times. When they were done eating, they all settled down in the living room to watch a movie. Paige and Jake spread out on the big couch, while Chloe and Henry shared the loveseat, and Caleb took his usual spot on the oversized chair with his long legs draped over the side.

The kids were pretty worn out from spending the day in the sun and the excitement of the engagement conversation, so it didn't take long before they were fast asleep in their seats. Jake carried Henry to bed upstairs and then came back for Chloe. Paige watched as he took such care with her children. She gently nudged Caleb awake, and he wandered groggily to what used to be the guest room, but he had claimed it as his own. It made Paige happier than he could ever know that he felt so at home after such a short time.

"Are you ready for bed, wife?" Jake asked, holding out his hand to lead Paige upstairs to their bedroom. He was thrilled that he would get to sleep next to her every night and wake up next to her every morning since they finally told their kids that they were getting married.

"Now hold on just a minute, sir. I'm not your wife yet," Paige teased, pretending to hesitate at the bottom of the staircase.

"As far as I'm concerned, you are," he said seductively, guiding her up the stairs, moving his hands all over her body and under her clothes as they took each step.

"Is that right?" Paige savored the feeling of anticipation that was warming her from the inside.

"Mmmhmm," Jake mumbled as he scooped Paige up at the top of the staircase and carried her to bed. After nudging the bedroom door shut, he gently laid her down and started peeling off clothes.

"Time to claim what's mine," he growled as he towered over her on the bed, lowering his mouth to hers.

They spent the next hour exploring every inch of the other intimately. Paige fell asleep on Jake's chest exhausted, completely satisfied, and her skin was flushed all over. Jake ran his fingers through her hair as she slept, thinking how he had never known he could love so deeply.

Not wanting the peaceful and loving feelings flooding through her to end, Paige decided to host a big brunch for her family and friends the next day. Her parents, Sadie, Faith, Travis, and John were all in her house sipping on mimosas and bloody marys while Jake showed the younger two kids how to make stuffed French toast, eggs, grits, bacon, sausage, and hashbrowns. Breakfast food had always been Paige's favorite and Jake wanted to spoil her.

In the middle of everyone working on their second helping of food, there was a knock on the front door. Since they all knew there was a police officer outside on watch, John excused himself from the table to see what his fellow officer needed.

"The flower delivery guy just came by to drop these off. Everything looks normal to me," the officer reported, still eyeing the bouquet warily like it was a bomb that could go off at any second.

John looked over the flowers arranged in a pink mason jar vase and didn't notice anything unusual about it. Paige's mom, Sherry, walked over to join John in the entryway and looked it over as well.

"Looks like a beautiful bouquet of peonies, daffodils, and daisies," she said, eyeing the flowers expertly.

John nodded his head, still looking at the pink, yellow, and white flowers, checking the bottom of the vase. He handed the arrangement to Sherry and took the little card that was attached to a plastic pronged holder and read it to himself silently.

"Sherry, can you and Mr. Hawkins take the kids outside for a few minutes?" John asked, looking up from the small card, keeping his poker face in place.

"Of course." Sherry placed the flowers on the bench in the foyer and herded her husband and the three kids out the back door. Sherry was dying to know what the card said, but she knew her daughter's first priority would always be the children's well-being; so, if John didn't want them present for whatever was about to go down, she would comply with his wishes.

When the back door closed behind her parents and the kids, Paige turned in her seat to face John and asked, "What is it, John?"

When he didn't answer her right away, Paige rose up from where she was seated next to Jake and went to take the card from John's hand. His eyes never left Jake's, even when Paige was pulling the card from his grasp. She read it a few times and then started pacing. The others were asking her what it said repeatedly, but she stayed silent and kept pacing.

John wouldn't say anything either, would give them no hint about what was going on. Paige's anger was building. She was furious. She had never felt so much rage in her entire life, and it was all directed at Jake Bennett.

CHAPTER TWENTY-SIX

"**Y**ou sorry son of a bitch!" Paige screamed once she finally stopped pacing.

She tried to calm herself down before speaking. It didn't worked. A part of her knew she was being irrational. All of the stress from death threats, being attacked, then the card with the flowers, and hurts from the past made her anger boil over like a volcano spewing hot lava. She was facing Jake, and he had a look of absolute panic on his face.

"Paige, what are you talking about? What does the card say?" Jake asked, rising up from where he was seated, looking back and forth between Paige and John. He was looking for some kind of hint as to what in the world was going on.

Paige stomped towards Jake and got in his face. With barely contained rage she said, "You and your dick always causing problems. Just like last time. You must have put it on the psycho bitch real good for her to be so damn obsessed with you."

Paige shoved the card at Jake's chest as hard as she could. He tried to hold on to her hand, but she pulled away and put plenty of space between them. Jake looked down at the little white card. Typed in flower shop script was the message:

Congrats on being pregnant with his child.

I am too.

But only one of us will have his baby.

See you soon.

"Paige, there is no way this is true," Jake argued, holding out his hands to her, silently pleading for her to believe him. When Paige wouldn't look at him, he went over to her and grabbed her by the shoulders. Faith and Sadie started to come around the table to intervene, but John shook his head and motioned for them to stay put. He would step in if needed, but he knew Jake would never be rough with Paige.

"Paige, you have to believe me. She's trying to upset you and break us apart. She must have followed us to the doctor's office the other day and figured it out. Paige, please talk to me," Jake pleaded in earnest.

Paige kept shaking her head back and forth. She wouldn't look him in the eye. Tears were streaming down her flushed face. Jake racked his brain for the right thing to say. After a few seconds, something Paige had said came to the front of his mind.

"What did you mean when you said just like last time?" Jake asked warily. He sensed that something bad was coming.

Paige finally turned her head to look at him. The fury he saw in her green eyes scared him. She shoved him away hard. "I was pregnant too," Paige said through gritted teeth.

"What?" Jake was confused, he thought maybe he hadn't heard her right.

"I was pregnant before Rachel," Paige said in a deceptively calm voice.

Jake shook his head trying to make what he'd just heard make sense. As soon as the meaning of what Paige said clicked in his mind, he sank down to his knees on the floor. Faith and Sadie gasped and put their hands up to their faces to try to help keep their emotions in check. Travis put a comforting hand on his wife's shoulder.

"That's right. I was seventeen and pregnant and alone," Paige said standing over him with an icy stare.

"I never knew," Jake whispered, looking back up at her.

"Yes, I know. I was working up the courage to tell you that I was pregnant with your child. Before I could, I got a phone call informing me that Rachel was pregnant too, and that you were going to marry her." Paige started sobbing as the memories overwhelmed her, unable to keep up the false calm detachment. "I was so distraught. I felt like my life was hopeless. And then I lost the baby."

Jake stood up and grabbed her hands gently, but firmly. "You should have told me."

"Like you would have fucking cared," Paige said coldly.

Paige tore her hands out of his and stepped back away from him. Faith and Sadie were full blown crying, holding onto each other for dear life. John leaned back against a wall with his arms crossed over his chest, complete shock on his face. It wasn't too often something caught him so off guard.

"What would have been the point of me telling you, Jake? I lost the baby, and you were with her. What would you have done? Nothing. You didn't want me anyways. She had your baby, and I didn't," Paige yelled, returning to anger so her despair could not consume her.

Jake tried once again to pull Paige to him so he could comfort her, but she was not having it. He wanted so desperately to hold her. His heart was breaking over what she told him, and he couldn't bear to see her so upset. "Paige, please baby," he begged, not sure what to say.

"Don't you dare baby me. Get out of my house. GET OUT!" she screamed at the top of her lungs.

Before he could try to plead his case again, Sadie came up to him and put both of her hands on his chest, stopping him from moving any closer to Paige. "Jake, I think you should leave now. She needs to calm down or she could lose this baby too." Sadie said in her firm, but not judgmental, doctor tone.

It was probably the only thing anyone could have said to get Jake to listen and walk away from Paige. He looked hopelessly at Sadie and when she nodded, he whispered, "I'm sorry," and walked out the front door.

Jake didn't leave though. He sat down heavily on the front porch steps and put his head in his hands and let the tears he had been holding back stream freely down his face. *A baby. With Paige. All those years.* He knew it didn't make much sense to mourn an unborn baby he didn't know about from so many years ago. It would have made his life extremely difficult; two babies with two different women at around the same time. But he did mourn that loss. His heart broke for what he had put Paige through.

***

Sadie and Faith had not seen the card for themselves yet, but they could guess what it said by how things went down. Sherry came inside to check on things, but after she spoke to Sadie, went back outside to take her grandkids and Caleb to her house.

John, who had stayed quiet during the showdown said, "Paige, I'm going to take the flowers and the card to the station as evidence. We'll contact the flower shop and try to trace the sender." As Paige silently nodded her head up and down, he scooped up the card from where Jake had let it fall to the floor, grabbed the offending flowers and went out the front door. He didn't necessarily have to take the bouquet with him, but he didn't want the sight of it causing Paige more pain. It had done enough damage.

John sat down on the porch next to Jake and put his hand on his friend's shoulder. He told Jake the same thing he told Paige about taking the evidence to the station.

Jake lifted his head, wiped his eyes, and cleared his throat. "Thanks, John," Jake said hoarsely.

"What I didn't mention to Paige is that more than likely the flowers were ordered online, not in person or even over the phone. A fake name and address and a prepaid credit card were probably used, so it might not be much help. Be prepared for that," John explained reluctantly.

"Okay," was all Jake managed to choke out.

"You told me before that the last woman you slept with was about two months before you and Paige got together. Any chance she isn't lying, and she is three months pregnant?" John asked. "That might help us figure out who she is. She would start to show soon, if she's not already, and that would stand out, even in an office building of three-hundred or so."

Jake cleared his throat so he could answer the question. "I highly doubt it. I was always careful. I used protection and like they say about professional athletes I took it with me when I left if you know what I mean." Jake was embarrassed to be talking about his past private habits, but he needed at least one person to believe he hadn't knocked up "The Psycho."

"Have you been able to remember anything about her?" John pushed.

"Physically, just the same stuff we know from her attack on Paige. She's shorter than Paige, less curvy. Nothing really specific about her appearance is standing out in my mind. I remember we had a conversation clarifying it was just a casual one-time fling and she consented. I don't even think I told her my name. I certainly didn't ask hers. We had sex. I showered and then I left. The house was in Charleston, I might be able to find it, but honestly, I don't even know what bar I drank at that night. I intentionally didn't dwell on the details of my casual hookups like that one." Jake was so frustrated with himself.

"Okay, Jake. That's fine. You gonna head home now?" John asked.

"No. I know you have an officer here watching the house, but I can't make myself leave. I'm too worried about her. She is in this mess because of me. She's hurting so much, John. I can't leave her. I'll sleep out here on the porch if I have to. I saw the kids head out with

Paige's parents, so it won't cause any trouble for them. I would never do anything to upset them," Jake said sadly.

John knew there was no point in trying to convince Jake otherwise, so he sighed and patted Jake on the shoulder one more time. He made his way down the driveway to his car to take the flowers down to the station, lost in his thoughts. He would do everything he could to track down the sender so at least his friend could focus on fixing his family.

***

Inside the house, Faith and Sadie got Paige to settle down on the couch. Faith wrapped her in her favorite blanket and Sadie got her a cup of decaf tea with a little honey in it. They each settled into their usual spots, Faith in the oversized chair and Sadie on the loveseat.

"Sweetie, why did you never tell us about the miscarriage?" Faith asked after a few silent minutes passed. Faith had discussed her infertility issues with Paige at length in the past. She figured it must have been really hard for Paige not to confide her secret to Faith during those heartbreaking conversations.

"I figured that if Jake didn't know, no one else should," Paige explained simply.

"What did your parents say about the pregnancy when they had to take you to the hospital?" Sadie asked.

"I didn't go," Paige replied softly.

"What do you mean you didn't go to the hospital? Did you at least go to your primary care?" Sadie was shocked. Her medical mind could not understand what Paige was saying.

Paige took a minute to get herself together. She didn't want to bawl her way through explaining what happened. "No, I didn't go to any doctor. I was too scared. If I had told my parents about it, they would have known it was Jake's baby. I was worried they would want to talk to him or something and I didn't want him to know about it. I also didn't want my parents to be disappointed in me."

"But honey, didn't it hurt?" Faith asked gently.

"Yes, it was extremely painful. I crawled into my bathroom and laid on the rug, biting my fist during the worst of it to keep from screaming out loud. I cried until I ran out of tears. When the bleeding slowed and the cramping eased up some, I got up, threw the rug in a trash bag, changed clothes, put on a giant pad, and went to Wal-Mart to buy a new rug so my mom wouldn't notice."

Faith came over and sat on the couch next to Paige, and Sadie sat on the floor by her side. "Paige, to have gone through that all alone must have been absolutely terrible. You should have told someone," Faith said as she patted Paige's hand to try to comfort her friend.

"I wasn't sure what to say, I guess. Sometimes I would be relieved that I wasn't going to be a teen mom, then that would make me feel ashamed because it was like I was glad my baby didn't make it. Sometimes I would be overwhelmed with such a feeling of loss that I couldn't breathe. I felt like there were no words adequate enough to express what I was going through. And I was only seventeen years old, you know? Jake was having a baby with someone else and getting married. After a while, I just wanted to forget it ever happened," Paige explained as she felt her eyes start to water again.

"But you and Jake became friends again later after his marriage ended. You never wanted to tell him?" Sadie asked softly. Sadie didn't want her friend to think she was judging her. She personally would not have been able to keep something like that to herself.

Paige nodded her head as she picked at the blanket. "Yeah, I wanted to quite a few times. But since I didn't go to a doctor and get checked out, there wasn't any proof the pregnancy had happened at all. I was worried that maybe he wouldn't believe me, or he would tell someone else, and they would say I made it up because I was in love with him. I didn't feel like going through all that drama after already having to go through losing a baby by myself."

"I may not be Jake's biggest fan, but he doesn't seem like the type that would demand proof for something like that from you," Faith said.

"No, he's not. That was a mindset leftover from my manipulative boyfriend before him. By the time I realized that, it was too late. I wasn't about to call him out of the blue and be like hey funny story, I was pregnant with your baby back in the day, but then I lost it, so I didn't tell you. Okay, have a nice life!" It was something Paige had given a lot of thought to over the years.

Faith chuckled and said, "No, I guess that wouldn't have been very realistic."

The three friends sat in quiet reflection for a few minutes, processing everything about the bizarre situation.

"What are you going to do now?" Faith asked, breaking the silence.

"I know I can't really fault Jake right now. There is always drama around that man, though. It's just so *exhausting*. I think I'll take a few days to be by myself and rest, and then me and him can work it out."

Paige had said all she needed to say and felt like pigging out. "Enough with the sad stuff. I need a brownie, like yesterday."

"Yes, that's what I'm talking about! Coming right up." Sadie hopped up and went to the kitchen to satisfy her best friend's pregnancy craving.

They ate junk food and watched funny movies and relaxed together until it got really late. Around midnight, Paige insisted that she was going to be alright, so Sadie and Faith returned to their own homes.

As soon as the two women were out the door, the temporary relief provided by the company of Paige's friends was overtaken by a heavy weight settling on her chest. Her thoughts started going crazy again with old painful memories and current worries. Faith texted her to let her know Jake was fast asleep on the front porch and he was snoring. Paige went up to bed alone, hoping the pregnancy tiredness would override her overactive brain and the loneliness of an empty bed.

CHAPTER TWENTY-SEVEN

Paige woke up early the next morning to the perky sound of the alarm on her cell phone, feeling like she had been hit by a Mack truck. She had slept for a few hours but did not feel rested at all. The last thing she wanted to do was get up to get ready for work at the butt crack of dawn; but since she was a responsible adult, that was exactly what she was going to do.

After Paige's makeup failed to fully cover the dark circles under her eyes, she decided to cut her losses and went downstairs to make a healthy breakfast, *maybe something with spinach*. She was growing a baby after all.

"We'll get all this figured out, little one. You'll be safe. Mommy promises," she whispered while rubbing her lower abdomen..

When Paige opened her front door to leave, she saw Jake asleep sitting on the top step with his legs straight out in front of him, arms crossed, and his chin down on his chest, his back resting against the railing. He was lightly snoring. His white t-shirt wrinkled. Even in sleep, he seemed on edge. She stepped out on the porch and shut the door behind her with a little bit more force than she normally did. Jake startled awake.

Jake looked up at Paige and saw the resolve in her tired eyes. It frightened him. He stood up to face her ire and beg for her forgiveness. "Paige, please. I am so sorry you are going through all this. I accept full responsibility and I promise that I'm going to do everything I can to make it right. Please baby.... don't leave me," he choked back a groan as his plea escaped his lips.

Jake noticed Paige wasn't wearing her engagement ring, but she hadn't been wearing it to work anyway because of "The Psycho". However, it still made him sad to see it missing from her left ring finger.

"Jake, go home. I just need a few days to myself, okay? We'll figure it all out then. I don't have the energy to deal with this right now."

Paige squeezed Jake's hand as she walked past him, memorizing the sensation of touching him to get her through the next few days. Then she walked down the front porch steps, got into her borrowed truck, and drove away.

Jake watched Paige drive off in her dad's truck. It took all his inner strength to not run to his own truck and go after her. He would respect her wishes even though it felt like his world was shattering. Still, he didn't go home right away. He went inside Paige's house and gathered up a few things he would need while he let Paige have her space for a few days. Then, he went around the house and made sure all the doors and windows were locked up tight, stalling as long as he could. He dreaded going back to his quiet, empty house.

On her drive to work, Paige could not stop her mind from racing. She had handled Jake for the time being, but she still had "The Psycho" to worry about. Since Brenda always got to work before her, Paige decided to be productive and call Brenda to get her mind focused on work related topics instead of crazy stalkers and man problems.

"Hey Brenda, what do you have for me this morning?" Paige asked when her assistant picked up.

"Well, I know you usually don't like to hear the office gossip, but I got something real juicy for you," Brenda whispered, cupping her free hand around the phone and her mouth so she wouldn't be overheard on her end.

"Ooh, tell me," Paige said, internally acknowledging that office gossip wasn't exactly what she was hoping for, but since she was eager for any kind of distraction, she'd take what she could get.

"It would seem that Stacey and that freelance photographer in Myrtle Beach really hit it off. She called this morning to say that she was staying up there one more day so he could show her a few more places, if you know what I mean," Brenda said scandalized.

"Good for her," Paige said with a smile. "What about Cora Rae? Anything from her yet?" Paige asked nervously.

"No, not yet. But that doesn't necessarily mean anything. Cora Rae is usually not in this early. And she hasn't called out. Guess she didn't get as lucky as her buddy Stacey in Myrtle Beach," Brenda joked.

"Okay then. I'm on my way in, so I'll see you in a bit." Paige hung up and turned up the radio. She sang along enthusiastically to Carrie Underwood to distract herself from unwanted morbid thoughts for the rest of her drive to work.

When Paige pulled into her designated spot at the office and parked, she expected Officer Romero to walk up to the truck like she normally did. Paige waited a couple of minutes inside the cab of the truck and then started scanning the parking lot and the street for the officer. She finally spotted Officer Romero's squad car parked on the side of the building in an alley. Paige could make out the form of the officer's body sitting in the driver's seat, so she decided to be proactive and go to Officer Romero for a change. She grabbed her purse, still a little heavier than normal, and stepped out into the muggy early summer air and headed towards the windowless side alley street.

As Paige approached the police car window, she went to knock on it, but stopped when she noticed something wasn't quite right. It almost looked like Officer Romero was asleep in the driver's seat. She used her hands to shield from the glare off the glass and peered in. She could see a little trail of blood trickling down the side of the officer's face.

"OFFICER ROMERO! OFFICER ROMERO!" Paige screamed as she banged on the window glass frantically trying to wake up the unconscious woman.

Paige was making so much noise that she didn't hear the footsteps of the person coming up directly behind her. By the time she saw the reflection of a gloved hand and an arm reaching for her in the window, it was too late. She was grabbed from behind and a cloth was held over her mouth. Paige struggled against the surprisingly strong grip pinning her arms to her torso, but then her world went dark. Again.

***

Jake dawdled at Paige's house for over an hour going from room to room securing everything until he couldn't find any more excuses to stay. He knew he should try to get some work done. He had gotten behind with everything going on, but he needed to get his mind right first.

Jake pulled into his driveway, parked and sat in his truck for a few minutes. He was dreading going inside a house that had no trace of Paige or the two young kids in it. Still stalling a bit, he got out and went to check the mailbox, there was a few days' worth of mail, and then he finally headed inside. He paused as he stepped through the front doorway. His house didn't feel like home anymore. Home was Paige's house with all of their children together.

Jake showered quickly and tried to eat a little something. When he couldn't put it off any longer, he sat down behind his home desk to get some paperwork done. He started by looking through the mail to see if there was anything that needed his immediate attention. There were the usual bills, junk mail, and a couple of things he would take to the office later and let Marie handle. And then there was the South Carolina Society Magazine.

Yes, Jake had a subscription to the magazine Paige worked at. He subscribed as soon as he heard she'd started working there almost ten years ago. Back when she first started, he only read the travel articles she had written. Once she became Editor in Chief, he only read her introduction letter at the beginning of the magazine and then passed the magazine on to Marie.

Jake opened up the newest issue and for a few moments stared at the picture of Paige that accompanied the editor letter. She was sitting behind a modern desk, with a magnificent view of Charleston in the window behind her. She looked chic and scholarly. To him, she was the most beautiful woman in the world. He took in every feature of her lovely face, imagined cupping her soft cheek with his hand. He missed her so much already. How was he supposed to make it a few days without her?

After spending most of his adult life without a loving partner, the hole Paige's absence left was that much more obvious. He finally felt that his life was full, and he was in danger of losing everything. What he wouldn't give to be able to call her up and tell her that he loved her. His eyes were starting to burn and water because he was staring so hard at the picture, so he blinked fast a few times to clear away the moisture that seemed quick to come to his eyes lately. He may look tough on the outside, but when it comes to the people he cared about, he was a big ol' teddy bear.

Jake let his aching eyes wander to the right of her letter to the magazine's table of contents. A miniature photograph of a cottage in the woods caught his eye. It looked almost magical nestled in the trees like it was. The title was "Hideaway Cottage: The Best Airbnb in Charleston". As he looked at it closer, he realized that it looked familiar.

Jake turned to the page the article was on to see if there were more photos. Sure enough, there were pictures of the inside as well as the outside. He had been there before. It was the house the last woman he slept with before Paige took him to. He jumped up ecstatic to finally have some useful information to give John and the Charleston police. They should be able to figure out who the renter was and then they would have the identity of Paige's stalker. At least he hoped so. If not, the wild goose chase felt like it would never end. He looked down to the little picture next to the writer's name and stopped in his tracks.

"Oh shit."

CHAPTER TWENTY-EIGHT

Paige struggled to open her eyes as she gradually regained consciousness. She couldn't seem to get her brain to work right. After a few minutes of silently willing her eyelids to open, she was able to look at her surroundings. She was confused as to how she got there.

Paige took in the cozy room around her. There was a whitewashed stone fireplace with two buffalo plaid armchairs facing it, a fluffy white rug between them to her left. There was also a deep-set cream-colored couch covered with giant buffalo plaid pillows to match the chairs. The room opened to the dining room on her right, a rustic oak wood table and four matching hard backed wood chairs at the center.

Paige tried to move her limbs, and pain shot through her arms. She looked down and saw that her arms were tied behind her back around a wooden support beam in between the living and dining rooms. She was sitting on the freshly polished hardwood floor with her legs out in front of her. Her feet were not tied, so she gritted her teeth through the pain, bent her knees to get her feet planted, and slowly started standing up, sliding her tied up hands up the beam as she went while shuffling her feet backward. Paige felt a little less helpless standing up. She started moving her hands behind her back, trying to loosen the rough, thick ropes that were cutting into her wrists.

The front door was about fifteen feet directly in front of Paige, so when it opened, she could immediately see who her captor was as she stepped through the door frame. "Stacey," was all Paige said when the woman walked in carrying Paige's purse on her shoulder.

The attack in the stairwell replayed in Paige's head. She pictured Stacey's face in place of the masked one; remembered the angry primal screams the woman yelled as she tried her best to kill Paige.

"Glad to see you're finally awake, bitch. Now the fun part can start," Stacey sneered creepily.

Paige put on a brave face, but inside she was panicking. She looked around her surroundings as details began to fall into place in her mind and recognized the Airbnb Stacey had written her latest article about. "Hideaway Cottage: The Best Airbnb in Charleston", the romantic cottage in the woods she had thought about bringing Jake to for some alone time. She could have chuckled at the irony of it all. But then it occurred to her that no one would know to look for her there. Her heart sank. She forced herself to acknowledge that she probably wasn't going to make it out of there alive. But she refused to give Stacey the satisfaction of seeing her scared, so she shored up her resolve to not give in to the fear.

Paige watched silently as Stacey went over to the dining room table and dumped Paige's purse out. The contents scattered across the wood and her twenty-two-caliber magnum landed with a loud thud. Stacey picked up the pistol and looked it over methodically.

"I must say I'm very disappointed, Paige. After the fight you gave me in the stairwell, I would have expected you to be carrying something more impressive than this little pea shooter," Stacey mocked as she pointed the gun at Paige. She smirked and set the gun back down on the table.

Stacey reached around to her back and pulled out a bigger gun. "As for me, I prefer a nine-millimeter Glock. Gets the job done in one shot," Stacey continued as she pointed the larger gun at Paige. "You are not going to die that easy though. I have other plans for you."

Stacey put her gun down on the table next to Paige's and went into what Paige assumed was the kitchen. She came back out with a butcher knife and grinned devilishly at Paige. She set the big knife down next to the guns, scraping the blade across the wood for effect. It wasn't quite as bad as nails on a chalkboard, but it made Paige cringe just the same.

"Stacey, you don't have to do this. We can get you counseling. The magazine will help you get help. I'm sure of it," Paige tried to reason with Stacey. She honestly didn't think it would work, but she had to give it a shot.

"Why would I need counseling? There is nothing wrong with me. You are the pathetic widow who has to use her sad story to get a man to be with her. Trying to steal him from the woman he really wants to be with," Stacey quipped back angrily.

Paige couldn't stop herself from rolling her eyes, enraging Stacey. Stacey stomped over to her and slapped her hard across the face. Paige felt her back teeth rattle but managed to not cry out. She turned her head back to face Stacey and smiled. On the outside Paige was hard as steel, on the inside her heart was breaking for the baby she was carrying who would never get the chance to be born. *There is definitely no way I'm getting out of here alive,* Paige thought with despair.

"Stupid slut, thinking that you could steal my man by trapping him with a baby. He would never fall for that shit," Stacey shrieked, and then she slapped Paige again.

"He doesn't even know who you are. Doesn't even care to know what your name is. You are nobody to him," Paige answered levelly as she turned her head once again to face Stacey. She was thankful her voice didn't shake.

"Oh yeah, bitch? You see that couch over there? We made sweet passionate love on it. We connected in a way only soulmates do. And then we did it again, over there on that rug by the fire. It was so romantic. The rug felt so soft on my back while his hard body was on top of me, inside of me. Once I get rid of you, I'll remind him of our love, and he'll forget all about you." Stacey had a dreamy look about her as she remembered her time with Jake in that very room.

"It was a one-night stand you delusional psychopath and there is no way you are going to get away with this," Paige spat. Paige felt like throwing up as she couldn't help but visualize Jake with the other woman in the romantic setting.

"Oh, is that what you think?" Stacey sneered hatefully.

Then Stacey laughed maniacally and went down the hall that Paige remembered from the photos led to the master bedroom, a snug little guest room, and a small bathroom. Paige could hear Stacey grunting and dragging something down the hall when she returned. Stacey brought her heavy load in front of Paige and let go of her burden unceremoniously. Paige looked down and it was a body. Stacey kicked the body over and Paige saw that it was Cora Rae.

"Is she dead?" Paige asked around the lump in her throat.

"Not yet, but she will be. I'm going to put a few strategic holes in her with your little toy gun," Stacey chirped gleefully. "If it doesn't kill her right away, there will be plenty of time for her to bleed out before y'all are found."

"Why? What does Cora Rae have to do with anything?" Paige asked cautiously.

Paige thought the two women were friends. They were almost always together in the office and often went to lunch together. Paige started to wonder how Stacey could hurt someone she cared about, but then remembered what kind of person she was dealing with; an unhinged, violent person, not the sweet and smart writer she pretended to be.

"Don't you see? You idiot! I'm going to frame her. Finally, the dimwit can be useful," Stacey said as she kicked Cora Rae again. "I rented this cabin using her name and credit card, so when they find y'all dead here, they will think it was her all along and that y'all killed each other. I thought you were supposed to be smart," Stacey scoffed.

"How would that work exactly? I'm guessing she's never slept with Jake and the card with the flowers you so sweetly sent to me said you are pregnant. Or was that a lie?" Paige was sure she already knew the answer, but she was stalling. She didn't want to see Stacey shoot Cora Rae.

"Well, I'm not pregnant with his child *yet*," Stacey admitted, setting a hand over her stomach. "But I will be when I console him from the loss of the bastard you are carrying, and he remembers that he is madly in love with me. Everyone knows Cora Rae is obsessed with love and marriage and will just assume she's crazy and fabricated a romance with *my* Jake in her head after seeing him somewhere. He does catch the eyes of women. You yourself called this cottage romantic, so the only connection to me is that I wrote an article about it after renting it months ago and inspired her madness. Honestly, they can use their imaginations with that part for all I care," Stacey explained.

"A fabricated romance, huh? You mean like the one you've made up in your head? Sounds like you've got a few screws loose up there yourself," Paige baited. She didn't want whatever Stacey had planned for her to be drawn out, better to get it over with. Stacey's eyes bulged in anger, and she went over to the table and got her butcher knife. She charged at Paige and held the knife up to her throat. Paige could feel the tip of the cold unbending metal on her skin.

"Watch it, bitch." Stacey took the knife off of Paige's throat and ran it over her cheek, applying slight pressure. Paige felt the sting of metal piercing her skin, and the blood that started trickling down the side of her face from the shallow cut.

Stacey started wandering around the room, waving the knife around as she spoke. "I have my alibi all set up. It's not the strongest, I know, but when I am finished with you, I'll sneak back to my hotel in Myrtle Beach and pack up my stuff and check out. I'll make sure I'm seen on as many cameras as I can as I'm leaving. I put all of the negatives of the photos I have taken of you and Jake in Cora Rae's suitcase. I'm a bit of an amateur photographer, you see, and have taken many pictures of my lover over the past few months. He's so damn handsome. The camera loves him," she sighed dreamily like a woman deep in love.

Paige followed Stacey with her eyes as she moved around the room during her rant, but all the while she was wiggling her hands, maneuvering to try to loosen the ropes; and it was working. She almost had her left hand out. Stacey turned and started making her way back over to Paige and she had to stop her efforts. Stacey came up to Paige again and lifted the knife to Paige's chest.

"Time to have some fun, bitch."

***

As Jake bolted out the front door of his house towards his truck, jumping over the three front steps of the porch to the ground, he tried to call Paige's cell phone. There was no answer. He didn't bother with leaving a voicemail. The sinking feeling in his gut told him it was too late to warn her, but he still tried to convince himself that she wasn't answering because she was upset with him. He called the main number for the magazine, and the receptionist connected him to Paige's assistant Brenda. It sounded like absolute chaos in the background when she picked up the phone.

"Brenda, this is Jake, I'm Paige's fiancé, where is she?" he asked hurriedly, holding on to the last shred of hope that his gut feeling was wrong. Officer Romero was supposed to be with Paige, so it wasn't like she was unprotected.

"Oh Jake, I'm so sorry I didn't know how to reach you. Charleston P.D. is here. I called them earlier when Paige didn't show up. I had spoken with her while she was driving to work. Her dad's truck was in her parking spot, but she never came in the office. I alerted security and the cameras showed her walking into the side alley, and they found Officer Romero's squad car there. She had been hit over the head with something and knocked unconscious, maybe even drugged. They think whoever did it must have moved her squad car and put her in it to lure Paige over to the alley where there are no cameras and then abducted her." Brenda was crying uncontrollably by the end of her story. Her tears dripping off of the phone as she held it to her face.

Jake was about to ask Brenda to put a police officer on the phone when John came flying into his driveway with his police lights on, blocking him from backing out. Jake hung up on Brenda and jumped out of his truck to tell his friend that he knew who had taken Paige.

"Jake, I'm so sorry, I just found out. There was a delay in them telling me..." John started but Jake cut him off.

"I know who has her, John." Jake showed John the article and explained the connection between the writer, himself, and the cottage featured in the magazine. Jake listened as John went to his car and got on his radio to relay the information to the dispatcher. He paced back and forth next to his friend's patrol car with his hands on top of his head, trying not to go crazy.

"Let's head towards Charleston while we wait for them to get back to me with our suspect's home address. Charleston P.D. will take point on this Jake. They might not let us near the scene," John warned his friend as they got in his patrol car.

Jake nodded, he couldn't seem to find his voice. He was terrified by the thought that the woman could be hurting Paige, and he had no idea where she was. He was also starting to feel extremely angry. So angry he could kill.

On the drive to Charleston, John tried to talk to Jake, but he couldn't process anything his friend was saying. His brain was going wild picturing what was possibly happening to Paige. What if she was already dead? His heart couldn't bear the thought. His knee was hopping up and down shaking the whole passenger side of the vehicle. He felt caged in the car. He needed to get out. He needed to do something, anything to get to Paige. Over the past fifteen minutes the helpless feeling had started to creep in on him in a big way.

Jake heard static and then the dispatcher's voice suddenly came through the police radio and Jake went perfectly still. His brain instantly went on hyperfocus. "The suspect owns a home on the edge of Charleston, Officer Avery, but Charleston P.D. went over there as soon as we contacted them with her name, and no one was there. They are going through the house now collecting evidence. It's obvious the suspect is involved," the dispatcher reported. "I gave the officer in charge your direct phone number so they can keep you updated on the search quicker."

"Thank you," John said into his radio.

John looked over at Jake to gauge his reaction to what he'd heard from the dispatcher. "You were right about the writer. We'll head to Paige's office to wait. We'll find her Jake. It's just going to take some time. Paige is a tough lady." John tried to reassure his friend, but knew they were empty words.

Jake was overcome with despair. They had no idea where his Paige was and the more time that passed, the more harm could be done to her. To their unborn child. Chloe and Henry would technically be orphans if they lose their mom. He was going to be their father for the rest of their lives no matter what the outcome was. They would never have to be alone, but they needed their mom. He needed her.

Jake looked down to his hands where he had been twisting the magazine in angst. He smoothed it out on his lap. It was still open to the article that crazy woman who is obsessed with him had written about the cottage where they hooked up. As he looked over the glossy pictures, a thought hit him. "Do you think she would take Paige to this cottage?" he asked, holding up the magazine towards John.

"Couldn't hurt to check it out. Unfortunately, I don't think they have any other leads yet," John answered.

John got back on his radio and relayed Jake's hunch to the dispatcher so she could contact Charleston P.D. After a few minutes, the dispatcher got back to him. "Officer Avery, the Hideaway Cottage has been rented for the week by a Cora Rae Summers. Charleston P.D. is on their way out there to check it out now," she relayed.

"Cora Rae works with Paige at the magazine too," Jake said to John as soon as the dispatcher went silent.

"She might be an accomplice. Or another hostage. Guess we will find out soon enough," John said levelly. He turned on his police siren and sped towards the Hideaway Cottage.

Jake prayed they got there in time.

CHAPTER TWENTY-NINE

When Cora Rae woke up, some innate survival instinct told her to stay quiet and to keep her eyes closed. At first, she simply listened to what was going on around her. Every part of her body hurt, and she was lying on a hardwood floor. She could hear someone's feet moving around close by her head. Cora Rae assumed it was that crazy bitch, Stacey; the woman she had begun to think of as her best friend.

Cora Rae was so confused by Stacey's complete change in personality. They had been sitting in her car in the hotel parking lot Saturday night, about to go get some dinner, when Stacey started saying the meanest things to her. Then, Stacey pointed a gun at her face! Up until that point, they had been having a great time hanging out and discussing how their days went. Stacey made her drive back to Charleston to the Hideaway Cottage. Recognizing the cottage from the magazine photos was the last thing she remembered.

Cora Rae took a chance and partly opened one eye. She could see Stacey's bright blue running shoes a few feet away and a pool of what looked like blood. Stacey was facing away from her, so she chanced opening both eyes and looked up. What she saw made her heart ache. Paige was tied with her hands behind her back to a wood support beam and there were cuts all over her. Her sleeveless pastel green blouse was cut open and her chest, arms, and stomach were covered in wounds slowly seeping blood. Her practical white bra was still intact, but ruined, nonetheless.

Cora Rae caught a glimpse of Stacey's face, and she barely recognized her. She looked crazed, like a rabid animal. Cora Rae looked back up at Paige. Her eyes were open, and she had gashes on both cheeks. Those must have been the first cuts Stacey inflicted; the blood was congealed and no longer dripping. They briefly made eye contact and Paige subtly shook her head at Cora Rae and looked away. *Okay then. If Paige can be brave, so can I. I'll just bide my time until the moment is right,* thought Cora Rae, and she closed her eyes.

***

Thank God, Paige thought when she saw that Cora Rae was awake. *At least she might have a chance to escape.* Stacey hadn't tied Cora Rae up, so maybe she would be able to get out the front door if Stacey ever left the room again.

Paige wasn't sure how much more torture she could take. She was so dang tired. The room seemed to be spinning and undulating, but she knew it was because she was dizzy and weak. As she looked down, she noticed all of the blood she had lost collecting beneath her. *Yup, that'll do it,* she thought. She was about to lose the fight. Stacey was close to succeeding in slowly killing her. How long had Stacey been torturing her? Minutes? Hours? Days?

Paige's ears were starting to ring. *Maybe I'll get to pass out now,* she hoped for the sweet relief of unconsciousness. The ringing noise grew louder and louder. She realized the trill sound was actually police sirens and a new hope bloomed in her chest. Had they actually been able to find her?

When there was no doubt that the police cars were indeed coming to the Hideaway Cottage, Stacey paused her mutilation of Paige and went over to the dining room window to peek out at the new arrivals.

Charleston P.D. squad cars and a black SWAT van were coming down the long dirt drive. Paige could hear the tires crunching over rocks and even in her injured state could see the huge dust cloud the speeding cars left behind them.

Stacey walked over to the dining room table and without looking down picked a gun up from the table and started to pace frantically, mumbling to herself.

"Stacey Brock, this is Chief Harper with Charleston P.D. We have you surrounded. Come out with your hands up," an authoritative voice boomed through a megaphone. The Charleston police officers scrambled into position while the SWAT team geared up for action.

Stacey let out a high-pitched laugh and yelled, "does that shit actually ever work on anyone? I have a gun and hostages, you moron." She waved the gun in front of the dining room window, closed the thick light blocking curtains in both front rooms so no one could see in and went back to pacing the floor.

Paige shored up her remaining energy and used the distraction to work on get her hands free. She looked down at Cora Rae, they made quick eye contact and gave each other brisk nods, and then Cora Rae closed her eyes again. Paige ignored the burning of the rope on her skin and eventually pulled her left hand free. She kept it behind her back but made little movements to bring back the feeling and stretch what muscles she could. She had been in one position way too long and her nerve endings started screaming in sharp stinging pain.

All of a sudden, they heard a huge commotion outside. It sounded like fighting, but that didn't make any sense. Paige watched as Stacey walked back over to the dining room window and pushed the curtain aside a little with the barrel of the gun to sneak a peek at what was happening in the front yard. Paige used that time to move her left shoulder a bit. Stacey giggled and Paige went back to standing still.

"How sweet! My lover was trying so hard to get in here to me they had to tackle and handcuff him. He put up quite a fight! Looks like it took three guys to restrain him! They should have just let him come in. I would never hurt him," Stacey cooed.

Stacey started walking back towards Paige and looked down at Cora Rae's limp body. "Leave it to her to sleep through so much fun," she said, and she kicked Cora Rae again.

Paige was so proud of Cora Rae for not making a sound when that kick had to have hurt. "Why do you hate her so much?" Paige asked.

She was stalling again. She couldn't believe Jake was outside! She prayed and prayed she would get to see his face again. To hold him and kiss him. To tell him how sorry she was that she let this horrible woman come between them even for a second. But first the police would have to figure out a way to get inside the cottage that wouldn't end with Stacey slitting her throat. She felt so guilty that his last memory of them together would be her telling him to stay away. Oh, how she wished she could tell him how much she loved him.

"Because ever since I caught you touching my man in that shitty little back woods restaurant, I've had to pretend to be friends with this complete waste of space to learn more about you. Boy does that girl blab," Stacey rolled her eyes.

Stacey took a quick break from her ranting to give Cora Rae's still body the side eye and a sneer. Then she returned her attention to Paige, waving the gun around in one hand and the butcher knife in the other as she spoke.

"I typically prefer my own company, which is why I hadn't made an effort to make any friends at work until then. So, imagine my surprise when I followed Jake from his house to meet his friends that night and there you were, putting your filthy hands all over him.

I'd been following him for a couple months, you see, so I could get to know him better. I hadn't seen him with anyone else and knew it meant that I was right about him being madly in love with me. I just knew he was searching for me, the mysterious woman from the romantic cottage. I was waiting for the perfect time to reveal myself to him."

Stacey pressed the barrel of the gun to Paige's forehead and declared, "He's mine." Then she turned sharply on her heel and started walking away from Paige. "Now be quiet. I need to come up with an escape plan. Then I'm going to stab you in the belly and lay low until my lover comes for me."

Paige went back to wiggling her right hand behind her back. It was bad luck that Stacey had tied her hands in separate knots, but she was making progress. Stacey made her way over to the couch to lay down. *Torturing someone must be exhausting,* Paige thought sarcastically. Stacey set the blood-stained knife on the floor but kept the gun resting on her chest. She was caressing the fluffy throw pillows like a lover. Paige could imagine what she was remembering, and it made her angry. She pulled harder at the rope and used her free hand behind her back to stretch the rope. She almost had her hand free when a different voice from outside called out over the megaphone.

"Stacey Brock, this is Charleston SWAT. Release the hostages or we are coming in."

Paige took a deep breath. They must have figured out from Stacey's earlier refusal to cooperate that Cora Rae was in there too. Paige wasn't sure why that brought her so much relief, but it did. She felt it somehow increased Cora Rae's chances for survival.

Stacey jumped up from her supine position on the couch and went over to the thick wooden front door. "If I hear anyone come near this house, I'll shoot the pregnant one," Stacey screamed.

A deep-toned yell of protest could be heard from outside and then it was muffled, the sounds of a scuffle were followed by a car door slamming shut.

Stacey turned to look at Paige, who had abandoned all subtlety and was frantically using her free left hand to get her trapped right hand out of the rope. Paige felt a sudden last hail Mary type rush of adrenaline and in the blink of an eye she had both hands free. She quickly stood up straight to face Stacey, even though the stabbing pain from the nerves in her hands and arms made her dizzy. Stacey pointed the gun at her.

"Guess the game is over. You have to die now," she said, taking a step closer to Paige.

"You think you can kill me with that little pea shooter?" Paige asked and looked down at the gun Stacey was pointing at her.

Paige noticed earlier that in her manic state of mind, Stacey hadn't realized she picked up the wrong gun, even though the weight difference should have been obvious. *Guess she doesn't use it as much as she says,* Paige thought to herself at the time.

Stacey lowered the gun and noticed that even though it was black like hers, it was indeed smaller. Then she screamed at the top of her lungs and started to lift the weapon back up aiming it at Paige once again. Cora Rae chose that moment to swing her leg out at Stacey's ankles, kicking Stacey's feet out from under her and causing her to tumble down on top of Cora Rae. Paige took advantage of the distraction and sprinted to the dining table, willing herself to not pass out. Stacey sat up and hit Cora Rae over the head with the gun, knocking her out again. She watched as blood started pouring from Cora Rae's head and ran across the floor and mingled with the pool of Paige's blood. When Stacey looked up Paige had her hand on the bigger gun and was lifting it up to take aim at her.

Paige felt the heavy weight of Stacey's gun in her palm and had to use two hands on the grip to hold it up and still. Her arms and shoulders protested with sharp shooting pains. Her strength was draining, and she was running on pure adrenaline. Stacey was back to standing over Cora Rae with a maniacal look in her eyes and a twisted sneer. She lifted the gun, Cora Rae's blood dripping from the grip. The two women took aim at each other. Gunshots rang out.

Cora Rae jolted to consciousness at a noise so loud it made her ears ring. Her head was pounding ferociously. Then she heard two almost simultaneous loud thumps, like something heavy hitting the floor, immediately followed by the sounds of metal objects clanging on the hardwood. *Gunshots*, she thought as the sound that had revived her registered in her groggy brain. *Oh no! Stacey shot Paige!*

Desperate to see what had become of Paige and to try to get ready to defend herself against Stacey, she attempted to open her eyes. She managed to open them a tiny bit, enough to realize her vision was blurred by blood. Frantically, she swiped at her eyes to get the blood out. A choked cry escaped past her lips at the thought that the blood might actually be coming from her eyeballs, and she would be blind.

A few seconds later Cora Rae was able to see enough to spot Paige sprawled on the floor next to her. Paige's eyes were closed, and she was perfectly still. One of her hands looked as if it was reaching for Cora Rae. There was so much blood on the floor around them and covering Paige. Cora Rae struggled to call out to her to wake up, but her brain did not to want to cooperate. She felt warm tears streaming down her face, helping to clear the blood out of her eyes, but her eyelids were too heavy to keep them open any longer. Despair washed over her as she gave up the fight and closed her eyes.

Another loud sound made Cora Rae's head throb even harder, but she welcomed it. Someone was battering down the front door. Maybe she would be saved after all. She wasn't sure she wanted to be though. The guilt at not being able to save Paige was overwhelming. If what Stacey said was true, then Paige was pregnant. She felt so stupid for not seeing through Stacey's façade from the beginning. Maybe she really was the dimwit everyone thought she was. She sensed movement around her and felt someone touching her neck.

"These two over here are alive!" a deep voice called out from the space in between her and Paige.

"This one is dead," another deep voice answered from the other side of her.

"The house is clear, weapons secured. Send in the paramedics," a third man yelled to someone outside.

Cora Rae got a rush of adrenaline as her heart bloomed with hope. "Save Paige," she managed to croak out as she was transferred to a stretcher and covered with a thin blanket. She hollered at the sudden increase in pain from being touched and moved.

"You just take it easy, ma'am. We're going to get you two to the hospital," the first voice she had heard said gently as a paramedic covered her mouth and nose with an oxygen mask.

Cora Rae started to silently pray harder than she had ever prayed before in her thirty-three years. After they wheeled her out of the house and she was in the ambulance with EMTs fussing over her, she heard yelling.

"That's her fiancé and he has every right to go to the hospital with her," a very frustrated man boomed. The shutting of the ambulance doors and the starting up of the sirens prevented her from hearing the reply.

As Cora Rae was being transported to the hospital, to try to keep her mind off of the pain, she pictured the handsome man who had stopped by the office the other day to take Paige to lunch. He must be the father of her baby. She imagined covering their wedding for the magazine. She was doing her best to mentally manifest a happy ending for them.

Unfortunately, after a few minutes, Cora Rae's attempt at escapism started to fail her because the pain was refusing to take a back seat in her brain. The rest of the ride in the ambulance to the hospital was such a blur. Strange voices were calling out her vitals, but she had no idea what they meant. Was she dying? In her mystery novels she indulged in on the weekends, the characters who were close to death always said they could feel the pain fade away into numbness. That was definitely not happening to her. Cora Rae had never been in so much pain in her life. Every inch of her body ached, but the pain in her head was unbearable and it felt so heavy. She had never been one to demand drugs, but if they didn't give her some pain killers soon, she was going to beg them to put her out of her misery.

Once they got her to the hospital, the bright lights overhead stung her eyes through her closed eyelids and made her head hurt even worse. New voices were calling out orders as she was being rushed down what had to be a hallway. She wanted to pass out. She had never known such agony. Someone was moaning like a wounded cat, and she heard a gentle female voice whisper in her ear, "Don't worry sweetie, we'll make the pain stop very soon." Cora Rae realized then that she was the one moaning.

Cora Rae wanted to scream that she couldn't take the pain anymore when she heard the words, "Medically induced coma", come from an authoritative female voice to the left of her head. In normal circumstances, those words would have scared her to tears, but at that moment they brought her sweet relief. The last thing she heard was, "Start the pentobarbital", before she slipped into deep oblivion.

CHAPTER THIRTY-ONE

Inside the squad car Jake had been stuffed into after his outburst, he was shuffling side to side in the backseat trying to find the best view of the cottage. The cops had left him handcuffed sitting on the ground after he arrived on the scene and tried to run past them to get inside to rescue Paige.

When that crazy woman threatened to shoot Paige, he got his feet under him and tried once again to get to the cottage's front door. He hadn't cared that he couldn't use his arms. That time the police threw him in the backseat of a police car. The car had been pulled up in front of the small house kind of slanted, not facing the cottage head on but also not parallel to it either. The frames of the car windows were getting in the way of him having a clear view of what was happening. The moving bodies of the police officers weren't helping either. He could hear the communications coming through the police radio, but nothing gave him any insight as to what was going on inside.

It was a good thing the officer left the car running with the air conditioning on; between the warm and humid South Carolina weather in June and all his frantic movement, Jake would have passed out from heat exhaustion in no time.

Jake was losing his mind with worry and guilt. He was convinced it should be him in there, not his Paige. Why didn't that psycho come after him if she was so obsessed with him? Did she honestly think he would have anything to do with her after she hurt his beloved Paige? His thoughts were immediately cut off by the sound of gunshots from inside the house.

Jake went wild inside of the cop car. He threw his body weight at the door trying to get out. He needed to get in the cottage to Paige. The car door would not budge, but he did not stop trying to force it open. His left shoulder screamed in pain as he bruised it against the door over and over, but he ignored it. SWAT went running by with a battering ram and he paused smashing into the door to position himself the best he could to watch them break down the cottage's front door.

Time seemed to slow down as he watched the front door of the house splinter open under the pressure from the battering ram. SWAT swarmed inside the cottage in full gear with guns drawn. To Jake it seemed like it took forever for them to let the paramedics in.

"Please let Paige be okay. Please dear Lord, I will do anything, just let her and our baby be okay," Jake begged out loud as he waited impatiently to see who would come out.

Someone has to be alive for them to send the paramedics in, he reasoned to himself. As soon as the thought crossed his mind, he saw the coroner's van pull up to the side of the house. He started praying the coroner wasn't there for his Paige as his foot bounced around from an overabundance of frantic energy.

Two paramedics emerged from the house pushing a raised stretcher with one of the SWAT guys with his helmet shield open walking next to them. It appeared to Jake that the officer was trying to soothe whoever was being taken to the ambulance. Jake scooted to the right side of the back seat trying to get a look at who it was. He didn't recognize the deep chestnut brown hair lying against the white sheet on the stretcher, some of it matted with what looked like blood. *That must be Cora Rae*, he thought. That Stacey bitch's hair was a dull lighter brown in her picture in the magazine, and it would be hard to miss Paige's raven hair. The blanket covering Cora Rae did nothing to hide the fact that she was seriously injured. Jake's heart rate picked up even more and it felt like his heart was going to explode out of his chest. What had that psycho done to his Paige if she had hurt Cora Rae so badly, when she wasn't even the one involved in a relationship with him?

Jake scooted back over in the seat to watch the front door to see who they brought out next. There was another stretcher being pushed out, but it was completely surrounded by the SWAT officers. He couldn't see who they were bringing out. Was it Paige? He was desperate to know her fate right that second. John went running by and up to the stretcher. He must have been wondering the same thing Jake was. Luckily, he hadn't been restrained as well when Jake had his not so little outburst. Jake kept waiting for John to give him some kind of signal or something to let him know if it was Paige. There was another stretcher emerging from the cottage, it was laden with a zipped-up body bag, heading for the coroner's van.

Just as Jake thought he was going to lose his mind he heard a voice come over the police radio, "Two female hostages alive but in critical condition. Being transported to MUSC by ambulance now. Suspect is deceased."

Jake allowed himself one deep breath and a thank you to the Lord above before he started yelling at the top of his lungs for them to let him out of the damn car. He was successful in getting John's attention at least. John finally turned and came running back to the squad car. The officer whose car it was had come back to stand by the car and John was charging at him.

"That's her fiancé and he has every right to go to the hospital with her," John yelled at the Charleston police officer, jabbing his finger toward where Jake was trapped in the car for emphasis.

"Yes please! Let me out!" Jake screamed through the window, pulling at the door handle with his wrists still in handcuffs behind his back, like it had somehow magically become unlocked.

The handcuffs bit into his wrists at the awkward movement, but he couldn't care less. He saw the officer hold out his hands to John like he was trying to calm him down. Anger flared in John's eyes for a brief second before the other officer said something too low for Jake to hear. John nodded and took off running towards his own squad car. *What the hell,* Jake thought as the Charleston officer opened the driver's door and climbed in.

"Mr. Bennett, I'm Officer Jameson. I'm going to drive you to the hospital. They are going to need all of the room in the ambulance to work on your fiancé. She's unconscious and in critical condition."

Jake didn't know what to say. Of course, he would rather be with Paige, but he would never interfere with any chance she had of survival. It had not slipped his mind that the voice over the radio said the survivors were in critical condition, but Paige being unconscious was new information to him.

Officer Jameson threw on his blue lights, blared his siren, and pulled in front of the ambulances to escort them to the hospital. Jake turned around in the seat, never taking his eyes off the ambulance where Paige was fighting for her life. He acknowledged to himself that they had most likely lost their baby and he was overwhelmed with grief. Not only for himself, but Paige and their family as well. He vaguely noticed John pulling up the rear of their speeding caravan with his police lights on and sirens blaring as well.

Even though the ride to the hospital seemed to take forever to Jake, they actually made very good time. The long line of emergency vehicles had drivers moving out of the way in a hurry. When they pulled up to the emergency department doors at MUSC, Jake had to wait to be let out of the back of the patrol car and uncuffed. Officer Jameson worked quickly, but Jake couldn't bear one more second of being cooped up away from Paige.

CHAPTER THIRTY-TWO

Normally, Sadie would never go into the hospital on one of her days off. Until that day, she hadn't needed to. She usually was OCD about keeping up with her charts and always managed to get any extra things the hospital threw at her done by staying late on the days she was already there. She was all about work/life balance. With all of the stuff going on with Paige, however, she had fallen a little behind.

So, there she was, sitting at her desk pretending to watch a mandatory webinar on how to properly dispose of biohazardous materials, something she already knew frontwards and backwards, when her cell phone rang. Her stomach plummeted when she saw on the screen that it was Paige's assistant, Brenda, calling. Sadie had made sure to save the contact information in her phone after Paige was attacked in the office stairwell.

"Brenda? Is everything okay?" Sadie asked as soon as she answered the call.

Sadie silently hoped Paige had all of a sudden gotten hoity-toity and was having her assistant call to schedule her personal lunches.

"Dr. Jennings, Paige is missing," the other woman cried into the phone.

Sadie felt chills run through her, but she called on all of her training as a surgeon and tried to remain calm and focused. "How long? What happened?" Sadie asked the upset woman, keeping her questions simple to help the lady focus through her obvious turmoil.

"I spoke with her when she was on her way to work, so when it seemed like too much time had passed, I looked out the window to the parking lot below and saw the truck she has been driving in her spot. I called security to check it out and that is when they found Officer Romero knocked unconscious in the side alley and Paige is nowhere to be found," Brenda explained rapidly.

Sadie's heart began to race as she tried to think of what to ask Brenda next and of what she could do to help find her best friend in the whole world. "Have the police been notified? What about her fiancé, Jake?" Sadie asked.

"The police just arrived and are searching for her inside the building again. I'm sorry, I didn't know that she was engaged. I don't know how to get in touch with him," Brenda replied hurriedly.

"That's okay, Brenda. I'll figure that part out. Just please, please keep me updated with whatever is going on with the police there. Keep your ear to the ground," Sadie pleaded.

"Of course, Dr. Jennings. I'll be in touch." Brenda said, feeling better that she at least had a task she could carry out that would benefit Paige in some way.

Sadie ended the call and stood up from her chair to start pacing. The webinar completely forgotten on her computer. *What to do first,* she thought to herself as she moved around her office. She dreaded what she had to do, but she picked her cell phone back up and called her other best friend in the whole world to let her know what had happened.

"Hey Sadie, what's up?" Faith answered cheerfully when she saw who was calling her. The happiness Faith was sporting quickly disappeared as Sadie relayed her conversation with Brenda.

"Oh my gosh, Sadie. What are we going to do?" Faith asked her level-headed best friend. It was taking all of Faith's fortitude to not break down in tears. As it was, she had plopped down into her desk chair and was clutching her chest. She felt like her heart was breaking.

"I think you should come here to the hospital. If she has been taken by her stalker, we have to face the fact that she'll more than likely be injured. When the police find her, they will probably bring her here; unless she's been taken somewhere far away, but we'll just have to pray that won't be the case. We can wait for news in my office, that way we'll already be close by," Sadie answered as a plan started to formulate in her mind. Sadie refused to even think that Paige might not make it out of wherever she was alive.

"Okay, that sounds good. I'm going to call Travis and we'll be on our way," Faith replied, relieved to know what her next step would be.

"Drive careful. Love you, Faith."

"Love you too, Sadie."

Sadie ended the call with Faith and immediately dialed Paige's mom. Sadie couldn't reign in her tears as she heard Sherry break down over the news. She could hear Paige's dad come running up to Sherry begging her to tell him what was wrong. When she couldn't seem to answer him, he picked up the phone his wife had dropped, and Sadie repeated the story to him.

"We'll go get Chloe and Henry from school and bring them back here to our house. Let us know as soon as you have any news on Paige," Mr. Hawkins said roughly, barely holding it together himself.

"Of course, you'll be my first call. I promise." Sadie ended the call and allowed herself to have a good shoulder heaving cry. She needed to get it out of her system so she could focus on the best way to help Paige.

About thirty minutes later, Faith and Travis knocked on her office door. She hadn't bothered to try to hide the fact that she had been crying. Faith knew her too well to get anything past her.

"I called Paige's parents and let them know what was going on. It was heartbreaking," Sadie confided to Faith.

"I bet. What about Jake?" Faith asked.

"Oh, I can't believe I forgot. I got so overwhelmed after speaking to the Hawkins's." Sadie was so mad at herself for dropping the ball on notifying Jake. *He's Paige's fiancé for crying out loud,* she thought.

"Sweetie, it's okay. We should probably have John Avery do it anyways because you know Jake is going to be a handful and a half when he finds out," Faith reassured her. Faith also had a good cry fest in the car on the way over while Travis drove. She was ready to focus on helping Paige too. Faith pulled up John's number on her phone and put the call on speaker.

"Damnit, how did she get the jump on Romero? Damnit! Damnit! Damnit!" John's frustration came through loudly over the speaker phone.

Sadie and Faith knew John was venting out loud to himself, so they didn't even try to answer his question. Instead, Faith said, "I thought it would be best if you told Jake in person. You know he is going to go bananas. I'm betting he's at home. I doubt he went into work today after everything that went down yesterday with the flowers. He was asleep on Paige's porch when we left last night after midnight."

"Yeah, you're probably right. I'll head over to his place now."

Faith heard a sound over the phone, like John's call waiting had sounded.

"And that would be my buddy over at Charleston P.D. beeping in. I'll call you if I learn anything new." John switched over to the other line without saying a formal goodbye to Faith and Sadie. He knew they would understand.

"Okay, he's going to tell Jake. What do we do now?" Faith asked as she set her cell phone down on Sadie's desk.

Sadie came over and held her hand. Travis came over from where he had been leaning against the wall and put his arms around both women.

"Now we wait," Sadie replied simply.

Over the next couple of hours Faith and Sadie went through a rollercoaster of emotions. They took turns being the strong one when the other one would lose hope that Paige was going to be found. Travis was their rock through it all. Finally, Sadie got a call on her cell phone and the caller I.D. said it was one of the emergency department doctors.

"Hey, Dr. Jennings, we just got a call that two ambulances are on their way in with two female criticals. One of them is your friend Paige Collins. Thought you would want to know," the doctor informed Sadie.

"Yes, thank you so much. I'm on my way," Sadie replied gratefully. She hung up the call and turned to face Faith and Travis.

"Sadie, what is it? Is it Paige?" Faith asked urgently.

"Yes, she's on her way here in an ambulance. I have to warn you Faith, she's in critical condition. There is another female in critical condition on the way as well, but I'm not sure who it is. I didn't even think to ask once he said Paige's name," Sadie answered as she started heading towards her office door.

"Wait a second," Faith blurted out. "Why didn't John give us a heads up?"

Travis put his hands gently on Faith's shoulders and answered, "Baby, he might have been involved in the rescue. Who knows, but I have a feeling we'll get all of our questions answered soon."

"I hate it when you're so darn reasonable," Faith mock reprimanded her husband. In truth, Faith needed the calmness Travis always brought to even the most hectic situations. They balanced each other out quite nicely.

Faith and Travis followed Sadie through the maze of the hospital to the emergency department. Waiting at the doors to the exit outside where ambulances unload were two teams of doctors and nurses waiting with equipment for the incoming ambulances to arrive. Sadie told Faith and Travis to go have a seat in the waiting room while she spoke with the doctor who had called her to let her know Paige was on the way to the hospital.

"Any new information?" Sadie asked as she approached the medical team.

The doctor pulled her aside and whispered, "Your friend is unconscious. The other woman is still conscious, but both have severe injuries."

"Is the other woman her attacker?" Sadie quietly asked.

"I believe the other woman is another victim," he replied.

"What? That doesn't make any sense. Who...." Sadie was interrupted by another doctor approaching them. The Chief of Medicine for the hospital. Someone must have alerted him to the situation.

"Dr. Jennings, may I speak with you?" her superior asked politely.

Just as Sadie was going to try to protest, the sirens of the ambulances could be heard, and the vehicles came to a screeching halt right in front of the doors. Sadie started to take a step to go to Paige, but the Chief of Medicine blocked her way.

"Dr. Jennings, I have to insist that you not get involved. This is too personal for you." When Sadie went to go around him, he gently grabbed her arm. "Sadie, listen to me. It's clear that you are upset. It won't do your friend or this hospital any good to have an obviously distraught doctor in the way. Let your colleagues take care of her and you can be the liaison between the hospital and the family. That way you'll be first to know what is going on, okay?" he reasoned compassionately.

When Sadie nodded her agreement, he gave her shoulder a little squeeze. He stood by her as they wheeled Paige past and Sadie saw how badly her friend had been hurt. He was not standing there as a guard, but in solidarity with his fellow doctor. Sadie's knees started to buckle, but he held her up.

The next person rolled in through the doors was Cora Rae. Sadie had met her a few times, the most recent being the last Christmas party for the magazine. *What the hell happened?* Sadie thought as they rushed Cora Rae past. The poor woman was in an extreme amount of pain and looked as bad as Paige. Sadie could not fathom the amount of hate and evilness someone had to have in them to intentionally cause that level of suffering. *How will they ever recover from this?* she wondered sadly.

Chapter Thirty-Three

Jake sprinted into the hospital trying to catch up to the medical staff who were rushing away with his Paige. As he entered through the doors the stretchers had gone through, he noticed Sadie standing off to the side wearing regular clothes. She was having as bad a day as he was. She caught sight of him and rushed over to him, stopping him from following Paige.

"I'm sorry, Jake. You can't go back there," Sadie said, her voice full of sadness.

John ran up from behind them and stood next to Sadie, blocking Jake's path in case he ignored Sadie and tried to follow after Paige. Not knowing what to do, Jake brought both his hands up to rub them through his hair while he tried to think.

"Jake, those need to be treated," Sadie said, noticing that his wrists were rubbed raw and bleeding in a couple of spots.

Jake brought his hands down to look at his wrists, the discomfort hadn't even registered. He was too preoccupied by Paige's predicament. "I can deal with it later," he said dismissively.

"Why don't I go ahead and take care of it now? It's better than just sitting around while we wait for news," Sadie urged. Sadie looked over at the Chief of Medicine to see if it was okay with him that she treat Jake's wounds, and when he nodded his approval, Sadie turned to John. "John, Faith and Travis are in the emergency department waiting room. Can you go update them and let them know me and Jake will join y'all shortly?" Sadie asked, but her tone implied she wasn't really asking.

"Yes, of course. Faith has to be a ball of nerves waiting for news," he answered, his eyes still on Jake. "I have a strong feeling you can handle Jake here just fine on your own," John added. After nodding at Sadie, he turned and rushed to the waiting room.

Sadie led Jake to a small treatment room and started gathering the supplies she needed to bandage his wrists. She took a seat on a rolling stool and took a minute to look at Jake, really look at him. He looked, for a lack of a better word, haunted. "What happened to them Jake?" she whispered, as if speaking too loudly would cause him harm.

Jake took a minute to try to get himself together enough to tell Sadie the parts of what happened that he knew, but he couldn't seem to start talking while she was looking at him. He didn't know why, maybe because it was all so terrible. Sadie must have read his mind because she dropped her gaze to his wrists and got to work on cleaning them and spreading some kind of ointment on them. It was soothing, even though it stung a bit, so he was able to begin.

He told her about the connection between himself, Stacey, and the cottage and how he finally figured it all out. Explained that Cora Rae must have gotten caught up in the whole mess somehow, but he wasn't sure how that happened. By the time he finished telling her what it was like when the paramedics and officers brought Paige out of the cottage, they both had tears running down their faces.

Sadie silently stood up and went to put the remaining unused medical supplies on a counter. When she faced Jake again, they both seemed to know what the other needed and they embraced each other in a friendly, comforting hug.

When Jake and Sadie joined the others in the waiting room, it was apparent to Sadie that John told the same story to Faith and Travis that Jake had told her. Faith had fresh tears in her eyes and Travis was comforting her. They both wore the look of someone who had just heard a horror story.

"Poor Paige and Cora Rae," Faith lamented. "I can't even imagine how scared they must have been." Faith noticed Jake look away as she said the words. He was feeling guilty. "Oh Jake honey, I didn't mean to upset you. This is not your fault," Faith said as she went over to Jake and hugged him.

"It should have been me in that cottage being harmed, not Paige," he said as he hugged her back tightly.

Before Faith could think of something to say in response to Jake, a Charleston police officer walked up and joined their group.

"From what we found in Miss Brock's house, you're not wrong Mr. Bennett," the officer said. Everyone turned to stare at the newcomer in shock.

CHAPTER THIRTY-FOUR

"Officer Sanders, what did you find?" Jake asked, recognizing the friend of John's he'd met outside of Paige's office building weeks ago.

They all gathered around in a tight circle to hear Officer Sander's story. The answers they had been searching for were about to revealed.

"I'm not supposed to officially say anything yet, so this is strictly off the record. The deceased Miss Brock had a makeshift dark room in her house. There were many photos of you, Mr. Bennett, hanging around the room. We found her negatives in Cora Rae Summer's things. It appears the Brock woman was trying to frame her. There were also pictures of you that were printed off of social media." Officer Sanders took a minute to catch his breath. He'd been having a busy day.

Faith took his pause as a chance to comment, "That's so scary, feels like a complete invasion of privacy, and I'm not even the one she was stalking."

"That's not all," Officer Sanders continued, "it appears she has done this before. We found a box with similar pictures of other men, so while she was holding Mrs. Collins and Miss Summers hostage, we had a forensics team doing some digging on her to see if there was anything we could use to convince her to release the women."

"What did they find?" John asked, his professional curiosity peaked. The whole group was on edge as they learned more about the woman behind the violence.

"Well, she's originally from Mobile, Alabama. There are three similar unsolved cases in towns around that area and there are two more here in South Carolina. One only a few months ago, actually. The reason the connection was never made to Mrs. Collins's case during the investigation is because she usually ends up murdering the men. Their bodies found out in the woods mutilated or washed up on a riverbed or in the case of the last one, behind a Charleston office building sliced up."

"Why did she go after Paige then? This makes no damn sense. It really should have been me in there. Why the hell was it different this time?" Jake questioned, getting upset. He would have given anything to have traded places with Paige in that cottage.

"Her journals answered that question. She was convinced that you were her one true love and you had been searching for her during the time after your, uh, rendezvous, since she never saw you with another woman until Mrs. Collins. She believed you were only with Mrs. Collins out of pity and that she would be freeing you from that burden," Officer Sanders explained.

Jake had to sit down. He couldn't wrap his head around how someone could get things so misconstrued that they would torture and try to kill someone over a one-night stand who they didn't even exchange names with.

"Well, she was delusional. Good grief," Faith summarized what everyone else was thinking.

"How is Officer Romero?" John asked, concerned about his fellow officer.

"She's pissed off at herself that the Brock woman snuck up on her. Miss Brock put a gun to the back of her head and then chloroformed her. Hit her over the head with the butt of the gun for good measure, I reckon. She's got a mild concussion and is still a little groggy, but she's going to be just fine." Officer Sanders yawned. "If y'all don't mind, I'm going to head out before I fall asleep standing up. It's been a long day."

They each took a turn shaking hands with Officer Sanders and thanking him for the update. Sadie excused herself to go check on the status of Paige and Cora Rae. The remaining four sat in quiet contemplation, processing everything they had learned about the woman who had been tormenting Paige for the last month or so and apparently stalking Jake for even longer than that.

John went outside to notify Paige's parents that she had been found and was in the hospital, at Faith's request. He unfortunately had more experience at delivering hard news. Her parents were relieved she had been found, but the uncertainty of her fate was still unknown and that was difficult for them to handle. John found out that Caleb had also ended up with Paige's parents when he couldn't get in touch with his dad and had called around looking for him. Jake was relieved to hear it when John told him. All of the kids should be together to comfort each other.

A short while later, they all stood up as they spotted Sadie coming back to the waiting area. "Sadie, how are they?" Faith asked pleadingly.

"Come with me and I'll explain what's going on," Sadie said, beckoning them with her hand to follow her. She led them down a few hallways and into a family counseling room in the intensive care unit.

"Paige is still unconscious. They did the initial assessment, and it appears she has lost a lot of blood. They are preparing to give her a blood transfusion. She was shot in the arm, but it was more of a graze, so alone that is not life-threatening. The problem is she is covered with deep gashes that are consistent with having been made by a knife. She also has injuries around her wrists from being tied with rope and they are concerned about nerve damage. She has a long road ahead of her, but thankfully she's going to make it," Sadie reported.

Everyone took a deep breath.

"And what about our baby?" Jake questioned softly, scared to hear the answer.

"I'm sorry, Jake, I don't know yet," she replied sadly.

Jake nodded his head. He was pretty sure he already knew the answer.

"What about Cora Rae?" Faith asked.

"They put her into a medically induced coma. She has swelling on her brain that they need to get under control. She has a nasty gash on her head from being hit with something heavy. She also has giant bruises on her back and front torso, so they are worried about internal bleeding. Her prognosis is unclear at this moment. I called Paige's assistant Brenda and asked her for Cora Rae's emergency contact information. Someone is getting in touch with them now."

"Oh Sadie, that poor woman. Well, when her family arrives just have them brought here so we can all be there for each other," Faith declared.

Sadie left the room to be closer to where Paige and Cora Rae were being treated. It was weird to be wandering around the hospital in her street clothes. Her white doctor's coat was like armor when she went to go talk to families. She felt exposed without it, like she couldn't steel herself against the onslaught of other people's emotions or compartmentalize hers.

Jake sat in the counseling room for hours with John, Faith, and Travis. Only leaving long enough to call Caleb for a few minutes to give an update. He was so proud of his son for stepping up for his new younger siblings. Jake wished he could go see Chloe and Henry, but he didn't want to leave where Paige was. John was keeping himself busy making sure they all had drinks or food when they needed it. Jake didn't feel much like eating but knew that he needed to keep his strength up to take care of Paige when the time came.

When Cora Rae's parents joined them in the family counseling room, Jake became consumed with guilt again. It was inadvertently his fault Cora Rae had been harmed by that unhinged woman. Faith must have been able to tell what he was thinking after he had been introduced to them because she came over and sat next to him and patted his hand like he had seen her do to Paige when she was showing support. She sat there in companionable silence with him. Jake was relieved that at least she didn't seem opposed to him anymore.

Every time Sadie came back to give an update Jake felt like his heart had fallen into his stomach. *Please, Please, Please,* would run through his head the whole time she was speaking. For hours it was much of the same. Paige's body seemed to have responded well to the blood transfusion, but she was still unconscious. Sadie didn't mention the baby and Jake didn't ask. He knew it was cowardly, but he couldn't face hearing that their unborn child was gone before it even had a chance to be more than an embryo because of such hate-filled violence against its mother.

Cora Rae was still fighting for her life in the coma and Jake's heart broke for her parents. They were absolutely distraught. It blew their minds that the woman their daughter had been telling them all about had hurt her when she was supposed to be her best friend. Faith would go over and hug them after Sadie would leave again. She would speak quietly with them and listen earnestly to the childhood stories Cora Rae's mom would tell.

Midnight came and went. Jake didn't know if it was the exhaustion or grief, but he was starting to lose hope that there would be any good news coming his way.

CHAPTER THIRTY-FIVE

Paige knew she was dreaming, but it felt so peaceful she didn't care that it wasn't real. Jake was fishing on the bank of a creek, sitting on a cooler, holding his rod and reel. He was wearing a plain white t-shirt, her favorite on him, and khaki shorts. His worn-out baseball cap protecting his eyes from the sun. The muddy brown water of the creek started to shimmer, and she emerged from it like some sort of shallow water mermaid, but she had legs. She was wearing a very sparkly emerald-green dress that hugged snugly to her curves. Dream Paige was sauntering seductively through the shallow water towards Jake. He was giving her his sweet and sexy smile she loved so much. The one that could make her insides melt. As she was about to place a kiss on that irresistible mouth of his, she woke up.

The first thing to cross Paige's mind as she came to was that she must really be outside in the sun. It was so dang bright. She blinked repeatedly until she could open her eyes and look around. Relief flooded through her as she realized that she was alive and in the hospital. She hurt all over, but it didn't matter. She was going to get to see her children again. She would get to marry Jake.

Quietly consulting by the door to her hospital room was Sadie and another doctor. Paige's eyes flooded with tears at the sight of her friend. She tried to call out, but no sound escaped. She cleared her throat and with the barely audible sound Sadie's head jerked to look at her and they made eye-contact. Sadie rushed to the bedside and gently took ahold of Paige's hand.

"By the look on your face, I guess I must look pretty bad," Paige said jokingly, her throat felt like it had cotton balls in it.

"You're still as gorgeous as ever, but you might have some battle scars," Sadie answered, her voice catching on a sob.

"Cora Rae? Is she alive? I tried to get to her after Stacey went down, but I don't remember if I ever made it across the floor to her," Paige wondered.

"Cora Rae is alive, but she's in a medically induced coma. She has suffered a lot of head trauma, and they are trying to control the swelling. The neurosurgeon had to put in a shunt. Her prognosis is unclear at this point. Her parents are here. Faith is helping to take care of them."

"She was so brave, Sadie. If it hadn't been for her, I wouldn't have had time to get loose and get to the gun. She saved me," Paige said in awe.

She would personally make sure everyone knew that Cora Rae was a hero. Paige was quiet for a minute, reflecting on all that had happened.

Then she continued, "What kind of recovery am I looking at Sadie?"

Sadie gave her friend the rundown of her injuries and what they would mean for her over the long run. When Sadie finished, Paige shook her head as tears fell from her eyes.

"I want to see Jake. I need to tell him," Paige whispered.

***

Around two a.m., Jake looked down into the bottom of his fourth cup of hospital coffee. It was hands down the nastiest coffee he had ever consumed, but he desperately needed the caffeine. He didn't want to miss any updates about Paige or Cora Rae. He was about to ask Faith for another piece of gum to get the burnt tree bark taste out of his mouth when Sadie came back to the family counseling room.

Sadie gave Faith a quick, reassuring smile and then turned to Jake and said the words he was desperate to hear, "Jake, Paige is awake and she's asking for you."

Jake knew it was taking all Faith had to not push him aside and run to Paige first. He went over and hugged her on his way out, his way of letting her know that he understood.

"Tell her I love her, and I'll see her soon," Faith told him as they pulled apart.

Jake nodded and followed Sadie to go see the love of his life.

When Jake entered Paige's room, his heart started pumping overtime. The parts of her not covered with hospital blankets were covered in cuts that had been sewn up. She kind of looked like a patchwork doll. It made him think of that creepy Christmas movie Tim Burton had made. Paige loved that movie, but he didn't understand the fascination. He wanted to throw himself on the bed with her and take her into his arms, but instead he approached slowly and took her hand in his gently.

"Paige, I'm so sorry," he started, but his voice went hoarse as his emotions caught up with him.

"Sadie said I'm going to be fine, Jake, don't worry sweetie. It's over now, for real this time," Paige assured him and squeezed his hand.

"Can I ask you for something?" she asked shyly.

"Anything baby, you know that," Jake promised as he leaned closer to hear better what he could do for his magnificent woman who had suffered so much because of him.

"Kiss me," Paige whispered as she pulled him down to her.

Jake touched his lips to hers gently, but that wasn't good enough for her. She pushed her tongue into his mouth and deepened the kiss. After all she had been through, she wanted to relish in the things that made her feel alive and joyous. Kissing Jake definitely got her feeling alive. Her senses heightened with every touch. It also let the pain of her injuries in, but it was totally worth it.

After a few minutes, Jake pulled away chuckling, "Don't start nothing you can't finish, baby."

He pulled a chair up to the bed and sat down, never letting go of her hand. He set his other hand on her belly and as he realized what he had done, his smile faded.

"Paige, when you're ready," he hesitated, "we can try for another baby if you want. I would understand if it's too much after losing two babies, though." Jake wasn't sure if that came out right, but he needed her to know that he wanted whatever would make her happy.

"But honey, we still have this one," Paige answered, putting her hands on top of his on her stomach.

"But I thought, I mean I assumed because Sadie didn't say anything. Honestly, I didn't ask because I was scared of the answer, but...that's so great," Jake rambled as he started crying happy tears in earnest.

For once lately, Paige did not start crying. Somehow, seeing him vulnerable made her strong. That was a part of what made them such good friends before. They always stepped up when the other one needed it.

"Well, Sadie told me they didn't say anything because it was, and still kind of is, a big possibility that we may lose this child. I have a good feeling though. This pregnancy is going to stick, I just know it," Paige declared confidently.

"Hmm, he's a strong one," Jake mumbled into her tummy as he nuzzled it lovingly.

"What makes you think it's a boy, huh?" Paige teased back.

They stayed quiet for a few minutes, his head lying on her stomach while she ran her fingers through his soft hair.

Eventually, Paige spoke again, "We owe Cora Rae so much, Jake. Not only for my life, but for our child's. I was still half tied up when Stacey decided that it was time for me to die. Cora Rae had been pretending to still be unconscious and kicked Stacey's legs out from under her at the perfect moment. It gave me the time I needed to get loose and get to the gun. That's also how she got at least one of her head injuries. Stacey had stood back up and hit Cora Rae over the head with my gun. There is no telling what Stacey did to her before she had me to torture. I just can't get over how brave Cora Rae was. She knew the police were outside. She could have kept quiet. They would have rescued her after I was shot."

"You're right, baby. We do owe her. Forever. And we will be there for her when she wakes up."

Jake cleared his throat and asked, "How are you with everything that happened? Taking a life, no matter how psychotic, must be hard to wrap your mind around," Jake noted tenderly.

His intention was not to upset Paige, but to make sure she knew it was ok to talk about anything and everything if she needed to.

"In some ways it is hard to process. She was someone's daughter, maybe a sister. I feel bad for whoever is going to be missing her. But Jake, I aimed for right in between her eyes and pulled that trigger with the intent of ending her. I didn't want to die and that's what it was about to come down to. But I did it not only in defense of myself, but also Cora Rae and this child I'm growing. I already love it so much, Jake. I won't let anyone hurt it," Paige explained emphatically.

Jake took a minute before he said anything. Finally, he cupped Paige's cheek and rubbed his thumb gingerly along one of the knife wounds. Then he took his hand and placed it back on her stomach. He folded down the blanket that was covering her, pushed up the hospital gown and laid a delicate kiss on her stomach, wincing as he saw more knife wounds.

"A love to kill for," he whispered, his breath tingling along her stomach.

"Exactly," Paige said simply.

He understood her perfectly.

Epilogue

About eight months later....

"Push! Push! Push!" the doctor instructed from where he was sitting between her open legs. "I can see the head!"

"You're almost there, Mrs. Bennett!" the nurse encouraged, standing behind the doctor, looking over his shoulder.

"Yes baby, you're doing so great," Jake said to his wife as he kissed her sweaty forehead.

He held on to her hand as she crushed his fingers and worked to bring their precious baby into the world. He was so proud of her. She was the bravest woman he had ever known. His warrior.

"Okay, the head is out. One more big push with the next contraction and she'll be out, Paige. You got this!" Sadie cheered.

Another perk of working at the hospital was that Sadie got to be in the room when her new niece was born. She was holding Paige's other hand and was extremely impressed by her friend's strong grip.

Paige breathed in deep and pushed with all her might when the next contraction hit and screamed on an exhale at the top of her lungs. She didn't care who heard and what they thought about her.

"You did it, baby! She's here!" Jake said in wonderment. "Oh my God! She's so beautiful!"

Jake had tears in his eyes as he watched the doctor hold up his daughter. He took the medical scissors the nurse held out to him and cut the umbilical cord. He took his sweet baby girl from the doctor and laid her on his wife's chest. He put his forehead on Paige's and whispered every lovingly praise he could think of to say. He loved her so much and now she had given him such a special gift. He gently rubbed his daughter's back and silently thanked God for all of his blessings.

"Little Clara Rae, you're so perfect," Paige cooed to her daughter. Paige and Jake had decided to name her after her honorary auntie whose brave actions had saved her mother's life as soon as they found out they were having a baby girl.

Sadie came over and smiled down at her friend. "I'll go out and tell everyone she's here. I am sure they are anxious." She bent down and said, "Welcome little one," to the bundle on Paige's chest, then quietly left the delivery room.

The waiting room was filled with Paige and Jake's loved ones. "It's a girl!" Sadie cheerfully announced when she entered the crowd.

Faith and Cora Rae squealed and hugged each other at the joyous news. Cora Rae had become part of the family. No one thought of her as a dimwit anymore. She was a hero. Chloe and Henry jumped up and down and cheered. Caleb high-fived his little brother and sister. Paige's parents smiled at each other and hugged, then congratulated Jake's parents. John was there and shook hands with all of the men and hugged all of the ladies. The entire group had been on such a wild ride together and in that moment were overjoyed that Paige and Jake were getting their happy ending. Everyone went over to the nursery window, waiting for a chance to see the new addition to the family.

Paige was enjoying her skin-to-skin time with Clara Rae when the nurse came to take the baby to get cleaned up.

"Alright Mrs. Bennett, you need to rest. I'll take this beauty to get cleaned up and be examined by the pediatrician."

Reluctantly, Paige allowed her daughter to be lifted off of her.

"Go with her, Jake," Paige insisted, and when they were all out the door, the exhaustion of childbirth overtook her, and she drifted off to sleep. She had peaceful dreams full of love, joy, and family.

When the doctor and nurses were done with every check-up they needed to do with Clara Rae, Jake got to hold her again. She felt so perfect in his arms.

"You're going to be a warrior like your mama, I can tell," he whispered to his daughter.

"Now, there are some people who want to get a look at you."

Jake walked over to the nursery window to where his family and loved ones were waiting. The proud daddy held up his baby for them to see as happy tears streamed down his face.

About the author

This is Jen McGee's debut novel. She is a married mother to three beautiful children and two crazy dogs. She is a proud member of Romance Writers of America and Pitch to Published. When not writing, reading, or chasing kids, Jen has been known to stay up late binging Netflix and doing jigsaw puzzles.

Acknowledgements

There are so many people I need to thank for helping to make this book happen. First, my husband and kids who had to constantly hear, "Mommy is writing!" and for being my biggest cheerleaders. Thank you to Jessica, Hope, and Amber for reading pages over and over and for giving great constructive feedback. Thank you Amber for making the cover so beautiful! Also, a huge thank you to all of my other family and friends who supported me in this crazy quest to become a published author. There were many fellow writers in my P2P group who provided advice, feedback, and encouragement for which I will forever be grateful.